I SERVED
THE KING OF
ENGLAND

BOHUMIL HRABAL

I SERVED
THE KING OF
ENGLAND

TRANSLATED FROM THE CZECH BY
PAUL WILSON

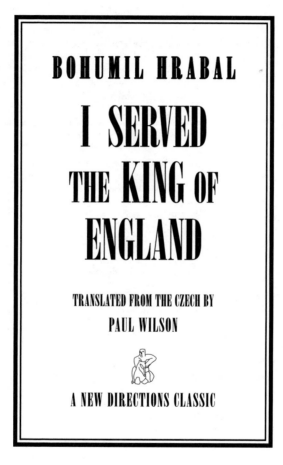

A NEW DIRECTIONS CLASSIC

PUBLISHER'S NOTE: New Directions wishes to thank Drenka Willen for her assistance in the publication of this edition.

Manufactured in the United States of America
First published in hardcover by Harcourt Brace Jovanovich in 1989
First published paperbound by Vintage International in 1990
First published as a New Directions Paperbook (NDP1067) in 2007
Published simultaneously in Canada by Penguin Books Canada Limited.
New Directions Books are printed on acid-free paper.

Library of Congress Cataloging-in-Publication Date to come

Hrabal, Bohumil, 1914-1997.
  [Obsluhoval jsem anglického krále. English]
  I served the King of England / Bohumil Hrabal ;
translated from the Czech by Paul Wilson.
      p. cm. — (A New Directions classic)
  ISBN-13: 978-0-8112-1687-6 (alk. paper)
  ISBN-10: 0-8112-1687-X (alk. paper)
  1. Czechoslovakia—History—Fiction.
I. Wilson, Paul R. (Paul Robert), 1941- II. Title.
PG5039.18.R2O2713 2007
891.8'635—dc22
                                        2007001145

New Directions Books are published for James Laughlin
by New Directions Publishing Corporation,
80 Eighth Avenue, New York, NY 10011

7 9 10 8

CONTENTS

I SERVED
THE KING OF
ENGLAND

A Glass
of Grenadine

◆◆◆◆◆◆◆◆◆◆◆◆◆

When I started to work at the Golden Prague Hotel, the boss took hold of my left ear, pulled me up, and said, You're a busboy here, so remember, you don't see anything and you don't hear anything. Repeat what I just said. So I said I wouldn't see anything and I wouldn't hear anything. Then the boss pulled me up by my right ear and said, But remember too that you've got to see everything and hear everything. Repeat it after me. I was taken aback, but I promised I would see everything and hear everything. That's how I began. Every morning at six, when the hotel-keeper walked in, we were lined up like an army on parade, with the maître d', the waiters, and me, a tiny busboy, along one side of the carpet, and along the other side the cooks, the chambermaids, the laundress, and the scullery maid. The hotelkeeper walked up and down to see that our dickeys were clean and our collars and jackets spotless, that no buttons were missing, and that our shoes were polished. He'd lean over and sniff to make sure our feet were washed, and then he'd say, Good morning, gentlemen, good morning, ladies, and after that we weren't allowed to talk to anyone.

The waiters taught me the proper way to wrap the knives and forks in napkins, and every day I emptied the ashtrays and polished the metal caddy for the hot frankfurters I sold at the station, something I learned from the busboy who was no longer a busboy because he had started waiting on tables, and you should have heard him beg and plead to be allowed to go on selling frankfurters, a strange thing to want to do, I thought at first, but I quickly saw why, and soon it was all I wanted to do too, walk up and down the platform several times a day selling hot frankfurters for one crown eighty apiece. Sometimes the passenger would only have a twenty-crown note, sometimes a fifty, and I'd never have the change, so I'd pocket his note and go on selling until finally the customer got on the train, worked his way to a window, and reached out his hand. Then I'd put down the caddy of hot frankfurters and fumble about in my pocket for the change, and the fellow would yell at me to forget the coins and just give him the notes. Very slowly I'd start patting my pockets, and the dispatcher would blow his whistle, and very slowly I'd ease the notes out of my pocket, and the train would start moving, and I'd trot alongside it, and when the train had picked up speed I'd reach out so that the notes would just barely brush the tips of the fellow's fingers, and sometimes he'd be leaning out so far that someone inside would have to hang on to his legs, and one of my customers even beaned himself on a signal post. But then the fingers would be out of reach and I'd stand there panting, the money still in my outstretched hand, and it was all mine. They almost never came back for their change, and that's how I started having money of my own, a couple of hundred a month, and once I even got handed a thousand-crown note.

Every morning at six and again in the evening before bedtime the boss would come around, checking to make sure I'd washed my feet, and I had to be in bed by twelve. So I began to keep my ears open and not hear anything and keep my eyes open and not see anything. I saw how neat and orderly everything was, and how the boss didn't like us to be too friendly with one another, I mean, if the checkout girl went to the movies with the waiter, they'd both be fired on the spot. I also got to know the regular customers who drank at a table in the kitchen, and every day I had to polish their glasses. Each of the regulars had his own number and his own special insignia, a glass with a stag and a glass with violets and a glass with the picture of a town, rectangular glasses and round bulbous glasses and an earthenware stein all the way from Munich with HB stamped on it. Every evening this select group would show up—the notary public and the stationmaster and the vet and the director of the music school and a factory owner named Jína—and I'd help them all out of their coats, and when I served them beer, the proper glass had to go into the proper hand, and I was amazed at how rich people could sit around for a whole evening talking about how just outside the town there was a footbridge and right beside the footbridge, thirty years back, there was a poplar tree, and then they'd really get going. One of them would say there was no footbridge there at all, just a poplar tree, and another would say there was no poplar tree and not even a proper footbridge, just a plank with a handrail. They'd keep this up, drinking their beer and talking about it and jeering and shouting insults at one another, but it was all a show, because soon they'd be on their feet yelling across the table that the footbridge had been there but not the poplar tree, and the other side would yell back that the poplar tree damn well was there and the footbridge damn well wasn't. Then they'd sit down again and everything was all right, and you could see they'd only been yelling at one another like that to make the beer taste better. Or they'd start arguing about which of the local Bohemian beers was the best, and one swore by the beer from Protivín and another by the beer from Vodňany and a third by the beer from Plzeň and a fourth by the beer from Nymburk and Krušovice, and pretty soon they were at it again. But they all liked one another and only shouted like that to make the evening eventful, to help kill the time. Or when I was handing him his beer, the stationmaster would lean back and whisper that the vet had been seen at Paradise's, with Jaruška, in a private room. Then the principal of the municipal school would whisper that he'd been there all right, but on Wednesday not Thursday, the vet, I mean, and with Vlasta not Jaruška, and then they'd talk about the girls at Paradise's for the rest of the evening, and who'd been there and who hadn't, and I lost all interest in whether there was a poplar tree and a footbridge on the outskirts of town or just a footbridge without the poplar tree, or the poplar tree alone, or whether the beer from Braník was better than the beer from Protivín. All I wanted to hear was what it was like at Paradise's. I worked out how much I would need and then sold those hot frankfurters so I could make enough money to go to Paradise's, and I even learned how to cry real tears at the station, and the customers would wave their hands and tell me to keep the change because they thought I was an orphan. And a plan took shape in my mind that one night, after eleven, after I'd washed my feet, I'd sneak out the window of my tiny room and pay a visit to Paradise's.

On the day I picked, things got off to a wild start at the Golden City of Prague restaurant. During the morning a group of well-heeled, well-dressed gypsies walked in, tinkers they were, and sat down at a table. Everything they ordered was the best, and each time they ordered something else they made sure we knew they had money. The director of the music school was sitting by the window, but the gypsies were shouting so loud that he moved back into the middle of the restaurant, still reading his book, which must have been pretty good because he kept his nose buried in it when he got up to move three tables over, and he was still reading when he sat down again, feeling around behind him for the chair. I was polishing the regulars' beer mugs, holding them up to the light, and we were still serving breakfast, just soups and goulashes to a handful of customers, and of course all the waiters were supposed to keep busy even if there was nothing to do, which is why I was polishing the glasses so carefully and the maître d' was standing by the sideboard straightening the forks and the waiter was rearranging the cutlery all over again. Anyway, as I was looking through a Golden Prague mug, I saw some angry gypsies run past the window, and the next thing I knew they had burst into the restaurant, and I suppose they must have pulled their knives out in the hallway, and then something awful happened. They rushed up to the tinker gypsies, but the tinker gypsies apparently were waiting for them because they jumped to their feet and backed off, dragging the tables, keeping the tables between themselves and the gypsies with the knives, which didn't help because two of them ended up on the floor with knives sticking out of their backs anyway, and the ones with the knives hacked and stabbed away, and soon the tables were covered with blood, but the director of the music school, with a smile on his face, went right on reading while the gypsy storm whirled around him, and they bled over his head and his book, and twice they stuck their knives into his table, but the director went on reading. I was under a table myself and crawled into the kitchen on my hands and knees while the gypsies screamed, and the knives flashed and reflections of sunlight flew around the Golden Prague like golden flies, then the gypsies backed out of the restaurant leaving an unpaid bill and blood all over the tables, two men on the floor and on one of the tables two severed fingers, an ear, and a chunk of flesh. When the doctor came to see the wounded, he said the chunk of flesh on the table was a slice of muscle from someone's arm, near the shoulder. The director simply put his head in his hands, his elbows resting on the table, and went on reading his book. All the other tables were jammed together at the entrance in a barricade to cover the tinker gypsies' escape, and the boss could think of nothing else but to put on a white vest with a honeybee print, post himself outside the restaurant, hold up his hands, and tell the customers that there'd been an unfortunate incident and we wouldn't be open till the next day. It was my job to deal with the tablecloths covered with bloody handprints and fingerprints. I had to carry everything into the courtyard and fire up the large boiler in the laundry, and the laundress and the scullery maid had to soak everything and then boil it. I was supposed to hang the tablecloths out to dry, but I was too short to reach the clothesline, so the laundress did it while I handed her the wet, wrung-out tablecloths. I only came up to her breasts, and she laughed and used the chance to make fun of me by pushing her breasts into my face as if it were an accident—first one breast, then the other, right into my eyes until the world went dark and everything was scented. When she leaned over to take a tablecloth out of the hamper, I could see down between her swinging breasts, and when she stood up and the breasts went horizontal again, she and the scullery maid laughed and asked me, How old are you? Have you turned fourteen yet, sweetheart? And when will that be? Then it was early evening, and a breeze came up, and the sheets in the courtyard made a screen, the kind we'd put up for weddings or private parties, and I had everything in the restaurant ready and spanking clean again, with carnations everywhere—they brought in a whole basket of flowers each day, depending on the season—and I went to bed. When it was quiet and I could hear the tablecloths flapping in the courtyard as if they were talking to one another till the yard was full of rustling muslin conversation, I opened the window, climbed out and slipped between the tablecloths past the windows to the gate, then I swung myself over and walked down the narrow street, edging along from lamppost to lamppost. If anyone approached, I would wait in the shadows until he was gone, and then from a distance I saw the green sign saying Paradise's.

For a while I just stood outside and waited, listening to the faint jangling of a mechanical music box coming from deep inside the building, then I mustered my courage and went in. There was a wicket in the hallway that was so high I had to pull myself up by my fingers, and Mrs. Paradise herself was sitting there and she said, What can I do for you, my little man? I said I'd come to be entertained, and she opened the door and I went in and there was a young woman with jet-black hair combed out sitting and smoking a cigarette. She asked me what I'd like. I said I'd like to have dinner and she asked, Would you like it here or in the bar? I blushed and said no, I wanted it in a separate room, and she stared at me, let out a long whistle, and then, already knowing the answer, she said, With anyone in particular? I pointed at her and said, With you. Shaking her head, she took me by the hand, led me along a dark corridor lit with soft red lamps, and opened a door. There I saw a small couch, a table and two plush chairs, and a light coming from somewhere behind a valance swept across the ceiling and down the walls like the branches of a weeping willow. I sat down, and after I'd patted my money I felt braver and said, Would you have dinner with me? And what will you drink? She said champagne, so I nodded, and she clapped, and a waiter arrived with a bottle, opened it, carried it over to an alcove, and filled two glasses, and when I drank it the bubbles tickled my nose and made me sneeze. The young woman drank one glass after another, then introduced herself, Jaruška, and said she was hungry and I said, Fine, bring on the best, and she said she loved oysters and they were fresh today, so we ate oysters and had another bottle of champagne and then another. She started stroking my hair and she asked me where I was from, and I told her from a village so small I'd never seen real coal until last year, and she thought that was funny and asked me to make myself at home. I was feeling hot, so I took off my jacket, and she said she felt hot too, and would I mind if she took off her dress? So I helped her out of it and folded her dress neatly across the chair, and then she unbuttoned my fly, and that was when I knew that at Paradise's it was not just nice or wonderful, but like paradise, and she took my head in her hands and pressed it between her breasts, and her breasts smelled sweet, and I closed my eyes and practically fell asleep, so intoxicating was her smell and her shape and the softness of her skin, and she pushed my head lower and lower, and I could smell her lap, and she sighed. It was all so wonderful and forbidden that I wanted nothing more in this world, and I resolved to save eight hundred and more a week selling hot frankfurters, because at last I'd found a beautiful and noble aim. My father used to say that if I had an aim in life I'd be all right because then I'd have a reason for living. But that was only half of it. Jaruška quietly slipped off my trousers, pulled down my underpants, and kissed the inside of my thighs, and suddenly I was so distracted by the thought of what went on in Paradise's that I began to tremble and I curled up into a ball and I said, Jaruška, what are you doing? And she stopped, but when she saw me she couldn't help herself and took me into her mouth, and I tried to push her away, but she seemed possessed and held me in her mouth and moved her head faster and faster till I stopped trying to push her away but instead stretched out to my full length and held her by the ears and felt myself gushing out, remembering how different it was from the times I used to do it to myself, because the girl with the beautiful hair drank the last drop from me, her eyes closed—drank what I had always tossed away with disgust into the coal bin in the cellar or a handkerchief in bed. When she got up, she said in a sleepy voice, And now for love. I was too shaken up and too limp, and I said, But I'm hungry, aren't you? I was thirsty too, so I took Jaruška's glass, and she rushed at me but couldn't stop me from drinking, and I put the glass down, disappointed, because what was in it was not champagne but some kind of pale fizz. She'd been drinking it from the start and I'd been paying for champagne. I laughed and ordered another bottle, and when the waiter brought it I opened it myself and filled our glasses. Then we ate again, and the music box tinkled away in the bar, and after we'd finished the bottle I felt tipsy and went down on my knees again and put my head in her lap and began to poke about with my tongue in that lovely muff of hair. But because I was light, the girl took me under my arms and lifted me onto herself and spread her legs. As smooth as butter, I slipped into a woman for the first time in my life, the very thing I'd been wanting and here it was. She held me tightly against herself and whispered, Hold back, take as long as you can, but I only moved twice, and the third time I gushed into her warm flesh, and she arched her back so that she was touching the couch with just her hair and the soles of her feet, with me on the bridge of her body right to the very end, before I got soft, and stayed there between her legs until finally I unwound and lay down beside her. She took a deep breath, fell back on the couch, and began to stroke and caress my body as if she knew it by heart. Then came the time for getting dressed, and the time for saying good-bye, and the time for paying, and the waiter added up this and that and handed me a bill for seven hundred and twenty crowns, and as I left I took out another two hundred crowns and gave it to Jaruška, and when I left Paradise's, I leaned against the first wall I came to and just stood there, leaning against the wall in the dark, dreaming, because now I knew what went on in those marvelous places where the young women are, and I said to myself, That was your lesson, now you'll come right back here tomorrow and be the gentleman all over again. I'd impressed them all, I'd come as a busboy who sells hot frankfurters at the station, but when I left I was bigger than any of the gentlemen who sat at the regulars' table at the Golden Prague, where only the rich, the upper crust of the town, are allowed.

The next day I saw the world a lot differently, because my money had opened the door to Paradise's and to respect. I forgot to mention that when Mrs. Paradise saw me toss two hundred crowns away, she reached down eagerly from her wicket and took my hand. I thought she wanted to know what time it was on the wristwatch I didn't have yet, but she kissed my hand. Of course the kiss wasn't really a kiss for me, a busboy from the Golden Prague restaurant, it was for those two hundred crowns and for all my money, because I had another thousand crowns stashed away in my bed and I could still have maybe not as much as I wanted but as much as I could earn every day selling hot frankfurters at the station. Anyway, that morning I was sent with a basket to buy fresh flowers, and on my way back I saw a pensioner crawling around on his hands and knees looking for some change that had rolled away from him. It was on this errand, by the way, that I realized that the florist and also the sausage maker and the butcher and the proprietor of the dairy bar were all among our regulars. In fact, the same men who supplied us with meat and baked goods got together at our restaurant, and often the boss would look into the icebox and say, Go straight to the butcher and tell him to come and remove this poor excuse for a side of veal right now, and by evening the veal was gone and the butcher would be sitting there as though nothing had happened. But the pensioner must have had poor eyesight because he was groping around in the dust with his hands, so I said, What are you looking for, old man? He said he'd lost twenty hellers, so I waited till some people walked by, took a fistful of change, tossed it in the air, then quickly sank my hands into the carnations, grabbed the basket handles, and walked on. Just before rounding the corner, I turned and saw several more people on their knees, each one was sure he had dropped the coins and was yelling at the others to hand over the money and there they were on their knees, arguing, spitting, and scratching at one another's eyes like tomcats, and I had to laugh, because I saw at once what moved people and what they believed in and what they would do for a handful of change. When I brought the flowers back to the hotel, I saw a lot of people standing in front of the restaurant, so

I ran upstairs to one of the guest rooms, leaned out the window, and threw down a fistful of coins, making sure they fell not directly on the people but a few meters away. Then I ran downstairs, cut back the stems of the carnations, and put two sprigs of asparagus fern and two carnations into each little vase—all the while looking out the window at the people crawling around on their hands and knees, picking up money, my coins, and arguing about who saw which twenty-heller piece first. That night and the nights after that, I would dream and dream, even during the day— when there was nothing to do and I had to pretend to be busy, polishing the glasses and holding one up to the light close to my eye like a kaleidoscope, looking through it across the splintered square at the sky and the clouds— even during the day I dreamed that I was flying over towns and cities and villages and that I'd take handfuls of coins from a huge, bottomless pocket and throw them down on the cobblestones, scattering them like a sower of wheat, but always behind people's backs, behind the pedestrians or bystanders. Almost no one could resist picking up those twenty-heller pieces and they'd butt one another's heads like rams and squabble, but I'd fly on. It made me feel good, and I'd take another fistful of coins from my pocket and toss them down behind another group, and the money would jangle to the ground and roll off in all directions, and I could fly like a bee into trains and streetcars and suddenly strum a fistful of coins to the floor and watch people bend over and bump into one another trying to pick up the change they pretended had fallen from their pockets alone. These dreams heartened me because I was small and had to wear a high, stiff rubber collar, and my neck was short and narrow, and the collar cut into it and into my chin as well, and to keep it from hurting me, I would carry my head high. And because I couldn't tilt my head forward without pain, I had to bend over from the waist, so my head was usually tipped back and my eyes half closed and I looked at the world almost as though I were scorning or mocking it, and the customers thought I was conceited. I learned to stand and walk that way too, and the soles of my feet were always as hot as irons, so hot that I'd look to see if I had caught fire and my shoes were burning. Sometimes I was so desperate for relief I'd pour cold soda water into my shoes, especially when I was working at the train station, but it only helped for the moment, and I was always on the verge of taking my shoes off and running straight into the river, tuxedo and all, and soaking my feet in the water, so I'd put more soda water into my shoes and sometimes a blob of ice cream as well. That's how I came to understand why the maître d' and the waiters always wore their oldest, shabbiest shoes to work, the kind you find thrown away on rubbish heaps, because that was the only kind of shoe you could stand in and walk around in all day. All of us suffered from sore feet, even the chambermaids and the checkout girl. Every evening, when I took off my shoes, my legs were covered with dust up to my knees, as if I'd spent the day wading through coal dust and not walking over parquet floors and carpets. That was the other side of my tuxedo, the other side of all waiters and busboys and maître d's the world over: white starched shirts and dazzling white rubber collars and legs slowly turning black, like some horrible disease where people start dying from the feet up.

Each week I managed to save up for another girl, a different one each time. The second girl in my life was a blonde. When I walked into Paradise's and they asked me what I'd like, I said I wanted to have supper but, I added right away, in a separate room, and when they asked me who with, I pointed to a blonde, and there I was in love with a beautiful fair-haired woman, and it was even better than the first time, unforgettable as that had been. And so I tested the power of pure money and I ordered champagne, but I tasted it first, and the girl had to be served from the same bottle. I'd had enough of them pouring wine for me and soda pop for her. As I lay there naked staring at the ceiling, and the girl lay beside me staring at the ceiling too, I suddenly stood up and took a peony from the vase, stripped the petals off, and garnished the girl's lap with them. I was astonished at how splendid it looked. The girl sat up and looked at her lap, but the peony petals fell off, and I gently pushed her back and took the mirror from its hook and held it up so she could see how beautiful she looked with her lap all decorated with peonies and I said, This is wonderful, if there are flowers here, I'll decorate your lap every time I come. And she said that this had never happened to her before, someone appreciating her beauty like that, and she told me that because of those flowers she had fallen in love in me. I said it would be wonderful when I picked up some fir boughs at Christmas and arranged them in her lap, and she said, Mistletoe would be even nicer. But best of all, and she must arrange it, would be to hang a mirror from the ceiling over the couch so we could see ourselves lying there, especially her, beautiful and naked with a wreath on her lap, a wreath that would change with the seasons, with the flowers that are typical for each month. How wonderful it would be to garland her body with moon daisies and virgin's tears and chrysanthemums and purple loosestrife and autumn leaves. I stood up and hugged myself, and as I left I gave her two hundred crowns, but she handed it back, so I put it on the table and left, feeling six feet tall. I even slipped two hundred crowns to Mrs. Paradise in her wicket as she leaned out and stared at me through her glasses. I went out into the night, and in the dark, narrow streets the sky was full of stars, but all I could see were hepatica and wood anemone and snowdrops and primroses scattered over the blonde girl's lap. The more I walked, the more astonished I was at where I'd got the notion to arrange flowers in a woman's pretty lap with its mound of hair in the middle, like garnishing a plate of ham with lettuce. Since I knew flowers, I went on with it and dressed the naked blonde in cinquefoil and tulip and iris petals, and I decided to plan it all out in advance, so I could have entertainment all year round. So I learned that money could buy you not just a beautiful girl, money could buy you poetry too.

Next morning, when we stood on the carpet and the boss walked up and down to see that our shirts were clean and all our buttons there, and when he'd said, Good morning, ladies and gentlemen, I looked at the laundress and the scullery maid and found myself staring so piercingly at their little white aprons that the laundress tweaked my ear, and I realized that neither of them would let her lap, her patch of hair, be wrapped in daisies or peonies, let alone sprigs of fir or mistletoe, like a joint of venison. So I polished the glasses, holding them up to the light from the big windows, and outside, people were walking past, cut off from the waist down, and I went on thinking about summer flowers, and I took them from their baskets one by one and lay blossoms or just petals in the lap of the beautiful blonde from Paradise's, while she lay on her back with her legs spread apart, and when the blossoms slipped off I would stick them back with gum arabic or gently tack them in place with a small nail or a pin. So I did a fine job of polishing the glasses, something no one else wanted to do, rinsing each glass in water and holding it up to the window to make sure it was clean, though thinking all the time, through that glass, about what I would do at Paradise's, until finally I ran out of garden flowers, field flowers, and forest flowers, and this made me feel sad, because what would I do in winter? Then I laughed and was happy, realizing that in winter the flowers would be even more beautiful, because I could buy cyclamen and magnolias, and I might even go to Prague for orchids. Or maybe I'd just move to Prague, for there must be restaurant jobs there too, and I'd have flowers all winter long. Then noontime came, and I set out the plates and napkins and served beer and raspberry and lemon grenadine, and right at noon, at the busiest time, the door opened and she stepped in, then turned to close the door behind her, that beautiful blonde from Paradise's. She sat down and opened her purse, pulled out an envelope, and looked around. I knelt down and quickly tied my shoe, my heart beating against my knee. When the maître d' came over and said, Quick, get to your place, all I could do was nod, my heart throbbing so hard that my knee seemed to merge and change places with it. But then I pulled myself together, stood up, and holding my head as high as I could, I threw a napkin over my arm and asked the girl what she'd like. She said she wanted to see me again, and a glass of raspberry grenadine. She was wearing a summer dress covered with peonies, she was surrounded by them, a prisoner of peony beds, and I caught fire and blushed like a peony, because I hadn't expected this. My money, my thousand crowns, was gone, and what I was looking at now was completely free. So I went for a tray of raspberry grenadine, and when I came back with it the blonde had put the envelope on the tablecloth and the corners of my two hundred-crown notes were casually sticking out of it. The way she looked at me set the glasses of grenadine rattling and the first one slipped to the edge of the tray, slowly tipped over, and spilled into her lap. The maître d' was right there, and the boss came running up, and they apologized, and the boss grabbed me by the ear and twisted it, which he shouldn't have done, because the blonde cried out so that everyone in the restaurant could hear her, How dare you! The boss said, He's ruined your dress and now I'll have to pay for it. She: What business is that of yours? I want nothing from you. Why are you mistreating this man? The boss, sweetly: He spilled a drink on your dress. Everyone had stopped eating now, and she said, It's none of your business and I forbid you to punish him. Just watch this. She took a glass of grenadine and poured it over her head and into her hair, and then another glass, and she was covered with raspberry syrup and soda-water bubbles. The last glass of raspberry grenadine she poured down the inside of her dress, then she asked for the bill. She walked out with the aroma of raspberries trailing behind her, out into the street in that silk dress covered with peonies, and the bees were already circling her. The boss picked up the envelope on the table and said, Go after her, she forgot this. When I ran out, I found her standing in the square surrounded by wasps and bees like a booth selling Turkish honey at a village fair, but she made no effort to brush them away as they ate the sugary juice that coated her like an extra skin, like a thin layer of polish or marine varnish rubbed on furniture. I looked at her dress and handed her the two hundred crowns and she handed them back and said that I'd forgotten to take them yesterday. Then she asked me to come to Paradise's that evening and said she'd bought a beautiful bouquet of wild poppies. I saw how the sun had dried the raspberry grenadine in her hair and made it stiff and hard, like a paintbrush when you don't put it in turpentine, like gum arabic when it spills, like shellac, and I saw that the sweet grenadine had stuck her dress so tightly to her body that she'd have to tear it off like an old poster, like old wallpaper. But all that was nothing to the shock I felt when she spoke to me. She knew me better than they knew me in the restaurant, she may even have known me better than I knew myself. That evening, the boss told me they'd be needing my room on the ground floor for the laundry and I'd have to move my things to the second floor. I said, Couldn't we do it tomorrow? But the boss looked right at me, and I knew that he knew and that I'd have to move at once, and he reminded me that I had to be in bed by eleven, that he was responsible for me, both to my parents and to society, and that, if a busboy like me expected to do a full day's work, he had to have a full night's sleep.

The nicest guests in our establishment were always the

traveling salesmen. Not all of them, of course, because some traded in goods that were worthless or didn't sell—warm-water salesmen, we called them. My favorite was the fat salesman. The first time he came I ran for the boss, who was alarmed when he saw me and said, What's the matter? Sir, I said breathlessly, some big shot's just arrived. He went to take a look, and sure enough, we'd never had anyone this fat before. The boss praised me and chose a room that this salesman always stayed in afterward, with a bed that the porter reinforced with four cinder blocks and two planks. The salesman made a wonderful entrance. He had a helper with him who looked like a porter at the station and was carrying a heavy pack on his back, something with straps around it, like a heavy typewriter. In the evening, when the salesman sat down to supper, he would take the menu and look at it as though there was nothing on it he liked, and then he'd say: Leaving aside the lungs in sour sauce, bring me every entrée on the menu, one by one, and when I'm finishing the first, bring me the next, until I tell you I've had enough. And he'd always polish off ten main dishes before he'd eaten his fill, and then he'd get a dreamy look on his face and say he'd like a little something to nibble on. The first night he asked for a hundred grams of Hungarian salami. When the boss brought it out to him, the salesman looked at the plate, then took a handful of coins, opened the door, and tossed them out into the street. After he'd eaten a couple of slices of salami, he appeared to get angry again, took another handful of change, and tossed it out into the street again. Then he sat down again, frowning, while the regulars looked at one another and at the boss. All the boss could do was get up, walk over, bow, and ask, Just out of curiosity, sir, why are you throwing your money away? The salesman answered, Why shouldn't I when you're the owner of this establishment and you throw away ten-crown notes every day, exactly the same way? The boss went back to the table and reported all this to the regulars, but that really got them going, so he went back to the fat man's table and said, Just out of curiosity, sir . . . of course you're entitled to throw away as much money as you like, but I don't see what that has to do with my ten crowns. The fat man stood up and said, Allow me to explain. May I go into your kitchen? And the boss bowed and motioned him toward the kitchen door. When the salesman came into the kitchen, I heard him introduce himself: My name is Walden and I represent the firm of van Berkel. Now, would you mind slicing me a hundred grams of Hungarian salami? So the boss's wife sliced the salami, weighed it, and put it on a plate. Suddenly we were all afraid he might be an inspector, but the salesman clapped and his helper came into the kitchen carrying the thing with a cover over it, which now looked like a spinning wheel, and set it on the table. The salesman swept off the cover, and there stood a beautiful red device—a thin, round, shiny circular blade that turned on a shaft, at the end of which was a crank and a handle and a dial. The fat man beamed at the machine and said, Now, the largest firm in the world is the Catholic church, and it trades in something that no man has ever seen, no man has ever touched, and no man has ever encountered since the world began, and that something is called God. The second-largest firm in the world is International, and you've got that represented here too, by a device now in use all around the world called a cash register. If you press the right buttons throughout the day, then instead of having to figure out the daily receipts yourself in the evening, the cash register will do it for you. The third-largest is the firm I represent, van Berkel, which manufactures scales used to weigh things with equal precision the world over, whether you're at the Equator or the North Pole, and in addition we manufacture a full range of meat-and-salami slicers. The beauty of our machine is this, if you'll allow me to demonstrate. And, after asking permission, he stripped the skin off a roll of Hungarian salami, put the skin on the scales, and then, turning the crank with one hand, pushed the salami against the circular blade with the other. The slices of salami piled up on the little platform till it seemed that he had sliced the entire piece, though not much of it had disappeared. The salesman stopped and asked how much salami we thought he'd sliced. The boss said a hundred and fifty grams, the maître d' a hundred and ten. How about you, squirt? the man asked me. I said eighty grams, and the boss grabbed me by the ear and twisted it and apologized to the salesman saying, His mother dropped him on his head on a tile floor when he was an infant. But the salesman patted my head and smiled at me nicely and said, The boy came closest. He threw the sliced salami on the scales, and the scales showed seventy grams. We all looked at one another, and then gathered around the miraculous little machine, because everyone could see there was profit in it. When we stood back, the salesman took a handful of coins and tossed them into the coal box and clapped, and his porter brought another package, and in its wrapping it looked like the glass bell my grandmother used to keep the Virgin Mary under, but when he unwrapped it, there stood a set of scales, like the kind you see in chemist's shops, with a slender needle that only showed up to a kilogram. The salesman said, Now, this scale is so precise that when I breathe on it, it will measure the weight of my breath. And he breathed and, sure enough, the needle moved, and then he took the sliced salami from our scale and threw it onto his, and the scale showed that the salami weighed exactly sixty-seven and a half grams. It was obvious that our scales had robbed the boss of two point five grams and the salesman worked it out on the table. That gives us . . . and then he drew a line under his figures and said, If you sell ten kilos of Hungarian salami a week, this scale will save you a hundred times two point five grams, that's almost half a salami. And he made fists of his hands and leaned his knuckles on the table, crossing one foot over the other so the toe touched the ground and the heel was in the air, and he smiled triumphantly. The boss said, Everybody leave, we're going to talk business. I'll buy all of this as is. Pointing at the porter, the salesman said, These are my samples. For a whole week we've been lugging them from chalet to chalet up in the Krkonoše Mountains, and in every decent chalet we've sold the salami slicer and a scale, and together they're a package I call a tax saver.

The salesman must have liked me—perhaps I reminded him of his youth—but whenever he saw me he'd pat my head and laugh, a pleasant laugh, till tears filled his eyes. Sometimes he'd ask to have mineral water brought to his room. Whenever I brought it to him I'd find him already in his pajamas, lying on the carpet, his enormous stomach beside him like a barrel. What I liked about him was that he wasn't ashamed of his stomach, he carried it proudly before him like a billboard, plowing forward into a world that came halfway to meet him. Sit down, my son, he'd say, and then he'd laugh, and it always felt as though my mother, not my father, was talking to me. Once he told me, You know, I started out when I was just a little guy like you, with Koreff's, the haberdashers. Ah, my child, I still remember my boss. He always said a good business-man has three things—property, a shop, and some inven-tory—and if you lose your inventory you've still got your shop, and if you lose your shop and your inventory at least you've got your property, and no one can take that away from you. Once I was sent out to pick up some combs, beautiful bone combs—eight hundred crowns, those combs cost—and I carried them on a bicycle in two enormous bags—here, have a sweet, go on, try this one, it's cherries in chocolate—and as I was pushing the bicycle up the hill— by the way, how old did you say you were? I told him fifteen and he nodded and took a sweet and smacked his lips and went on—and as I was carrying those combs up the hill, a peasant woman passed me, she was on a bicycle, too, and she stopped at the top of the hill in the woods, and after I'd caught up to her, she looked at me so intensely that I had to look away, and then she caressed me and said, Let's see if the raspberries are ripe. And I laid my bicycle with the load of combs down in the ditch, and she put hers—it was a woman's bike—on top of mine and took me by the hand, and behind the very first bush we came to she pushed me down and undid my fly, and before I knew it she was on top of me. She was the first to have me, but then I remembered my bike and my combs, so I ran back, and her bike was lying on top of mine, and in those days women's bicycles had a colored netting over the back wheel, like the kind horses sometimes wear over their manes, and I felt for the combs and to my relief they were still there. When the woman ran up and saw that my pedal was tangled in the netting of her bicycle, she said it was a sign that we weren't to go our separate ways just yet, but I was afraid—here, try this sweet, something they call nougat—so we rode the bicycles off into the wood and she put her hand into my trousers again and, well, I was younger then, and this time I lay on her, just the way we put our bicycles down in the bushes, with hers down first and mine on top, and that's how we made love, and it was beautiful, and just remember, my boy, if life works out just a tiny bit in your favor it can be beautiful, just beautiful. Ah, but go to bed now, you've got to be up early, my boy. And he took the bottle and drank the whole thing at once, and I heard the water splashing into his stomach like rainwater down a drainpipe and into a cistern, and when he turned onto his side, you could actually hear the water shifting to find its proper level.

I never liked the salesmen who sold food and margarine and kitchen utensils. They would bring their own food with them and eat it in their rooms, and some of them even brought little camp stoves that ran on alcohol, and they'd make potato soup in their rooms and throw the peels under the bed and expect us to polish their shoes for nothing, and then when they were checking out they'd give me a company lapel pin for a tip, and for that I had the privilege of carrying a crate of yeast out to the car for them, because they'd bring the yeast from the wholesaler they represented and then try to sell it on their rounds when the occasion arose. Some of the salesmen had so many suitcases with them, it looked as if they'd brought all the goods they expected to sell that week. Others were practically empty-handed. Whenever I saw a traveling salesman arrive with no suitcases, I was curious to find out exactly what he was selling. It always turned out to be something surprising. For example, one of them took orders for wrapping paper and paper bags, and he carried his samples behind his handkerchief in the breast pocket of his coat. Another one carried only a yo-yo and a top in his briefcase, which never left his side—the order forms were in his pocket—and he'd walk through town playing with the yo-yo or the top and go into a store, still playing with it, and the toy-and-notions merchant would leave the small-goods salesman standing there and walk over as if in a dream and reach out for the yo-yo and the top, or whatever was popular just then, and he'd say, How many dozen, how many gross can you deliver? The salesman would agree to twenty dozen and, if the merchant insisted, add a dozen or so more. Another season it would be a foam-rubber ball, and there'd be a salesman tossing it up and down on the train, on the street, and then in the shops, and the merchant would approach him as if hypnotized, watching the ball go up to the ceiling, back down into his hand, back up, then down, and he'd say, How many dozen, how many gross can you leave me? I never liked these seasonal salesmen, and the maître d' didn't either. They were one-shot men, real warm-water salesmen, and we could see from the moment they set foot in the restaurant that they were the kind who would rather eat their fill and then leave through the window without paying, which happened to us a few times. The nicest salesman who ever stayed with us was the Rubber King, the one who supplied the chemist's shops with those intimate rubber goods that people are ashamed to ask for. He represented the Primeros firm, and he always had some novelty items with him whenever he came. The regulars would invite him to sit at their table, because something would always happen that was unpleasant for one of them but hilarious for the rest, and the salesman would pass around condoms of all colors, shapes, and sizes. Though I was just a busboy, I was surprised and disgusted by our regulars, who seemed so gentlemanly on the street but when they started carrying on at the table they were like kittens, and sometimes as repulsive and ridiculous as monkeys. Whenever the Rubber King was there, they'd slip a Primeros into someone's food—under the dumplings or some such place—and when the victim turned his dumpling over they'd all roar with laughter, knowing that before the month was out the same thing would happen to them. They all loved playing practical jokes on each other, like Mr. Živnostek, who made false teeth and was always dropping loose teeth or dentures into someone's beer. Once he slipped his own teeth into his neighbor's coffee, but the neighbor switched cups on him, and Mr. Živnostek almost choked to death until the vet gave him such a whack on the back that the teeth flew out and dropped under the table. Mr. Živnostek thought they were teeth from his factory and stamped on them, but then realized too late that they were his own custom-made dentures, and then it was the dental technician Mr. Šloser who had the last laugh. He liked doing rush repair jobs because they brought in the most money, which is why his best time of the year was the start of the rabbit-and-pheasant season when the hunters would all get together after the day's shoot and dine on their kill and get so drunk that many of them would break their teeth on the pellets, and Mr. Šloser would have to work day and night to repair them so their wives and families wouldn't find out. But the Rubber King had other things with him as well. One day he brought in what he called the Widow's Consolation, though I never did find out what it was, because he kept it in what looked like a clarinet case. As the Widow's Consolation was passed around the table each of them would open it a crack, hoot with laughter, and then snap it shut and quickly pass it on, and even though I was serving them beer, I never found out what it was that consoled widows. Once the Rubber King brought an artificial woman made of rubber. It was winter, and the regulars were sitting in the kitchen instead of in the billiards room or by the window, where they sat in summer, divided off from the rest of the room by a curtain, and the Rubber King made a kind of speech to the dummy, and they all laughed, but I didn't find it funny at all. Everyone at the table got to hold the dummy, but as soon as anyone had it in his hands, he'd suddenly turn serious and blush and quickly pass it on to the one next to him, and the Rubber King lectured them as if they were schoolboys: This, gentlemen, is the very latest thing, a sexual object to take to bed with you, a puppet made of rubber. Her name is Primavera, and you can have your way with her, she's practically alive, and she's approximately the size of a fully grown young woman. She's exciting, close-fitting and warm and sexy, and there are a million men out there just dying for her, dying to blow her up with their own mouths. This woman, the creature of your own breath, will restore your faith in yourselves and make you potent again and give you longer erections and superb satisfaction. Primavera, gentlemen, is made of special rubber, and between her legs is the queen of rubbers, foam rubber, and her orifice is provided with all the tucks and turns a woman should have. A tiny battery-operated vibrator activates it with a gentle stimulating pulsation so the female organ has a natural action of its own, and everyone can attain climax as he desires, and every man is the master of the situation. To avoid the inconvenience of cleaning out the orifice, you may use a Primeros condom, which comes with a tube of glycerine cream to prevent chafing. Everyone around the table wore himself out blowing up Primavera, and when it was passed on to the next man, the Rubber King would pull out the little plug and the air would go out of her, so that each man would have to blow it up himself and feel her swell under his hands with the breath from his own lungs, while the others clapped and laughed, eager for their turn, and there was great hilarity in the kitchen, and the cashier fidgeted and crossed and recrossed her legs and got very restless, as though each time they blew the dummy up they were inflating and deflating her. They fooled around like that until midnight.

Another salesman showed up with something similar, but it was more beautiful and more practical. He represented a tailoring firm from Pardubice, and our maître d', who was always pressed for time, knew about him through an old army connection because he'd been orderly to a lieutenant colonel who recommended this salesman to him. The salesman would stay at the hotel twice a year, and I saw what he did but couldn't make any sense of it, because first he'd measure the maître d' for trousers, then he'd have him stand there just as he was, in his vest and white shirt, and he'd place strips of parchment on his chest and back and around his waist and then write measurements on them and cut them to shape while they were still on the maître d', as though he were making him a coat directly from the strips, except that he had no cloth with him. Then the salesman would number the strips of parchment and carefully put them in a bag and seal the bag and write the maître d's birthdate on the outside along with his name and surname, and he took a deposit and said that all the maître d' had to do now was wait for the finished jacket to arrive C.O.D. He wouldn't have to go for a fitting, which was why he'd had this company tailor his coat in the first place, because the maître d' was a busy man. It wasn't until later that I heard what I'd wanted to know at the time but was too shy to ask: What happens next? The salesman answered it himself, in fact, because as he was cramming the deposit money into an overstuffed wallet, he said quietly to the maître d': You know, this is a revolutionary technique my boss invented, the first in the republic, maybe even in Europe and the whole world, and it's for officers and actors and the kind of person who doesn't have a lot of time on his hands, like yourself, sir. I just measure them and send the measurements to the workshop, where they take those strips and sew them together on a kind of tailor's dummy with a rubber bladder inside it that's gradually pumped up until the parchment strips are filled out, and then they're covered with fast-drying glue so they harden in the shape of your torso. When they remove the bladder, your torso floats up to the ceiling of the room, permanently inflated, and they tie a cord to it, the way they do to babies in the maternity wards so they won't get mixed up, or the way they tag the toes of corpses in the morgues of the big Prague hospitals. Then when your turn comes, they pull your torso down and try the dresses, the uniforms, the suit coats, or whatever's been ordered, on those mannequins, and they sew and refit, sew and refit, unstitching the seams and sewing them again, without a single live fitting. Since it's all done on this inflated stand-in, of course the coat fits like a glove, and we can mail it out postage-free or C.O.D. with confidence, and it always fits, unless the client gains or loses weight. If that happens, the salesman can simply come again and measure how much you've lost or gained, and then the mannequin is taken in or let out at the appropriate places, and the clothes are altered accordingly, or a new coat or tunic is made. And a client's mannequin is up there among several hundred colorful torsos, until he dies. You can find what you're looking for by rank and profession, because the firm has divided everything into sections—for generals and lieutenant colonels and colonels and captains and lieutenants and headwaiters and anyone who wears formal dress—and all you have to do is come and pull on the right string and the mannequin comes down like a child's balloon and you can see exactly how someone looked when he last had a jacket or a tuxedo made to measure or altered. All this made me long for a new tuxedo made by that company, and I was determined to buy one as soon as I got my waiter's papers, so that I and my mannequin could float near the ceiling of a company that was certainly the only one of its kind in the world, since no one but a Czech could have come up with an idea like that. After that I often dreamed about how I personally, not my torso, was floating up there by the ceiling of the Pardubice tailoring firm, and sometimes I felt as though I were floating near the ceiling of the Golden City of Prague restaurant.

Once, around midnight, I took some mineral water up to the salesman from van Berkel's who sold us that pharmacy scale and the machine that sliced Hungarian salami so thin, and I went in without knocking. There he was, sitting on the carpet in his pajamas as he always did after eating his fill. He was sitting there on his haunches and at first I thought he was playing solitaire or telling his fortune with a deck of cards, but he was smiling blissfully like a little child and slowly laying down hundred-crown notes side by side on the carpet, and he had half the carpet covered and it still wasn't enough, because he pulled another packet of banknotes from his briefcase and laid them out neatly in a row, as precisely as if he'd had lines or columns drawn on the carpet. When he finished a row, and the rows were as exact as a bee's honeycomb, he looked gleefully at the money, he even clapped his pudgy hands together and stroked his cheeks and held his face in his hands, reveling like a child in those banknotes, and he went on dealing them on the floor, and if a note was the wrong side up or upside down, he turned it so it was like all the others. I stood still, afraid just to cough and leave. He had a fortune there in those notes, like identical tiles, and his enormous delight opened my eyes to what was possible.

Although I was just as fond of money, I had never thought of this before, and I saw a picture of myself putting all the money I earned, not into hundred-crown notes just yet, but into twenties, and then laying my twenties out just like that, and I loved watching this fat, childish man in his striped pajamas, knowing that one day I too would shut myself away like this and lay out on the floor a joyful image of my power and my talent. And once I surprised the poet Tonda Jódl that way. He lived in the hotel, and fortunately he could also paint, because instead of giving him a bill the boss would take a painting. Jódl put out a small book of poems in our town, called *The Life of Jesus Christ,* which he published privately. He took the whole edition to his room and laid the copies out side by side on the floor, and *The Life of Jesus Christ* made him so nervous he kept taking his coat off and putting it on again, and he covered the whole room like that with the little white books and still had some left over, so he continued along the corridor, laying those volumes down almost to the stairway. Then he took his coat off once more and a while later put it on again. Or, if he was sweating, he'd just throw it over his shoulders, but when the cold got to him he'd put his arms back in the sleeves, and pretty soon he'd be so warm that he'd take it off again, and cotton balls kept falling out of his ears, and he'd take them out or stick them back in again, depending on how much he wanted to hear the world around him. He preached a return to the simple country life and he never painted anything but country cottages from the Krkonoše region, and he claimed that the role of the poet was to seek the New Man. Our guests didn't like him, or rather they did, but that didn't stop

33

them from playing practical jokes on him all the time. It wasn't just that he was always taking his coat off and putting it on again in the restaurant, he'd also take off his galoshes and put them on, depending on his mood, which would change every five minutes because of this search for the New Man, and when he'd taken them off, the guests would pour beer or coffee into them, and then they'd all watch the poet out of the corner of their eyes, missing their mouths with forks full of food while he put his galoshes back on, and the coffee or the beer would slosh out, and he would thunder for all the restaurant to hear: You evil, stupid, and criminal sons of man! What you need is the simple life! His eyes would fill with tears, not tears of anger but of happiness, because he saw the beer in his galoshes as a gesture, proof that the town recognized him, and if it didn't exactly honor him, at least it considered him one of its own. The worst was when they nailed his galoshes to the floor. The poet would slip into them and then try to walk back to his table, and almost fall over. Sometimes the galoshes were nailed down so hard that he'd actually fall on his hands, and then he'd rant at the customers again and call them evil, stupid, and criminal sons of man, but then he'd forgive them right away and offer them a small drawing or a book of poems, which he got them to pay for on the spot so he'd have enough to get by on. Basically he wasn't bad. As a matter of fact he hung over the whole town in a way, and I often dreamed that just like the angel over the chemist's shop at the White Angel the poet would float above the town, waving his wings, and he had wings, I saw them myself, but I was afraid to ask the priest about it. When he took his coat off and put it on, and his beautiful face was bent over a quarto of paper, because he liked to write poems at our tables, and when he turned his head a certain way, I could see his angelic profile and a halo floating above his head, a little violet circle of flame like the flame on a Primus stove, as if he had kerosene inside his head and that circle glowing and sizzling above it, the kind you find in stallkeepers' lamps. And when he walked around the town square, Tonda Jódl the poet would carry his umbrella as no one else could, and no one could wear a topcoat tossed over his shoulders quite as casually as he, or wear a floppy fedora the way he could, even though he had white balls of cotton sprouting from his ears, and before he even crossed the square he'd have taken his coat off his shoulders and put it back on again five times, and have doffed his hat ten times. It was as though he was paying his respects to someone, yet he never actually greeted anyone except the old women in the marketplace, the stallkeepers, to whom he would always bow deeply, for these were his people as he searched for the New Man. When it was damp and cold or when it rained, he would order a mug of tripe soup and a roll and take it across the square to those frail old women, and as he carried it he seemed to be carrying more than just soup, because in that mug, as least that's how I saw it, he was taking those old women a piece of his heart, a human heart in tripe soup, or sliced and fried up with onions and paprika, the way a priest would carry the monstrance or the host to the last rites, with tears in his eyes at the thought of how kind he was to bring the old women soup.

Back then, when he was spreading copies of his new book on the floor and out into the corridor, the cleaning woman tramped over the white covers of *The Life of Jesus Christ* as she was carrying a bucket of water to the toilets. But Tonda Jódl didn't shout at her, You evil, stupid, and criminal daughter of man. He left each of her footprints just the way it was, almost like a boy's shoeprint, and he signed those copies and sold *The Life of Jesus Christ* with the imprint of a sole for twelve crowns instead of ten. But because the book was printed at his own expense, there were only two hundred copies, so he arranged for a Catholic house in Prague to publish ten thousand copies, and for days on end he would work on his calculations, taking off his coat and putting it on again, falling down three times when they nailed his galoshes to the floor. And there's something else I forgot to mention. Every five minutes he'd pour some medicine into himself, so he was always spattered with powdered medicine like a miller when a bag of flour rips open and spills over the lapels and knees of his black suit. One of the medicines, Neurastenin it was called, he drank straight from the bottle, so he had a kind of yellow ring around his mouth, as though he chewed tobacco. Those medicines he poured down his throat were what caused him every five minutes to feel hot enough to sweat and then cold enough to shiver so violently the whole table would shake. And so the hotel carpenter measured the area covered by *The Life of Jesus Christ* in the room and the corridor, and then Tonda Jódl worked it out that when the ten thousand copies were published, there'd be so many books that if you put them on the ground you could pave the road from Čáslav to Heřmanův Městec, or there'd be enough to cover the entire town square and all the adjacent streets in the historic part of our town, or if you laid them end to end they could form a strip, a white line down the middle of the road all the way from Čáslav to Jihlava. He got to me with those books. Whenever I walked over the cobblestones of our town, I felt that I was walking on them, and I knew that it must be wonderful to see your own name printed on every cobblestone. Tonda Jódl went into debt over those ten thousand copies of *The Life of Jesus Christ*, with the result that Mrs. Kadavá, who owned the printing shop, came and confiscated them, and two porters carried them away in laundry hampers while Mrs. Kadavá said or, rather, shouted, *Jesus Christ* will be in my printshop, and for eight crowns you can have one *Jesus Christ* any time you want. And Tonda Jódl took his coat off and took a swig of Neurastenin and thundered, Thou evil, stupid, and criminal daughter of man.

I coughed, but Mr. Walden lay on the floor beside a whole carpet of green hundred-crown notes. Lying stretched out with one fat arm under his head like a pillow, he gazed across the field of money. I went back out, closed the door, and knocked. Mr. Walden asked, Who is it? I replied, It's me, the busboy, I'm bringing you your mineral water. Come in, he said, and I entered. He was still lying on his back, and his head was resting in his hand, and his hair, curly and full of brilliantine, sparkled almost like the diamonds on his other hand, and he was all smiles again and said, Give me one and park yourself for a bit. I took a bottle opener from my pocket and removed the crown cap, and mineral water fizzed away quietly. Mr. Walden drank, and between sips he pointed to the bills and talked, as quietly and pleasantly as the mineral water, I know you've already been here, but I let you have an eyeful. Just remember, money opens up the whole world to you. That's what old Koreff taught me when I was an apprentice there, and what you see here on the carpet I made in a week. I sold ten sets of scales, and that's my commission. Have you ever seen anything prettier? When I get home I'll spread it out like this all over the apartment, my wife and I will spread it out on the tables and on the floor, and I'll buy salami, cut it up into chunks, and eat it all evening and I won't leave a thing for the next day, because I'd just wake up in the middle of the night and polish it off anyway. I'm crazy about salami, a whole salami at a time, and someday I'll tell you why, when I come again. Then he got up, patted my head, put his hand under my chin, looked into my eyes, and said, You're going to make good someday, remember that. You've got it in you, I can tell. You just have to know how to grab the handle. But how? I asked. And he replied, I saw you selling frankfurters at the station, and I'm one of the ones who gave you a twenty and you took so long making change the train pulled away before you could give it back. And now, said Mr. Walden—and he opened the window and took a handful of change from his trouser pocket, threw it down into the empty square, and waited, with a finger up, so I'd listen to the coins jingle and clatter across the cobblestones—now, he went on, if you can throw small change out the window like that, the C-notes will come waltzing in through the door, you see? And the wind rose and a breeze swirled into the room through the window and, as if on command, all the notes came alive, rose up, danced about, and were swept into the corner of the room like autumn leaves.

I looked at Mr. Walden the way I looked at all salesmen,

because whenever I looked at them enough, I'd find myself wondering what kind of underwear they had on, and what kind of shirts they wore. And I'd imagine that they all had dirty underpants with yellow crotches, and dirty shirt collars and filthy socks, and that if they hadn't been staying with us they'd have thrown those socks and underwear and shirts out the window, the way they used to in the Charles Baths, where I was sent to live for three years with my grandmother. My grandmother had a little room in the old mill, almost like a closet, where the sun never shone and where it couldn't have shone anyway, because the window looked north and besides it was right next to the mill wheel, which was so big that it entered the water at the first-floor level and reached the third floor at the top of its arc. My grandmother took me in because my mother had me when she was single and turned me over to her mother, that is, my grandmother, who lived right next to the baths. This little room that she sublet in the mill was her entire fortune in life and she praised the Lord for hearing her prayer and giving her this little room next to the baths, because when Thursday and Friday came around and the traveling salesmen and people with no fixed address came for a bath, my grandmother would be on the alert from ten in the morning on. I looked forward to those days, and to the other days as well, although underwear didn't come flying out of the bathhouse windows as often then. As we watched out of our window, every once in a while one of the traveling salesmen would fling his dirty underpants out of the window, they would hover for a moment in the air, displaying themselves, then continue their fall. Some of them fell into the water, and Grandma would have to lean down and fish them out with a hook and I had to hang on to her legs to keep her from falling out. Sometimes shirts that got thrown out would suddenly spread their arms like a traffic cop at an intersection, or like Christ, and the shirts would be crucified in midair for a moment, and then plunge headlong onto the rim or blades of the mill wheel. The wheel would keep turning, and the adventure of it was, depending on the situation, either to leave the shirt or the underwear on the wheel until the wheel brought it around again on its rim, around and up to Grandma's window, when all she had to do was reach out and pick it off, or to use a hook to unwind it from the axle. In this case it would be flopping about as the wheel turned, but Grandma would manage to rescue it even so, pulling it through the window into the kitchen on her hook. She'd toss it all into tubs, and that evening she'd wash the dirty underwear and shirts and socks, then throw the water right back into the millrace as it surged under the paddle of the mill wheel. Later in the evening, it was wonderful to see white underwear suddenly fly out of the bathroom window in the Charles Baths and flutter down through the darkness, a white shirt against the black abyss of the current, flashing for an instant outside our window, and Grandma would hook it right out of the air before it could float down into the depths to land on the gleaming wet blades. Sometimes, in the evening or at night, a breeze would blow up from the water, bringing a fine mist with it, and the water and the rain would whip Grandma's face so hard that she would have to wrestle the wind for possession of the shirt. Still, Grandma looked forward to each day, and especially Thursdays and Fridays, when the traveling salesmen changed their shirts and underwear because they'd made some money and bought new socks, underwear, and shirts, and then tossed the old ones out the window of the Charles Baths, where Grandma was lying in wait with her hook. Then she'd wash them, mend them, put them neatly in the sideboard, and eventually take them around to the building sites, to sell them to the masons and the day laborers. She lived modestly but well enough to be able to buy rolls for the two of us, and milk for her coffee. It was probably the most wonderful time in my life. I can still see Grandma waiting at night by the open window, which wasn't easy in the fall and winter, and I can still see that rejected shirt caught in an updraft, hovering for a moment outside our window and spreading its arms. Grandma deftly pulled it in, because in another second the shirt would fall akimbo, like a white bird shot out of the sky, down into the black gurgling waters, to reappear like a tortured thing on the rack of the mill wheel, without a human body inside it, rising in a wet arc and then coming back down the other side, and slip off the wheel and fall into the rushing black waters, to be swept down the millrace under the black blades and far away from the mill.

Hotel
Tichota

◆◆◆◆◆◆◆◆◆◆◆◆◆

I bought a new vulcanite suitcase and into the suitcase I folded away the new tuxedo made to measure for me by the tailor from Pardubice. The salesman had certainly been telling the truth. He had measured my chest, wrapped strips of parchment around me, jotted everything down, put it all into an envelope, and taken my deposit. When I went to pick up the suit in Pardubice, it fit like a glove, but what I really wanted to know was where my inflated figurine, my torso, was. The boss of the place was as short as I was, and seemed to understand that I wanted to be taller, and how important being up there among the other torsos near the storeroom ceiling was for me, so he took me there to see it. It was a magnificent sight. Up near the ceiling hung the torsos of generals and regimental commanders and famous actors. Hans Albers himself had his suits made here, so he was up there too. A draft from an open window made the torsos move about like little fleecy clouds in an autumn wind. A thin thread bearing a name tag dangled down from every torso, and the tags danced gaily in the breeze, like fish on a line. The boss pointed at a tag with my name and address on it, so I pulled it down. It looked so small, my torso. I almost wept to see a major general's torso beside mine, and Mr. Beránek the hotelkeeper's, but when I thought of the company I was in I laughed and felt better. The boss pulled on another string and said, I'm making a suit for this one here, the Minister of Education, and the smaller one here is the Minister of National Defense. I got such a lift from all this, I gave him two hundred crowns extra, a small gesture from a small waiter who was leaving the Golden Prague Hotel and going to work in the Hotel Tichota, somewhere in Strančice, where the salesman from the third-largest firm in the world, van Berkel's, had recommended me. I said my farewells and set off for Prague.

When I got out at Strančice with my suitcase, it was afternoon and still pouring rain. It must have been raining for several days, because the road was covered with sand and mud, and a brimming torrent the color of café au lait had flattened the nettles and oraches and burdocks beside the road, and I trudged up the hill through the mud, following the arrows that said Hotel Tichota. As I was walking past several large houses with trees in front of them broken by the storm, in one of the gardens some people were tying up a tree that was split down the middle. It was loaded with ripening apricots, and the owner, a bald fellow, was trying to tie the crown of the tree back up with a wire while two women, one on each side, were holding it steady for him. But a sudden gust of wind snapped the wire, the women lost their grip, and the crown split apart again and toppled over on the man, knocking him off his ladder and pinning him to the ground in a cage of branches where he lay with his head scratched and bleeding from the sharp twigs. I was standing by the fence. When the women saw their man so tangled up in the branches that he seemed nailed to the ground, crucified by the thick limbs, they burst into gales of laughter. The man's eyes blazed and he shouted, You goddamn whores, you bitches, just wait till I get out of here, I'll pound you into the ground like pegs. The women may have been his daughters, or his wife and daughter, so I doffed my hat and said, Excuse me, is this the way to the Hotel Tichota? The man told me to go to hell, then he thrashed about but couldn't get up, and it was beautiful, him trapped under a canopy of ripe apricots and the two women laughing their heads off. Finally they lifted the tree so the man could get up, and he struggled to his knees and then to his feet. The first thing he did was set his beret, the kind with the little stem on top, squarely on his bald head, so I thought it best to walk on up the road, which was an asphalt road with a gutter made of square granite cobblestones. I kicked the mud and yellow clay off my shoes, and as I came up to the top of the hill, my feet were slipping and sliding. Once I stumbled and fell on my knees, and the dark clouds blew over and the sky turned as blue as the chicory blossoms flattened by the water rushing down the ditch. Then, at the top of the hill, I saw the hotel.

It was beautiful, straight out of a fairy tale, or from

China, or the kind of villa a moneybags might build in the Tyrol or on the Riviera. It was all white with a roof that rose in waves of red tile and green louvered shutters on all three floors, and each story was narrower than the one below, but the top story resembled a pretty little summerhouse with a tiny structure made of iron shutters on the roof, like an observation post or a weather station with instruments inside and barometers outside. On top of it all, at the very peak, a red weathercock turned in the wind. Every window on every floor had a balcony you walked onto through a set of French doors with louvers, like the ones on the shutters. There wasn't a soul in sight, on the road, in the windows, or on the balconies, it was completely silent, and the only sound in the air was the wind, which smelled so sweet you could almost eat it with a spoon, like ice cream, like invisible meringue. I imagined myself dipping into the air with a bun or a slice of bread, as though it were milk, and nibbling at it. I walked through the gate. The pathways were covered with sand partly washed away by the rain, and the thick grass was cut and stacked in haycocks. As I walked through the pine trees, I caught glimpses of meadows stretching away, and the grass was thick and freshly cut with a scythe. To enter the Hotel Tichota you had to walk over an arching bridge and through a set of glass doors with fancy wrought-iron gates opened back against a white wall. The bridge had white railings on each side, and below it was a rock garden with alpine flowers. I began to wonder if I was in the right place, and, if I was, whether they would hire me, and whether Mr. Walden had arranged everything, whether I, a tiny waiter, would be the right person for Mr. Tichota. Suddenly I was afraid. There was no one anywhere, not a voice to be heard, so I turned, and was running back through the garden when I heard a piercing whistle, so urgent I had to stop. It blew three times as if it were saying, Tut tut tut, then gave a long blast that made me turn around, and a short blast that made me feel a line or a rope was reeling me in, pulling me back to the glass doors. No sooner had I walked through them than I was practically run down by a fat man in a wheelchair who had a whistle stuck in his mouth. As he grabbed the rims of the wheels firmly in both hands, the wheelchair came to a halt so abruptly that he practically shot out of his chair and his black wig, more like a toupee, slid over his forehead, and he had to shove it back in place. I introduced myself to Mr. Tichota and he introduced himself to me. When I told him how Mr. Walden, the salesman who was a big shot with van Berkel's, had recommended me to the Hotel Tichota, Mr. Tichota said he'd been expecting me since morning but had given up hope because of the rainstorm. He said I should go get some rest and then present myself to him in my tuxedo and he'd tell me what he expected of me. I tried not to stare, but I couldn't take my eyes off that huge body in the wheelchair. Everything about him was so fat, like the ad for Michelin tires, but Mr. Tichota, to whom the body belonged, seemed full of good spirits and he whizzed back and forth through the foyer, which had racks of antlers on the walls, as though he were playing in a meadow, and he could maneuver himself in his wheelchair almost better than if he'd been able to walk. Mr. Tichota blew the whistle again, but it sounded different this time, as if in a different key, and a chambermaid in a white apron and black dress ran down the stairs. Mr. Tichota said, Wanda, this is our number-two waiter, take him to his room. Wanda turned around, and I could see each half of her beautiful bottom, and with every step she took, the buttock opposite the leg she was moving forward would plump out. Her hair was combed up and twisted into a black bun on top that made me seem even smaller, so I decided that for this chambermaid I would save my money and make her mine, and garnish her breasts and her bottom with flowers, and the thought of money gave me strength, which I had always felt drain away in the presence of a beautiful woman. Instead of taking me upstairs, she led me out onto a kind of mezzanine and then down some steps into a courtyard and then past the kitchen, where I could see two white chefs' hats, and hear the knives working, and laughter. Then two greasy faces with large eyes swam up to the window, then there was more laughter, which faded as I hurried on, carrying my suitcase as high as I could to make up for my size. My double-soled shoes were no help at all, the only thing that helped was holding my head up to make my neck longer. We walked across the courtyard to a small structure that disappointed me, because in the Golden Prague Hotel I had lived like one of the guests, but here I would be living in a porter's lodge. Wanda showed me the closet, turned on the tap so that water flowed into the sink, and pulled back the bedspread to show me that the bed had been freshly made, then she smiled down at me and left. As she was walking back across the courtyard, I saw through the window that she couldn't take a single step that was not observed, she couldn't even allow herself the pleasure of scratching or picking her nose. Wherever she went, she was on stage, like in a big shopwindow, and I remembered once when I was on my way back to the Golden Prague with the flowers and I saw two girls putting a new display in Katz's shopwindow, tacking some fabric in place with nails. As they worked along on their hands and knees, one behind the other, the one in front used a hammer to nail the cheviot and corduroy down in pleats, and when she ran out of nails she would reach back and take another nail out of the mouth of the girl behind her and tack down another pleat. They seemed to be having fun, and I stood there on the street with a basket of gladioli in my hands and a basket of marguerites on the ground, watching those young window dressers crawling about on their hands and knees. It was noon. The girls must have forgotten where they were, because every so often they would reach back and scratch their behinds, or somewhere down there, and then crawl forward on all fours, right up to the glass, wearing cloth slippers, and they would laugh till the tears came, and then one of them sputtered, the nails popped out of her mouth, and they giggled and snarled at each other in sheer girlish exuberance, like two puppies. Their blouses were loose, and you could see their breasts swinging back and forth as the laughter shook them. By now a crowd had gathered and was staring at those four breasts swinging like bells in a church tower, but when one of them looked up and saw all those people staring at them, she covered her breasts with her arm and blushed. The second girl swam out of her tears of laughter and saw the first one pointing at the crowd in front of Katz's. She was so surprised that as she clapped her arms to her breasts she fell back on her behind and her legs flew apart and you could see the whole works, even though it was covered by lacy modern underwear. People were laughing, but when they saw this they sobered up and some walked away while others stood there staring long after the window dressers had gone to lunch at the Golden City of Prague restaurant and the shop assistant had pulled down the shutters. That's how strongly the beauty of a young girl's body can affect some people.

As I sat down and took off my mud-caked shoes and my trousers and opened my suitcase to hang up my suit, I somehow began to feel homesick for my old hotel, the Golden Prague, and for Paradise's, and I kept seeing a town of stone around me and crowds of people and the teeming square, though all I ever saw of nature in those three years were the flowers I went for every day, the tiny park, and the petals I used to garnish the young ladies at Paradise's. As I took the tuxedo out of my suitcase, I suddenly wondered who my former boss really was. He was even smaller than I was, and he believed in money the way I did, and he had beautiful women for money, and not just at Paradise's. He'd leave his wife and go after them all the way to Bratislava or Brno, and they say that he managed to spend several thousand crowns by the time his wife found him, and that before he set off on his little sprees he would pin enough money into his vest pocket to cover the trip back plus a tip for the conductor to take him home, and since he was so small the conductor would usually carry him home from the station like a child, asleep. The drinking seemed to diminish him, and for a week he'd be as tiny as a sea horse, but when the week was up, he'd get the itch again. I remember he loved to drink heavy wines—ports,

Algerian wines, Málaga—and he drank them all with great seriousness and so slowly he hardly seemed to be drinking, and each sip seemed to make him more handsome, and he'd roll the wine around in his mouth for a while and then gulp it as though he were trying to get down a chunk of apple. After each mouthful, he would quietly declare that the Sahara sun was in that wine. Sometimes he would sit at the table and get drunk with the regulars, and when he nodded off his friends would call his wife down to get him, and she would take the elevator from the fourth floor where they had a whole suite to themselves. She never made a fuss, since it was no discredit to her—on the contrary, everybody respected her. My boss would be lying under the table or sitting in his chair asleep and she would pick him up off the floor by the collar as easily as if he were an empty coat. If he was sitting, she might tip the chair over backward, but just before it hit the floor she would pick him out of it and swing him up through the air as if he were nothing at all, and the boss would usually come to and wave his little hand, as much as he could with his coat pulled so tight around him, and his wife would fling open the elevator door and toss him inside, and he would clatter to the floor, and she would get in and push the button. I could see the boss through the glass door, lying on the elevator floor with his wife standing over him as they went up to the fourth floor together as if ascending into heaven. The regulars told stories about how years ago, when my boss first bought the Golden Prague Hotel, his wife would join them at their table and they used to have a kind of literary salon there. The only one left from those days by the time I got there was Tonda Jódl, the poet and painter.

They'd have discussions and read books, and they even put on plays, but about every two weeks the boss's wife would get into passionate arguments with her husband, and they would disagree so violently about romanticism or realism or Smetana and Janáček that they would start pouring wine over each other and hitting each other. The boss had a cocker spaniel and his wife had a fox terrier, and when the master and mistress started to fight over literature the dogs would start fighting too, until they drew blood. Then the boss and his wife would make up and go for a walk by the creek outside town, with bandages on their faces or slings on their arms, and the battered fox terrier and cocker spaniel would traipse along behind with sticking plaster on their ears, perhaps, and the blood still drying on the wounds. Then everyone would make up, but a month later they'd be at it again. It must have been wonderful, and I wished I had seen it.

So there I was, in front of the mirror in my tuxedo, the new one, and I'd put on a white starched shirt and a white bow tie, and just as I was slipping into my pocket a new nickel-plated bottle opener with a knife blade in the handle, I heard the whistle. When I went out into the courtyard, the shadow of someone jumping the fence passed quickly over me, and I felt something brush my head, and a waiter in a cutaway coat landed in front of me, got up, and rushed on, reeled in by the whistle's signal while the tails of his coat flew out behind him like beetle's wings. When he kicked at the swinging doors, they banged open, then gradually swung to a stop, and the glass in the door reflected a miniature courtyard, then me, approaching, enlarging, and going through the door too. In two weeks I finally figured out who this amazing hotel had been built for. I'd already made several thousand crowns in tips and wages, and that was my spending money. But for two weeks, though I lived alone in this little room counting my money whenever I was off duty, I still felt as though someone always had an eye on me, and Zdeněk, the headwaiter who'd been here for two years, had the same feeling and was always ready to jump over the fence and run to the restaurant whenever the whistle blew, even though there was practically nothing to do all day long. When we'd straightened things up in the restaurant, which didn't take long, and got the glasses and the cutlery ready, and changed the tablecloths and napkins, and checked the supplies, I would go with Zdeněk, who had a key to the cellars, to make sure there was enough cooled champagne and Pilsner export beer, and we took the cognac into the serving room to bring it to room temperature and then went into the garden, which was really a park, put our aprons on, and raked the paths. We were always having to replace the haystacks, because every two weeks the old ones were taken away and bundles of freshly cut grass were brought in, or else we set out ready-made haystacks exactly where the old ones had been, and then we would rake the paths, though as a rule I did that myself while Zdeněk was off in one of the nearby villages visiting his wards, as he called them, but I think they were really his mistresses, either married women who spent the weekdays alone in their summer homes or someone's daughters who'd come out from Prague to study for the state exams. And I would rake the sand and look at our hotel from the rear, through the trees or from the open meadow. In the daytime it looked like a boarding school, and I was always expecting a crowd of young girls to come bursting out of the main entrance, or teenagers carrying book bags, or young men in knit sweaters followed by servants lugging golf clubs, or perhaps an industrialist with a servant who would carry out cane chairs and a table, and maids spreading tablecloths, and then some children running up and wanting to be cuddled by their father, and then a woman with a parasol arriving, slowly peeling off her gloves, and pouring coffee when everyone was seated. But no one ever walked through those doors all day long, and still the chambermaids did the dusting and changed the linen in ten rooms every day, and in the kitchen preparations were always under way for what looked like a wedding reception, with more dishes and courses than I had ever seen let alone heard of, and if I had, then it was only from something the maître d' of the Golden Prague Hotel might have told me when he talked about the time he'd been to sea as a waiter in the first-class section of the *Wilhelmina,* the luxury liner that had gone down. He had missed that sailing and when the liner sank he was on his way across Spain to catch the boat at Gibraltar with a beautiful Swedish woman, who was the reason he'd missed the boat, and from what he told me, the feasts they served in the first-class dining room of the *Wilhelmina* were something like what we served here off the beaten track in the Hotel Tichota.

Even though I had every reason to be satisfied, I was often caught off my guard. For example, I would finish raking the paths and put a deck chair out behind the trees and settle into it to watch the clouds go by—there were always clouds in the sky here—and I'd be dozing off when suddenly the whistle would blow as if the boss were standing right behind me, and I'd have to take a shortcut and undo my apron on the run, leap over the fence the way Zdeněk did, and go straight into the restaurant to report to the boss. He would be sitting there in his wheelchair and as usual something was making him uncomfortable, a rumpled blanket that needed smoothing out, so we would fasten a belt around his waist, like firemen have, with a ring on it. This was the same kind the miller Mr. Radimský's two children used to wear when they played near the millrace with a Saint Bernard who lay on the point of land where the millrace rejoined the river, and whenever Hary or Vintíř—those were their names—toddled toward the millrace, the Saint Bernard would get up, grab the ring in his mouth, and pull Hary or Vintíř back out of danger. That's exactly what we did with the boss. We fastened a rope to the ring and hauled him up with a block and tackle, not all the way to the ceiling but far enough so we could ease the chair out from under him. Then we would straighten his blanket out or give him a new one or an extra one and lower him back into his wheelchair, and he looked ridiculous suspended in the air, angled forward, his whistle dangling straight down from his neck, so you could tell the angle he was hanging at. Afterward he would zip around the dining room again and through the alcoves and rooms, arranging the flowers. Our boss was terribly fond of women's handiwork, so the rooms in the restaurant were more like rooms in a middle-class home or a small château, with curtains everywhere and sprigs of asparagus fern, and freshly cut roses and tulips and whatever happened to be in season. The boss would make beautiful arrangements in vases, he'd push his chair forward to adjust something, then back off and look at it from a distance, not just at the flowers but at how everything fit together, and he always put a pretty doily under each vase. When he had amused himself all morning sprucing up the rooms, he'd start in on the tables. There were usually only two tables, for twelve at the most. Again, as Zdeněk and I silently set the tables with all the different kinds of plates and forks and knives, the boss, full of quiet enthusiasm, would put flowers in the center of the tables and check to make sure there was enough freshly cut asparagus fern for us to put on the table just before the guests sat down. When the boss was satisfied that he'd managed to make the restaurant look not like a restaurant, and to bring into his hotel the charm and grace of a Biedermeier household, he would wheel up to the door our guests would come through, stop for a few seconds with his back to the dining room, concentrate, then whirl his chair around and roll forward into the room, looking at everything through the eyes of a stranger, like a guest who'd never been here before. He'd look about in wonder, he'd wheel himself from room to room, checking all the details with a practiced eye, making sure the curtains hung just right and everything was properly lit, all the lights on—and at that moment the boss was beautiful, as if he'd completely forgotten that he weighed three hundred and fifty pounds and couldn't walk. He'd wheel about and survey it all with a stranger's eyes, then discard those eyes and put his own back in again, rub them, and blow his whistle, and it sounded different again, and I knew that a moment later the two cooks would hurry out of the kitchen to report on the state of the crabs and the oysters and how the stuffing à la Suvaroff had turned out and how the salpicon was this evening. Once, when I'd been there for three days, the boss knocked the chef down with his wheelchair when he found out the chef had put caraway seeds in the *médaillon de veau aux champignons.* Then we'd wake up the porter, a giant of a man who slept all day, and he'd eat everything that was left over from the evening banquets, stupefying amounts of food, great bowls of salad that neither we nor the chambermaids could ever have eaten by ourselves, and drink everything left in the bottles. He was as strong as an ox. He would put on a green apron at night and split wood in the floodlit courtyard, just split wood with melodic blows of his ax, split what he'd cut earlier that evening, split wood all night long. But I soon realized, I could hear it clearly, that he only split wood when someone arrived, and people would come by car, diplomatic cars, groups of them, late in the evening or at night, and the porter split wood that smelled sweet, and you could see him from every window, and our floodlit courtyard with the wood stacked nearly around it made you feel safe, because here was a six-foot-five fellow splitting wood, a man with an ax, who had once nearly killed a thief and beaten three others so badly he himself had to take them to the police station in a wheelbarrow. If any of the cars got a flat tire, the porter would lift up the front or the rear end with his bare hands and hold it there till the tire was changed. But his real job was ornamental wood-splitting in the floodlit courtyard so our guests could see him, just like that waterfall on the Elbe: it would fill up, and they would wait until the guide brought the tourists around and, when he gave the signal, open the sluicegate and the tourists would get a good, long look at a waterfall.

But—to finish the portrait of our boss—I'd be in the garden, leaning against a fence, counting my money, when suddenly I'd hear the whistle, as if the boss were some kind of all-seeing god. Or I'd be with Zdeněk, and as soon as we'd sit down or lie back on a haystack where no one could see us, the whistle would blow, just a single warning blast to keep us working and not lazing about. We began keeping a rake, a hoe, or a pitchfork beside us, and when the whistle blew we'd jump up and start hoeing and raking and carrying forkfuls of loose hay. Then it would get quiet, but we'd no sooner put the pitchfork down than the whistle would blow again. So we took to lying behind the haystack and poking out at something with the rake or the fork, so it looked as if the tools were working by themselves, on invisible strings. Zdeněk told me that when the weather was cool like this the boss was like a fish in water, but during a heat wave he'd practically melt and couldn't go wherever he wanted but had to stay in a room with a lower temperature, in a kind of icebox. Still, he knew everything and saw everything that went on, even things he couldn't see, as if he had spies on every branch in every tree, in the corner of every room, behind every curtain. It's hereditary, Zdeněk told me as he lay back in the deck chair. The boss's father had an inn somewhere below the Krkonoše Mountains and he weighed three-fifty too, and when the weather turned hot he had to move to the basement, where he had a bed and a keg of beer, otherwise he'd have melted like butter in the summer heat. We got up and wandered down a path I'd never walked down before, and we thought about our boss's father moving into the cellar of his village inn for the summer so he wouldn't turn into a pool of butter, and the path took us among three silver spruce trees, and there I stopped and stared in amazement. Zdeněk seemed even more amazed than I was and he grabbed my sleeve and said, Well, I'll be . . . There before us was a tiny house, a kind of gingerbread cottage, just like a stage prop, with a tiny bench in front. The window was as small as a window in the closet of an old farmhouse, and the door was latched like a cellar door, and if we'd tried to go in even I would have had to duck, but the door was locked, so we stopped and stared in the window for five minutes. Then we looked at each other and began to feel almost alarmed, and I felt goose pimples tingling up and down my arms because everything inside this little cottage was an exact replica of one of our hotel rooms, except that everything seemed to be made for children. It had exactly the same table, only in miniature, the same chairs, even the same curtains and flower stand, and there was a doll or a teddy bear on every chair, and two shelves along the walls had all kinds of toys on them, just as in a store, a whole wall full of toys, tiny drums and skipping ropes, all neatly arranged, as if someone had tidied up just before we arrived, set everything up just for us, to startle us or touch us. Suddenly we heard the whistle, not the warning whistle telling us to get to work, to get off our behinds, but a whistle that meant an emergency, so we set off at a run across the meadow and, out of breath, took a shortcut and jumped the fence, one after the other.

Every night the Hotel Tichota was pregnant with expectation. No one came, no car drove up, but the entire hotel was ready to go, like a music box that starts playing when you drop a crown into it, or like a band: the conductor's baton is raised, all the musicians are ready, expectant, but the baton hasn't given the downbeat yet. We weren't allowed to sit down or relax, we had to keep busy, straightening things out or leaning gently against the station table, and even the porter in the spotlit courtyard was waiting, bent at the waist over the chopping block with an ax in one hand and a log in the other, waiting for the sign to set his ax melodically in motion. It was like a shooting gallery with all the springs wound up but no one's there, and then suddenly customers show up and load the pellets into the airguns and hit the target, those figures cut of metal and painted and jointed with pins, and the whole mechanism kicks into motion if someone hits the bull's-eye. It also reminded me of the tale of the Sleeping Beauty where all the characters freeze just as they are when the curse comes over them, but at the touch of the magic wand all the unfinished motions are finished and those about to start, start. That's what happened when a car was heard in the distance. The boss, sitting in his wheelchair by the window, gave a sign with his handkerchief, and Zdeněk dropped a coin into the music box, which began to play "The Harlequin's Millions," and the music box or orchestrion or whatever it was was muffled by eiderdowns and felt panels so it seemed to be playing far away, in another establishment, and the porter, looking tired and bent, as though he'd been splitting wood since noon, let his ax fall. I tossed a napkin over my arm and waited to see who our first guest would be. In walked a general wearing a general's cape with a red lining, and he must have had his uniform made by the same company that made my tuxedo. He seemed despondent. His chauffeur followed him in carrying a golden saber and he set it down on a table and left, while the general walked through the rooms, inspecting everything and rubbing his hands together. Then he stood with his legs apart, put his hands behind his back, and gazed out into the courtyard at our porter, who was splitting wood. Meanwhile Zdeněk had brought a silver wine cooler, and I put oysters and dishes of shrimp and lobster on the table, and when the general sat down, Zdeněk uncorked the champagne, Heinkel Trocken, and poured a glass. The general said, You are my guests as well. Zdeněk bowed and brought two more glasses and filled them, the general stood up, clicked his heels, shouted *Prost!* and drank. We emptied our glasses, but the general took only a sip from his and made a face, shuddered, and spat out, The devil! I can't drink this stuff! Then he took an oyster from the plate, threw his head back, and eagerly swallowed the delicate, slimy flesh sprinkled with lemon juice, and again he seemed to eat with gusto, but no, he shuddered and snorted with disgust, his eyes watering. He downed his glass of champagne and shouted, Aaaaaah, I can't drink this swill! He walked from room to room, and each time he came back he would take a piece of crabmeat or a leaf of lettuce or some salpicon from the plates, and each time he shocked me by shuddering in disgust and spitting out, The devil! This is completely inedible! Then he would come back and hold out his glass for a refill and ask Zdeněk a question, and Zdeněk would bow and tell him about Veuve Cliquot and all about champagne, though he considered what he was offering, Heinkel Trocken, to be the very best, and the general, his interest aroused, would drink again, sputter in disgust, but then he'd drain the glass and walk over to look out into the courtyard, where everything was dark except the floodlit porter and his work and the floodlit walls stacked with pine firewood. Meanwhile the boss wheeled about silently, he'd glide up, bow, and then glide away again, and the general's mood improved, as if his disgust with the food and drink had somehow whetted his appetite. He switched to brandy and drank a whole bottle of Armagnac, and every time he took a drink he would make a face and swear and sputter in Czech, and then in German: *Diesen Schnaps kann man nicht trinken!* It was the same with the French specialties. After every mouthful the general seemed on the point of vomiting and he swore he'd never take another bite or drink another drop, and he would roar at the headwaiter and at me: What is this you're giving me? Are you trying to poison me? Do you want me to die, you swine? But then he'd drink another bottle of Armagnac, and Zdeněk would lecture him on why the best brandy is called Armagnac and not cognac, because cognac comes only from the region called Cognac, and even though the best cognac comes from two kilometers outside the border of Cognac it still has to be called brandy, not cognac. By three in the morning—when the general predicted he wouldn't last because at two o'clock we had killed him by offering him an apple—he had eaten and drunk enough for five men, but still he complained that it wasn't filling him up, that he probably had cancer without knowing it, or stomach ulcers at least, that his liver was shot and he was sure to have kidney stones. It was around three in the morning that he really started to get drunk and he pulled out his service pistol and shot at a glass standing on the windowsill, and the bullet went right through the window, but the boss came gliding up on his rubber wheels, smiling and congratulating him, and asked if the general would like to try for the cut-glass teardrops on the Venetian chandelier and said that the last great feat of marksmanship he'd seen here was when Prince Schwartzenberg tossed a five-crown piece in the air, shot at it with a hunting rifle, and hit it just before it fell to the table. The boss rolled away, fetched a pointer, and pointed to a hole above the fireplace where the bullet had entered the wall after ricocheting off the silver coin. But the general said his specialty was cordial glasses and fired away, and no one got upset about it, and when he shot through the window and the bullet whistled past the porter, who was still bent over his block chopping wood, the porter just gave his ear a good shake with his little finger and went on working. Next the general had Turkish coffee, and he placed his hand over his heart and swore he wasn't supposed to drink this coffee at all, but then he had another cup and announced that if there was a roast capon in the house he'd like to have it before he died. So the boss bowed and whistled and a moment later the chef appeared, looking fresh in his white cap, and brought out the whole roasting pan. When the general saw the capon, he took off his tunic, unbuttoned his shirt and after saying wistfully that he wasn't supposed to eat chicken, took the capon, tore it to pieces, and ate it. After each mouthful he bemoaned the state of his health and said that he wasn't supposed to overeat, that he'd never eaten anything so disgusting. Zdeněk told him that in Spain they drank champagne with chicken, and that some El Córdoba might be nice, and the general nodded, then sipped away and nibbled at the chicken, complaining and making a face at each mouthful of food and drink: *Diesen Pulard auch diesen Champagner kann man nicht essen und trinken.* At four o'clock, after he'd complained his fill, he seemed greatly unburdened, and he asked for the bill. The headwaiter brought it to him with everything itemized and presented it on a small tray in a napkin, but the general made him read out loud how much he'd spent, every item, so Zdeněk read it to him, every item, and the general began to smile, and his smile grew broader and broader until at last he was laughing outright, cackling in delight, and he was quite sober now, he'd even got rid of his cough and seemed to be standing more erect. He spent a while adjusting his shoulders in his tunic and then, looking more handsome than before, his eyes sparkling, he ordered a parcel of food for his chauffeur, paid the boss in thousand-crown notes, rounding it off to the nearest thousand, which seemed to be the custom here, added a thousand for the shooting and the holes in the roof and the window, and asked the boss if that was enough, and the boss nodded that it was. I got a three-hundred-crown tip, then the general threw his cape over his shoulders, red lining out, picked up his golden saber, set a monocle in his eye, and strode out, his riding spurs jangling, and as he walked, he managed to kick the saber neatly out of his way with his boot so he wouldn't trip over it.

Next day the general came back, and he wasn't alone now but with some beautiful young women and a fat poet. This time there was no shooting, but they got into such a terrible argument about literature and trends in poetry that they were spitting into one another's faces. I was sure the general was going to shoot the poet, but eventually they settled down and began arguing about a woman writer, and they kept saying she didn't know her vagina from an inkwell, and anyone who wanted to could dip his pen in her ink. Then for almost two hours they gossiped about another writer and the general said that if the fellow would treat his own texts the way he treated other people's vaginas it would be a good thing both for the writer and for Czech literature. But the poet disagreed and said the man was a real writer and that if Shakespeare was the greatest creator next to God Himself then this writer they were talking about was right up there with Shakespeare. As soon as they arrived they made the boss send for some musicians, and a band played for them nonstop while they and the girls drank formidable amounts. The general cursed every mouthful of food and drink, and he smoked a lot, and whenever he lit up he would have a coughing fit, take the cigarette out of his mouth, look at it, and shout, What kind of rubbish are they putting in these Egyptian fags anyway? But he went on smoking and his cigarette glowed in the gloom while the musicians played and drank. Another remarkable thing was that the two guests had the girls sitting on their knees while this was going on, and every once in a while they would retire to a room upstairs and come back fifteen minutes later roaring with laughter. Only each time the general went upstairs, he would slip his hand between the girl's thighs as she walked up ahead of him and mutter, No, sir, I'm getting too old for love, and then he'd say, You call these real women? But he'd mount the stairs anyway and come back fifteen minutes later, and I could see how satisfied and in love the girl was and that she'd been given the same treatment as those two bottles of Armagnac the day before and the Heinkel Trocken and El Córdoba. Then they'd carry on about the death of poetism and the new trend called Surrealism, which was entering its second phase, and about committed art and pure art, and by this time they were shouting at each other again. Midnight went by, and the girls couldn't seem to get enough champagne and food, they were so ravenous. Then the musicians said it was over, they couldn't play anymore and had to go home, so the poet took a pair of scissors and snipped a gold medal off the general's tunic and tossed it to the musicians, who were gypsies or Hungarians, and so they played some more. Again the general went off with one of the girls, said on the stairs he was all washed up as a man, and fifteen minutes later came back, then the poet went up with the general's first girl, but before that the musicians started packing up to go home, so the poet took the scissors and cut two more medals off and threw them on a tray for the musicians, and the general took the scissors and cut the rest of his own medals off and threw them on the tray with the others, just for those beautiful young women. We said it was the most audacious thing we'd ever seen, and Zdeněk whispered to me that the medals were the highest English, French, and Russian decorations from the First World War. Now the general took off his tunic and began to dance, and he scolded the girl and told her to take it easy with him, because his lungs and his ticker weren't what they used to be, and he asked the gypsies for a czardas, and the gypsies started to play and the general started to dance. After he'd coughed and cleared his throat, he began to dance in earnest, and the girl had to dance faster, and the general let go of her and raised one arm up and let the other one drag along the floor like a rooster, and he danced faster and faster and seemed to grow younger and the girl couldn't keep up now but the general didn't slow down and he was dancing and kissing her on the throat at the same time and the musicians formed a circle around the dancers and you could see admiration and understanding in their eyes, you could see that the general was dancing for them and they were all joined together by the music, and they played faster or slower according to the dance and the powers of the general, but he was still ahead of his partner, who was flushing red and gasping for breath, and the fat poet and the girl he'd been in the room with were standing above them, leaning on the balustrade. Then the poet took her in his arms, and the first rays of dawn appeared, and the poet carried the beautiful girl down the stairs, past the czardas dancers and through the open doorway, and he held out this half-naked, drunk girl with a torn blouse as an offering to the rising sun.

In the early morning, as the trains were taking the workers to work, the general's automobile pulled up, a low, open six-seater Hispano-Suiza with leather-upholstered seats, and they settled the bill and the poet paid out the entire proceeds from his new book, ten thousand copies, like Tonda Jódl's *The Life of Jesus Christ*, but he paid gladly and said it was nothing, he would ask for another advance right away and go to Paris and write a better book than the one they had just drunk away. The general was bundled into the back seat, in his white shirt with the sleeves rolled up and the buttons undone, and fell asleep between the girls, while the poet sat in front, a red rose stuck in his lapel. In his lap, holding the general's golden saber and leaning her elbows on the windshield, sat the beautiful dancer, wearing the general's tunic, unbuttoned, its medals cut off, and the general's cap stuck on top of her long flowing hair. She sat so erect, with those two enormous breasts, Zdeněk said she looked like the statue of the Marseillaise. The group drove down to the station, and as the workers were catching the train, the general's car drove past the platform toward Prague, and the girl with her breasts hanging out pulled the saber from its scabbard and cried, On to Prague! And so they arrived in Prague and, the way we heard it later, it must have been a wonderful sight, the general and the poet and the girls, especially the one with her blouse ripped and her two breasts thrusting forward and the sword unsheathed, driving down Příkopy and Národní Třida while policemen saluted and the general slumped in the back seat of the Hispano-Suiza sound asleep.

Here, in the Hotel Tichota, I also learned that the ones who invented the notion that work is ennobling were the same ones who drank and ate all night long with beautiful women on their knees, the rich ones, who could be as happy as little children. I always used to think that the rich were damned, that country cottages and cozy little parlors and sour soup and potatoes were what gave people a feeling of happiness and well-being, and that wealth was evil. Now it seemed that all that stuff about happiness in poor country cottages was invented by these guests of ours, who didn't care how much they spent in a night, who threw money to the four winds and felt good doing it. I had never seen men so happy as those wealthy industrialists and factory owners and, as I said, they knew how to carouse and enjoy life like naughty little boys, and they had so much time on their hands that they would even play tricks and practical jokes on one another, and then, right in the midst of all the fun, one of them would ask another if he could use a wagonload or two of Hungarian hogs, or perhaps a whole trainload? Or another would be watching our porter chop wood, and all these rich fellows thought the porter must be the happiest man in the world, and they would gaze wistfully at him doing work they had never done themselves, but if they'd had to chop wood, they would have been miserable. Suddenly one of them would say, I've got a boatload of cowhide from the Congo sitting in Hamburg, any ideas about what I might do with it? And the other one would say, as if it wasn't a boatload but a single hide, What percentage will you give me? The first one would say, Five, and the second would say, I want eight, there's always the chance of worms because the niggers do such a bad job salting them. The first one would hold out his hand and say, Seven. Then they'd look each other straight in the eye for a few moments, shake hands, and then go back to the girls, to place those same hands on naked breasts and slide them down to fondle those neat little mounds of hair under their bellies, and kiss them with open mouths as if they were eating oysters or sucking boiled snails from their shells, because from the moment they'd bought or sold trainloads of pigs and shiploads of hides they seemed twice as young. Some of our guests would buy and sell whole apartment complexes, and at one point a castle and two châteaux changed hands, and a factory was bought and sold, and company directors would arrange shipments of envelopes to the rest of Europe, and negotiate loans to the tune of half a billion crowns for someplace in the Balkans, and two trainloads of munitions were sold, and arrangements were made to deliver enough weapons to arm several Arab divisions. It was always done the same way, with champagne, women, and French brandy, and a view of the courtyard where the floodlit porter was chopping wood, or during moonlit walks or games of tag and blindman's bluff ending up in the haystacks the boss had put out as part of the landscaping, as ornamentation, like the wood-chopping porter, and then at the first light of dawn they would come back to the hotel, their hair and their clothes matted with straw and dried grass, as happy as if they'd just come from the theater. Then they would hand out hundred-crown notes to the musicians and me, fistfuls of them, with significant looks as if to say, You didn't see or hear a thing, did you? though of course we'd seen and heard everything, and the boss would bow from his wheelchair, he'd been gliding silently from room to room on his rubber tires, making sure that everything was just so and every whim was satisfied. Our boss thought of everything. If someone felt a sudden urge for a cup of fresh milk or cool cream toward evening, that was available too, and we even had special devices for vomiting in our tiled washrooms, an individual vomitorium with strong chrome-plated handgrips on each side, and a collective vomitorium that looked like a long horse trough with a handrail above it, a bar guests would hold on to while they vomited in a group, egging one another on. I was ashamed whenever I vomited, even if no one saw me, but rich people vomited as if it was all part of the banquet, a sign of good breeding. When they were through, they'd come back, their eyes full of tears, and soon they'd be eating and drinking with more zest than ever, like the ancient Slavs.

Zdeněk was an honest-to-goodness headwaiter. He'd apprenticed in Prague, at the Black Eagle, under an old maître d' who'd been a personal waiter in a special aristocrats' casino where the Archduke d'Este himself was a regular. When Zdeněk was waiting on tables, he'd work in a kind of creative fever, and he always behaved just like one of the guests, and was usually treated like one of them too, and he had a glass at every table that he'd only take the occasional sip from, but he'd always drink to everyone's health and keep moving among the tables, bringing food. There was something dreamlike about the way he did it, with a kind of swirling movement, so that if anyone had got in his way there would have been a terrible collision, but he always moved gracefully and elegantly, and he would never sit down in odd moments, he'd just stand there, and he always knew what someone wanted and brought it even before the guest asked for it. I sometimes went drinking with Zdeněk. He had an aristocratic habit of spending practically everything he earned, and now and then he would treat himself the way our guests did, but he'd always have so much money left over that toward morning, when we came back by taxi, he'd arouse the innkeeper of the emptiest inn in the village and order him to go wake up some musicians to play for him. Then Zdeněk would go from door to door and invite the sleepers to come down to the inn and drink his health, and then the music played and there was dancing till dawn, and when they'd drained the innkeeper's bottles and barrels dry, Zdeněk would wake up the owner of the grocery store, buy a whole basketful of jars, and pass them out as gifts to all the old women and men. He paid not only for everything they drank in the pub, but for all the jams and jellies and everything he'd given away. Then, when he'd finally spent everything, he'd laugh and was satisfied. At that point, his favorite trick was to pat his pockets looking for matches, then he'd borrow twenty hellers from someone, buy matches, and light his cigarette. This was the same Zdeněk who liked to ignite rolled-up ten-crown notes at the pub stove and light his cigars with them. Then we'd drive off with the musicians still playing for us, and if there was time, Zdeněk would buy up all the flowers in the flower shop and scatter carnations, roses, and chrysanthemums. The musicians would follow us to the edge of the village, and the automobile, garlanded with flowers, would take us back to the Hotel Tichota, because that day, or rather that night, was our day off.

Once, when a guest was announced in advance, the boss was especially fussy. Ten times, twenty times, he made the rounds of the hotel in his wheelchair, and each time he found something that wasn't quite right. We were expecting a party of three, so the table was set for three, and although only two showed up, all night long we served the third person too, as if he'd be arriving at any moment, as if the invisible guest was actually sitting there, walking about, strolling through the garden, swinging on the swing, and so on. First a big fancy car brought a lady whose chauffeur spoke to her in French, as did Zdeněk. Then, at about nine in the evening, another big fancy car pulled up, and out stepped the President himself, I recognized him immediately, and the boss called him Your Excellency. The President dined with the beautiful Frenchwoman, who had come to Prague by plane. He seemed to change completely and look younger somehow, and he laughed and talked a lot and drank champagne and then brandy. As his mood became more animated, they moved to a little room with Biedermeier furniture and flowers, and the President sat the beautiful woman beside him and kissed her hand, and then her shoulders and her arms, which were bare because of the kind of gown she was wearing. They were having a lively conversation about literature when suddenly the President whispered something in the woman's ear and she shrieked with laughter, and the President laughed too and slapped his knee. Then he poured some more champagne, and they held their glasses out to each other by the stems, and they clinked them together and looked deep into each other's eyes and drank slowly. Then the woman gently pushed the President back against the armrest and kissed him herself, a long, slow kiss, and the President closed his eyes, and she ran her hands down his sides, and he caressed her as well, and I could see his diamond ring sparkling as it moved over her thighs. Then it was as though he had suddenly woken up, and he was leaning over her and looking into her eyes, and he kissed her, and for a while both of them were motionless in an embrace. When the embrace was over, the President took a deep breath and sighed, and the lady let her breath out, and a strand of hair came loose and fell across her forehead. They stood up, holding both hands like children when they want to dance ring-around-the-rosy, and suddenly they ran to the door and went outside, and hopped and skipped down the path hand in hand, and we could hear the President's clear, hearty laughter. He was so different from his portrait on postage stamps or in public places, and I had always thought that a president didn't do things like this, that it wasn't right for a president to do things like this, and yet here he was, just like the other rich people, running through the moondrenched garden where that same afternoon we had put out fresh mounds of dry hay. I could see the woman's white gown, and the white starched dickey of the President's tuxedo, and his porcelain-white cuffs drawing lines in the air, flitting here and there through the night, from haystack to haystack, as the President ran ahead of the white gown and then turned and caught it and lifted it up easily. And I saw the white cuffs lift the white dress and carry it, and they were strong enough for that, those cuffs that gathered up the white gown as though they had just fished it out of the river, or like a mother carrying a child in a white nightshirt to bed, that's how the President carried the beautiful woman into the depths of our garden, under the century-old trees. Then he ran out with her again and set her down on a pile of hay, but the white gown escaped, with the President in pursuit, and the two of them would fall into a pile of hay, but the white gown would be up again and running, until finally it tumbled onto a pile of hay with the President on top of it. Then I saw the gown grow smaller as the white cuffs turned it over, just as we would turn over poppy petals, and everything in the garden of the Hotel Tichota fell silent. I stopped looking then, and so did the boss, who let the curtains drop, and Zdeněk looked at the floor and the chambermaid, who was standing on the staircase in a black dress, so that all you could see of her in the dark was her white apron and the white wings of her serving cap, like a headband around her thick black hair—she looked down at the floor too. None of us watched but all of us were excited. It was as if we were out there on that scattered mound of hay with the beautiful woman who'd flown here in an airplane all the way from Paris just for this scene in the hay. We felt that it was happening to us and, most of all, that we were the only ones taking part in this romantic celebration, that fate had been good to us and asked no more in return than the secrecy you expect of the confessional, of a priest.

After midnight, the boss asked me to take a crystal jug full of cool cream, a loaf of fresh bread, and a small lump of butter wrapped in vine leaves to the children's playhouse in the garden. Carrying it in a basket, I trembled as I walked past the mounds of hay scattered everywhere, and I bent down and couldn't stop myself from picking up a handful of hay to smell it. Then I turned down the path leading to those three silver spruces, and I could see the small, lighted window. When I arrived at the playhouse, I saw sitting on a little chair, among the toy drums and jump ropes and teddy bears and dolls, the President in a white shirt, and opposite him, on a chair that was just as small, the Frenchwoman, and there they sat, the two lovers, face to face, gazing into each other's eyes, their hands resting on a small table between them. The tiny house was lit by a lantern with a candle inside. When he got up, the President cast a shadow across the window. He had to crouch to come outside to take the basket from me. Our President was so tall he had to crouch, whereas I was standing up and was still small. I gave him the basket and he said, Thank you, my boy, thank you, and then the white shirt retreated. His white bow tie was undone, and on my way back I tripped over his evening coat. When dawn came and the sun was rising, the President came out of the playhouse, and the woman followed, wearing a petticoat, dragging her wilted gown behind her, and the President carried the lantern, which had a candle still burning in it, a tiny point of light against the rising sun. Then the President reached down, took his coat by the sleeve and dragged it behind him through the dried grass and stubble and hay. The two of them walked dreamily side by side, smiling happily at each other. As I watched them, I suddenly realized that being a waiter wasn't so simple, that there were waiters and waiters, but I was a waiter who had served the President with discretion, and I had to appreciate that, like Zdeněk's famous waiter who lived the rest of his life on the strength of having served the Archduke Ferdinand d'Este in a casino for aristocrats. Then the President left in one car, and the lady in another. No one left in the third car, that invisible third party the banquet had been arranged for and the tables set for, and for whose uneaten food and unused room the boss had also charged.

When the July heat wave came, the boss stopped wheeling around through the rooms, alcoves, and dining rooms and stayed in his quarters, in a kind of icebox where the temperature had to be kept below sixty-eight degrees. But though he no longer wheeled himself along the garden paths, he still seemed able to see us and be all-powerful.

He attended to things and issued commands and prohibitions and interdictions with his whistle till it seemed to me that he could say more with his whistle than by talking. About that time, four foreigners came to live with us, all the way from Bolivia. With them they had a mysterious suitcase, which they watched like hawks and even took to bed with them. They all wore black suits and black hats, and droopy black mustaches, and they even wore black gloves. The suitcase they were keeping such a close watch on was black too and looked like a small coffin. Now the free-spending gaiety and debauchery of our nights became a thing of the past. But the foreigners must have paid well if our boss took them in. One of his peculiarities, and a peculiarity of the house, was that anyone who stayed here paid as much for garlic soup and potato pancakes and a glass of sour milk as he would have for oyster and crab washed down with Heinkel Trocken. And it was the same with the accommodations: even if a guest snoozed till morning downstairs on the couch, he still had to pay for a whole suite upstairs. That was one of the glories of our house, the Hotel Tichota. I kept wondering what they had in that suitcase until one day the leader of the group in black returned—he was a Jew, a Mr. Salamon—and Zdeněk told me that Mr. Salamon had connections in Prague with the Archbishop himself and that he was requesting the Archbishop, through diplomatic channels, to consecrate a small gold statue called the *Bambino di Praga*, the Infant Jesus of Prague, which was supposed to be tremendously popular in South America, so popular, in fact, that millions of South American Indians wore replicas of it on chains around their necks and had a legend that

Prague was the most beautiful city in the world and that the Infant Jesus had gone to school there. This is why they wanted the Archbishop of Prague himself to bless the Prague *Bambino*, who weighed six kilograms and was made of pure gold. From then on we all lived for the glorious moment when the statue would be consecrated. But it wasn't easy. Next day, the Prague police showed up, and the division head himself informed the Bolivians that the Prague underworld already knew about their *Bambino* and that a mob had come all the way from Poland to steal it. After talking things over, they decided it would be best to keep the real *Bambino* hidden until the very last moment, and to have another *Bambino* made of gilded cast iron, at the Republic of Bolivia's expense, and they could carry that around with them until the consecration. The very next day, they brought to the hotel a suitcase that was just as black as the first one, and when they opened it up, what they saw was so beautiful the boss himself came out of his specially cooled room just to look at it, to pay his respects to the *Bambino di Praga*. Then Mr. Salamon began negotiating with the Archbishop's consistory, but the Archbishop didn't want to consecrate the *Bambino*, because the real *Bambino* was already in Prague, and if he consecrated this one, there would be two of them. I found all this out from Zdeněk, who understood Spanish and German. Zdeněk was terribly upset, it was the first time I'd ever seen him so shaken. On the third day, Mr. Salamon drove up, and you could see all the way from the station that he was bringing good news because he was standing up in the car, smiling and waving his hands above his head. He said he'd been given a good tip. Apparently the Archbishop was fond of having his picture taken, so Mr. Salamon proposed that the entire ceremony be filmed as a Gaumont Newsreel special and then the ceremony could be seen around the world. Wherever there was a movie house, people would see not just the Archbishop but the *Bambino* and Saint Vitus's Cathedral as well and therefore, as Mr. Salamon rightly pointed out, the church would gain in popularity and its renown would spread to the ends of the earth. On the day of the ceremonial consecration, the police gave Zdeněk and me the job of taking the real *Bambino* to the cathedral. The idea was that the Bolivians, along with the chief of police in formal attire, would carry the imitation *Bambino di Praga*, and Zdeněk and I and three detectives disguised as industrialists would follow inconspicuously behind. The leader of the Bolivian Catholic group decided I should carry the real *Bambino* on my lap, and so we drove off from the Hotel Tichota. The detectives turned out to be very jovial fellows. They told us that when the royal treasury and crown jewels were put on display to the public they'd dressed up as deacons, wandered around by the side altars, and pretended to be praying. All the time they were packing revolvers in shoulder holsters like Al Capone, and when there was a break they had their pictures taken twice with the crown jewels, disguised as prelates. They couldn't stop laughing as they told us about it. I had to show them the *Bambino di Praga*, and eventually we said why not stop and have Zdeněk take our pictures behind a fence, all in a group with the *Bambino*, using a camera belonging to the plainclothes cops. Before we arrived, they also told us that whenever there was a state funeral that members of the government attended, they had to make sure no unauthorized persons were allowed in and that no one put a bomb in the flowers, and they had a special probe which they stuck into all the bouquets and wreaths before the funeral. They had their pictures taken there too, and they showed us snapshots of themselves on their knees around a catafalque, leaning on the probe they used to test the wreaths for hidden bombs. Now they were industrialists in morning suits, and they were going to kneel and work their way slowly toward the act of consecration so that they could observe it from three angles, to make sure nothing happened to the *Bambino di Praga*. We drove through Prague, and when we arrived at the Castle, the Bolivians were waiting for us, and Mr. Salamon took the suitcase and carried it into the cathedral, and everything was splendid, just like a wedding. The organ thundered and the prelates in their insignia of office bowed, and Mr. Salamon carried the *Bambino* down the aisle, and the camera whirred away and captured it all. The ceremony was like a High Mass, and Mr. Salamon knelt most devoutly of all, and we slowly approached the altar on our knees, and everything was alive with flowers and gold leaf and the choir sang the Missa Solemnis, and at the very climax the cameraman gave the sign, the *Bambino* was consecrated, and an ordinary object became a devotional article, because it was blessed by the Archbishop and now radiated supernatural power and could bestow grace. When the Mass was over and the Archbishop had retired to the sacristy, the vicar of the chapter led Mr. Salamon in after him. Mr. Salamon was just slipping his wallet back into his coat as he came back out, so he must have donated a large check in the name of the Bolivian government for repairs to the church, or perhaps there had also been a fee for the consecration. Then I saw the ambassador of the Bolivian Republic carrying the *Bambino* back up the aisle of the cathedral while the organ played and the choir sang. Again the cars arrived and the *Bambino* was put away, but this time we didn't take anything with us, and everyone, including the ambassador and the whole entourage, drove off to the Hotel Steiner, while we went home to get everything ready for the farewell banquet that night. When the Bolivians arrived at ten o'clock, it was the first time they could really relax, and they began to drink champagne and brandy and eat oysters and chicken, and at midnight three cars arrived with some dancers from the operetta, and we had more work and more people that night than we ever had before. The Chief of Police, who knew all about our place, left the counterfeit *Bambino* on the mantelpiece of the men's room, and he secretly took the real *Bambino*, the consecrated *Bambino*, away to the playhouse, where he casually placed it among the dolls, puppets, jump ropes, and toy drums. Then they all drank, and the naked dancers danced around the counterfeit *Bambino* until dawn, when it was time for the ambassador to go back to his residence and the representatives of Bolivia to go to the airport and head home. The Chief of Police brought the real *Bambino* back to the hotel, but luckily Mr. Salamon looked into the suitcase, because in all the fun and confusion the Chief of Police had put a beautiful doll in a Moravian Slovak folk costume in the suitcase by mistake. They all ran back to the playhouse, and there lay the *Bambino* among the toy drums and three other dolls, so they snatched up the consecrated *Bambino*, put back the doll, and drove off to

Prague. Three days later, we heard that the Bolivians had to delay their flight. To mislead thieves, they left the counterfeit *Bambino* outside the entrance to the airport. At first a cleaning lady stuck it among some box trees, but when the members of the delegation, led by Mr. Salamon, were safely on board the plane, they opened the suitcase and discovered that what they had with them was not the real golden *Bambino* blessed by the Archbishop but the gilded cast-iron one. They rushed out to look for the real *Bambino* just as a porter was asking people whose suitcase this was. When no one claimed it, he left the *Bambino* standing on the pavement, and just then the Bolivian delegation came rushing up and grabbed the suitcase. After they hefted it, they breathed sighs of relief, opened it up and saw that it was the real *Bambino*. Then they rushed back to the airplane to take off for Paris and, from there, back to their own country with the *Bambino*, who according to the South American Indian legend had gone to school in Prague, and Prague, according to the same legend, is the oldest city in the world.

I Served
the King
of England

◆◆◆◆◆◆◆◆◆◆◆◆◆

I was always lucky in my bad luck. I left the Hotel Tichota
in tears, because the boss thought I'd deliberately caused
the mixup between the real *Bambino di Praga* and the
counterfeit one, that I'd set the whole thing up just to get
my hands on six kilos of gold, though it hadn't been me
at all, and so another waiter showed up with a suitcase,
and off I went to Prague, but right there in the station I
had the good luck to run into Mr. Walden. He was setting
off to cover his territory, and his assistant was with him,
the sad man who carried the scale and the salami slicer in
a bundle on his back, and Mr. Walden wrote me a letter
of recommendation to the Hotel Paris. He must have been
fond of me because as I said good-bye to him again he
patted me on the head and kept saying, Poor little fellow,
just stick to it. You're small so you've got to try hard to

make something of yourself, poor lad. I'll look you up. By this time he was shouting, and I stood there waving until the train was long out of sight. So there I was, on the threshold of another adventure. As a matter of fact the Hotel Tichota had begun to scare me. It started when I noticed that the porter had a cat that would hang around, waiting for him to come back from his night labors, or she would sit in the courtyard and watch him split wood, and that cat meant the world to him, he even slept with her, but then a tomcat started coming around and she went off with the tomcat and didn't come home. The porter became thin and pale and he looked everywhere for his beloved cat, until finally she came home again. The porter had a habit of talking to himself. Whenever I walked past him, I could hear how the unbelievable came true, because from these soliloquies of his I learned that he'd been in jail, that he'd chopped up a gendarme who was having an affair with his wife and given the wife such a thrashing with a rope they had to take her to the hospital, and so he got five years. One of his cellmates was a thug from Žižkov who'd sent his little girl for beer and when the kid lost the change from a fifty he got so mad he took his daughter's arm, laid it across a block of wood, and chopped her hand off. That was the first time the unbelievable came true. His other cellmate was someone who had caught his wife with a traveling salesman and killed her with an ax, then cut out her vagina and told the salesman to eat it or else be killed with the ax, but the salesman died from the sheer horror of it anyway, and the murderer turned himself in, and so the unbelievable came true again. The third time the unbelievable came true was the porter's own case, because he'd trusted his wife, but when he saw her with the gendarme he split the gendarme's shoulder open with an ax, and the gendarme shot him in the leg and our porter got five years. Anyway, one time the tomcat came right up to the porter's cat, and the porter held the tomcat against the wall with a brick and chopped through its spine with his ax. His cat began to mourn, but the porter squeezed the tomcat into kind of a screened-in grilled window and left it there dying for two days, then he threw his cat out. The cat paced up and down by the wall, but he wouldn't let her come home, and finally she disappeared. I suspect the porter killed her too. He was a gentle and sensitive soul, and therefore had a short temper, which is why he went straight after everything with an ax, both his wife and the cat, because he was horribly jealous of the gendarme and the tomcat. At his trial he said he was sorry he hadn't split the gendarme's head open helmet and all while he was at it, because the gendarme had been in his wife's bed with his helmet on, wearing his holster and pistol. It was this same porter who invented the story that I'd tried to steal the *Bambino di Praga*, and he told the boss that I hadn't a thought in my head except to get rich quick, even if it meant committing a crime. The boss was upset because whatever the porter said was gospel and, besides, no one would ever challenge him since he was as strong as five grown men. One afternoon I had found the porter sitting in the children's playhouse doing something, playing with the dolls and teddy bears, perhaps, and he told me he didn't want to see me go into that playhouse again, the way he'd seen me there once with Zdeněk, because he wouldn't want the unbelievable to come true for the fourth time. Then he told me how the tomcat had lain in agony for two days with a severed spine right next to my little room, and every time I passed by he'd remind me, pointing at the tomcat's mummified corpse, that this was how everyone who sinned in his eyes—and he gestured with two fingers at his own eyes—ended up. If there wasn't any other reason, he'd get me because I'd played with his dolls, and for that he might not kill me on the spot, but I'd be sure to die a slow death, just like the tomcat. Now, at the railroad station, I realized just what a creature of habit my six months at the Hotel Tichota had made me, because the conductors blew their whistles, the passengers climbed aboard, the conductors whistled signals to the dispatcher, and I found myself running from one conductor to another asking what my orders were. And when the dispatcher blew his whistle to alert the conductors, and all the doors were closed, I ran up to him and asked politely, May I be of service? So the train carried Mr. Walden away, and I walked across the intersections of Prague, and twice a traffic cop blew his whistle so loudly that I ran up, put my suitcase down on his foot, and asked, May I be of service? And so I walked on until I came to the Hotel Paris.

The Hotel Paris was so beautiful it almost knocked me over. So many mirrors and brass balustrades and brass door handles and brass candelabras, all polished till the place shone like a palace of gold. There were red carpets and glass doors everywhere, just like in a château. Mr. Brandejs gave me a warm welcome and took me to my temporary quarters, a little room in the attic with such a pretty view of Prague that I decided, because of the room and the view, to try to stay there permanently. After I'd unpacked my suitcase to hang out my tuxedo and my underwear, I opened a closet and saw it was full of suits, and a second closet was full of umbrellas, and a third was full of topcoats and inside, hanging on strings nailed to the wall, were hundreds of ties. I pushed the hangers together and hung up my clothes, and then looked out over the rooftops of Prague, and when I saw the shimmering Castle, the home of Czech kings, I was flooded with tears and forgot all about the Hotel Tichota, and I was glad they'd suspected me of trying to steal the *Bambino*, because if my boss hadn't believed it, I'd still be raking the paths and tidying the haystacks, nervous, wondering where the next whistle would come from and who would be blowing it, because by that time I'd figured out that the porter had a whistle too and was acting as the boss's eyes and legs, and he'd watch us and then whistle just like the boss. When I went downstairs, it was noon, and the waiters were changing shifts and having lunch, and I saw they were eating croquettes—boiled potato croquettes with fried bread crumbs—and everyone in the kitchen was served this, including the boss, who was eating in the kitchen just like the cashier. Only the chef de cuisine and his assistants had boiled potatoes in their skins. I was served croquettes with bread crumbs too. The boss had me sit down beside him, and while I ate, he ate too, but rather delicately, as if to say, If I, the owner, can eat this, then you, my employees, can eat it too. Soon he wiped his mouth with a napkin and took me out into the restaurant. My first job was to serve the beer, so I picked up the full glasses in the taproom and arranged them on my tray, putting a red glass token in a box for each beer, which was how they kept track of them here, and the old headwaiter pointed with his chin to where I was supposed to take the beer. From then on he just used his eyes, and I never made a mistake. Within an hour I could tell the old headwaiter was stroking me with his eyes, letting me know he liked me. He was class itself, a real movie actor, born to the tuxedo. I'd never seen anyone look better in a formal suit, and he seemed right at home in this hall of mirrors. Even though it was afternoon, all the lights were on, candle-shaped lamps with a bulb in every one and cut-glass crystal pendants everywhere. When I saw myself in the mirror carrying the bright Pilsner beer, I seemed different somehow. I saw that I'd have to stop thinking of myself as small and ugly. The tuxedo looked good on me here, and when I stood beside the headwaiter, who had curly gray hair that looked as though a hairdresser had done it, I could also see in the mirror that all I really wanted was to work right here at this station with this headwaiter, who radiated serenity, who knew everything there was to know, who paid close attention to everything, who filled orders and was always smiling as though he were at a dance or hosting a ball in his own home. He also knew which tables were still waiting for their food and would see that they got it, and he knew who wanted to pay, though I never saw anyone raise his hand and snap his fingers or shake the bill. The headwaiter would gaze out over the restaurant as if he were surveying a vast crowd of people, or looking out over the countryside from an observation tower, or scanning the sea from the pilothouse of a steamship, or not looking at anything, and every movement a guest made told him at once what that guest wanted. I noticed right away that the headwaiter didn't like the waiter and would reproach him with his eyes for getting the plates mixed up and taking the pork to table eleven instead of table six. When I'd been serving the beer for a week, I noticed that whenever this particular waiter brought the food from the kitchen on a tray he would stop before he went through the swinging door and, when he thought no one was looking, lower the tray from the level of his eyes to the level of his heart, look hungrily at the food, and take a pinch of this and a pinch of that—just a tiny amount each time so it looked as if he'd accidentally dipped his finger in the food and was licking it off. I saw the headwaiter catch him at it but say nothing, just watch. Then the waiter would wave his hand, hoist the tray over his shoulder, kick open the door, and rush into the restaurant. He always ran as though the tray were falling forward, his legs a-flurry, but it was a fact that no one else dared carry as many plates as Karel (that was his name). He could get twenty plates on his tray and lay eight along his outstretched arm as if it were a narrow table, and hold two more in his outspread fingers, and three plates in the other hand. It was almost like a vaudeville routine, and I suspect that Brandejs, the boss, liked the waiter and thought that the way he served the food was one of the attractions of the establishment. So almost every day we employees had potato croquettes for lunch, sometimes with poppy seeds, sometimes with a sauce, or with a toasted roll or covered with butter and sugar or with raspberry juice or with chopped parsley and melted lard. Each time, there would be the boss himself eating those potato croquettes with us in the kitchen. He never ate very much, because he said he was on a diet. But at two o'clock Karel the waiter would bring him a tray, and judging by the silver covers over the food it must have been a small goose or a chicken or a duck, or some kind of game, whatever was in season. He always had it brought into one of the private chambers, to make it look as though it was for someone else, a member or a broker from the Fruit and Vegetable Exchange, because the brokers always went on conducting their business after hours in the Hotel Paris. But when no one was looking, our boss would slip into the room, and when he came out he'd be glowing with satisfaction, a toothpick stuck in the corner of his mouth. I suspect that Karel the waiter had some kind of arrangement with the boss. When the main day at the exchange, which was Thursday, was over, the brokers would come to our hotel to celebrate over champagne and cognac the deals they'd closed. On each table would be trays laden with food, or really only one tray, but full enough to make it a real feast, and every Thursday, from eleven o'clock in the morning on, some brightly painted young ladies would be sitting in the restaurant, the kind I'd met at Paradise's when I was working at the Golden City of Prague, and they'd be smoking and drinking vermouth and waiting for the brokers to show up. When the brokers did show up, the girls would split up and go to separate tables, and the men would select them for the private chambers. Then I could hear the sounds of laughter and the tinkling of glasses through the curtains as I walked past, and this would go on for hours, until finally the brokers would leave in high spirits and the young ladies would come out and comb their hair, redo their kiss-smeared lipstick, tuck in their blouses, and glance behind them, almost putting their necks out of joint trying to see if the stockings they'd just put back on had the line, the seam, running straight down the middle of their legs into their shoes to the exact center of their heels. When the brokers left, neither I nor anyone else was ever allowed to go into the private chambers, and we all knew why. Several times, through a half-drawn curtain, I saw Karel lifting the cushions, and that was his little business on the side, picking up lost coins and bills, and the occasional ring or watch chain. It was all his, the money that fell out of the pockets of the brokers' trousers, coats, and vests as they dressed or undressed or were writhing about.

One morning Karel loaded up his tray with twelve main dishes and as usual stopped just inside the door to pinch a bit of sirloin tip and a touch of Brussels sprouts to go along with it, topping it off with a morsel of dressing from the veal. Then he lifted the tray as if the food had given him new strength and with a smile on his face struck out into the restaurant. But a customer who was taking snuff, or had a cold, inhaled abruptly through his nose, and as he inhaled it was as if the force of the intake pulled him straight up by the hair, because he suddenly rose to his feet, sneezing loudly, and caught the corner of the tray with his shoulder. Karel, leaning forward at the waist, had to run to catch up to the loaded tray, which now was sailing through the air like a flying carpet, because Karel always carried his food high. Either the tray was too fast or Karel's legs were too slow, but in any case when he reached for it the tray slipped away from his upturned hand, his fingers scrabbling desperately for it as all of us in the business watched, including the boss, who was entertaining a group from the hotel owners' association. Mr. Šroubek himself was at the banquet table, and he saw what then happened, just as we had foreseen it would. Karel took one more mighty leap in the air and managed to catch the tray before it fell, but two plates slid off one after the other, and first pieces of beef roll à la Puzsta, then dumplings poured over a guest who was just raising his eyes from the menu to ask if the meat was tender and the sauce warm enough and the dumplings light. It all slid off the plates and onto the guest, and as he rose to his feet dripping with sauce, the beef roll à la Puzsta and the dumplings tumbled off his lap and fell under the table. One dumpling remained on his head like a small cap, a yarmulke, the kind a rabbi wears, or a priest's biretta. When Karel, who had managed to save all the other ten plates, saw that and saw Mr. Šroubek, who owned the Hotel Šroubek, he raised the tray even higher, gave it a little toss, flipped it over, and flung all ten plates onto the carpet, demonstrating, as if he were in a play or a pantomime, how disgusted he felt about those two plates. He undid his apron just as theatrically, flung it at the floor, and stomped out in a fury, then changed into his street clothes and went out to get drunk. I didn't understand it yet, but everyone in the business said that if you dropped the two plates like that, the other ten had to end up on the floor too, because of a waiter's honor. But the matter was far from over. Karel came back, his eyes flashing, and sat down in the kitchen, glowering out into the restaurant. Suddenly he jumped up and tried to pull the large cupboard down on himself, the one that held all the glasses. The cashier and the cook rushed over and pushed the cupboard back upright, while the glasses clattered out of it and crashed to the floor, but those two plates had given Karel such power that he almost managed to pull the cupboard over three times. Each time the cooks, who by now were all red in the face, slowly pushed it back upright, and just when everyone had got his breath back, Karel jumped up and grabbed the kitchen stove—which was so long that when you added wood at one end, the fire would almost be out by the time you got to the oven at the other—and gave the stove such a yank that he pulled the stovepipe out of the wall, and soon the kitchen was full of smoke and fumes and everyone was choking. With great effort they got the pipe back in place, and the cooks, all smeared with soot, collapsed in their chairs and looked about to see where Karel was, but he was gone. Just as we all heaved sighs of relief, suddenly we heard a tinkling sound. Karel had kicked a hole in the glass of the air shaft over the stove and smashed his way down into the kitchen, and he landed with one leg up to his knee in the lunchtime special, which was tripe soup, and the other leg in a pot of goulash combined with sauce for the filly-on-mushroom. There were splinters of glass everywhere, so the cooks gave up, and they ran for the porter, who was a former wrestler, to take Karel out by force, since they decided he must have some kind of grudge against the Hotel Paris. The porter set his legs firmly apart and spread his huge paws as though he were holding a skein of wool to be wound into a ball and said, What's it going to be, you horse's ass? But Karel slugged the porter so hard that the porter fell over, and the police had to be called in. By the time the police arrived Karel was docile, but in the corridor on the way out he knocked down two of them and kicked a dent in the helmet of a third while the policeman was still wearing it. So they dragged him into one of the private rooms and beat him up, and each time he screamed, all the guests in the restaurant looked at one another and shrugged their shoulders. Finally the policemen took him out, all bruised up, but as he passed the cloakroom he told the girl that those two plates would cost some more yet, and he was right, because word had barely come back that he'd settled down when he suddenly kicked a hole in the porcelain sink and yanked the pipes out of the wall so that everything in the room, including the policemen, was soaking wet before they managed to stop up the holes with their fingers.

And so I became a waiter on the floor under the guidance of the headwaiter Mr. Skřivánek, and there were two other waiters, but I was the only one allowed to lean against the table in the alcove when things slowed down in the early afternoon. The headwaiter told me that I'd make a good headwaiter but that I had to train myself to fix a guest in my memory as soon as he came in and be aware when he was leaving—not necessarily at lunchtime, when a customer would have to pick up his coat from the cloakroom, but in the afternoon, when meals were served in the café and the cloakroom was closed—so that I would learn to spot those who wanted to sneak out without paying. I was also supposed to be able to estimate how much money a guest had with him, and whether he would spend accordingly, or should spend accordingly. That, Mr. Skřivánek said, was what being a good headwaiter meant. And so when there was time for it he would quietly describe to me what sort of guest had just arrived or was just leaving. He trained me for several weeks, until I felt ready to try it on my own. I would look forward to the afternoon as though I were setting out on some adventure, and I'd be as excited as a hunter waiting for his quarry to appear. The headwaiter would either smoke, his eyes half closed, and nod contentedly, or he would shake his head, correct me, and then go to the guest himself and show me that he'd been right, and he always was. And that was how I first found it out, because when I asked the headwaiter a basic question—How do you know all this?—he answered, pulling himself up to his full height, Because I served the King of England. The King? I said, clapping my hands. You mean you actually served the King of England? And the headwaiter nodded his head in satisfaction. And so the second phase of my training began. It was exciting, something like the lottery, when you're waiting to see if your number will come up, or hoping to win the door prize at a masquerade ball or some public celebration. A guest would come into the restaurant in the afternoon, the headwaiter would nod, we'd go into the alcove, and I'd say, Italian. The headwaiter would shake his head and say, Yugoslav, from Split or Dubrovnik. And we'd look each other in the eye for a moment, then nod, and each put twenty crowns on a tray in the alcove. I would go to ask what the guest wanted, and when I'd taken his order, and was on my way back, the headwaiter would see my expression, sweep up both twenty-crown notes, and slip them into his enormous wallet, for which he'd had one of the pockets in his trousers bordered with the same kind of leather, and I'd be astonished and ask, How did you know that? And he'd answer modestly, I served the King of England. And so we'd bet like that, and I'd always lose. But then he said that if I wanted to be a good headwaiter I had to be able to recognize not just the nationality but also what the guest was likely to order as well. So when a guest came into the restaurant, we'd nod, go into the alcove, and lay our twenties on the sideboard, and I'd say, Goulash soup or the tripe-soup special. The headwaiter would say, Tea and fried toast, no garlic. Then I'd go for the order and say, Good morning and what would you like? And the guest would say, Tea and fried toast, no garlic, and as I walked back the headwaiter was already scooping up both twenties, and he'd say, You have to learn to recognize a gallbladder case when you see one. Just take a look at him. His liver is probably doomed as well. Another time, I thought the guest would have tea with bread and butter, and the headwaiter said, Prague ham with a pickle and a glass of Pilsner beer, and of course he was right, and when I'd taken the order and was coming back with it, the head-waiter saw me coming, raised the little window, and called the order into the kitchen for me: One Prague ham. And when I got there, he added, And a pickle on the side. I was glad to be learning, even though I wasted all my tips, be-cause we bet whenever we could and I'd always lose, and each time I asked him how he knew, he'd slip the twenties into his big wallet and say, I served the King of England.

So there I was in Karel's place. I thought of Zdeněk, the headwaiter who liked waking up a whole village and spend-ing all his money like a bankrupt aristocrat, and then I thought, for the first time in a long time, of the maître d' from the Golden City of Prague, my first maître d', Malek was his name. He was incredibly stingy and no one knew where he kept his money, though everyone knew he had a lot of it and was saving up for a little hotel of his own, and that when he retired he would buy or rent a hotel somewhere in the Bohemian Paradise district. But the truth was quite different, because once we got drunk at a wedding and he grew very sentimental and confessed that eighteen years ago his wife had sent him with a message for a friend of hers, and when he rang the doorbell and the door opened, there stood a beautiful woman who blushed, and so did he as they both stood there in the doorway thunderstruck. She was holding some embroidery, and he went in and didn't say a word but put his arms around her while she went on embroidering, and then she slipped down onto the couch and went on embroidering behind his back while he took her like a man—those were his words. From then on he was in love and saved his money, a hundred thousand crowns in eighteen years, so that when he left his family, his wife and children, they would have some security. He would buy them a little house and then, though his hair was gray, go find happiness with his gray-haired beauty. After he told me all this, he unlocked his writing desk and showed me the hundred-crown notes he had stashed away to buy his happiness with, and looking at him I never would have guessed it, because one of his trouser legs was hiked up and he was wearing old-fashioned long underwear that came down to his ankle and was tied there with white lace sewed inside the cuff of his trouser leg. It was underwear straight out of my childhood, when I lived with my grandmother in the mill where the traveling salesmen would fling their underwear out of the window of the Charles Bath, the very same kind of long underwear that had once hung for a moment in the air. So each of the headwaiters was different, and Malek from the Golden City of Prague suddenly appeared to me, alongside the headwaiter of the Hotel Paris, like a saint of some kind, like the painter and poet Tonda Jódl who sold *The Life of Jesus Christ* and was forever putting his jacket on and taking it off again, covered with powder from his medicine, and with his mouth stained yellow from drinking Neurastenin. And I wondered what kind of headwaiter I would make. Now it was I who served the brokers every Thursday, because Karel never came back. Like all rich people, the brokers were as cheerful and playful as puppies, and when they closed a deal they would throw their money around like butchers who'd won at cards. Of course, butchers who played cards would occasionally lose their shirts and get home three days later minus their buggy, minus their horses, minus the livestock they'd bought, with nothing left but a whip. Sometimes these brokers would lose everything too, and then they'd sit in the private chambers looking at the world like Jeremiah watching Jerusalem burn. Gradually I gained the confidence of the young ladies who waited in the café until the exchange closed and then went down to the private chambers, and it didn't matter whether it was eleven in the morning or late afternoon or dusk or late at night, because at the Hotel Paris the lights were always on, like a chandelier you've forgotten to switch off. Best of all I liked the private chambers the young ladies called the Clinic, or Diagnostics 100, or the Department of Internal Medicine. The brokers who were still at the height of their virility would try to get the women tipsy as fast as possible, then slowly remove their blouses and skirts until they were rolling around with them on the upholstered couches and chairs as naked as God made them, and the brokers would end up completely worn out, so exhausted from making love in unusual positions that they looked as if they'd just suffered a heart attack. But in the Department of Internal Medicine or Diagnostics 100 things were merrier. Entertaining the older gentlemen was the most popular job, because this was where the girls raked in the most. The older brokers would laugh and make jokes and treat the undressing of a young woman as a collective game of strip poker, removing her clothes little by little, right on the table, while they sipped their drinks from their crystal champagne glasses and savored the bouquet. The girl would then lie back on the table, and the old brokers would gather around her with their glasses and plates of caviar and lettuce and sliced Hungarian salami, and they'd put on their spectacles and study every fold and curve of her beautiful female body, and then, as if they were at a fashion show or a life-study class in some academy of art, they'd ask the girl to sit, or stand up, or kneel, or let her legs dangle from the table and swing back and forth as though she were washing them in a stream. These brokers would never worry or argue among themselves about who had what part of her body closest to them, but their animation was like the animation of a painter transferring what excites him in a landscape to his canvas, and so these old men would peer through their glasses at the crook of an elbow, a strand of loose hair, an instep, an ankle, a lap, and one would gently part the two beautiful cheeks of her behind and gaze with childish admiration at what was revealed, and another would shriek in delight and roll his eyes to the ceiling, as if thanking the Lord Himself for the privilege of peering between the open thighs of a young

woman and touching whatever pleased him most with his
fingers or his lips. This private chamber was always filled
with light, not only with the strong light from the ceiling
funneling down through a parchment lampshade but also
with the glitter of wineglasses and four pairs of spectacle
lenses moving back and forth like tiny veiled fish in an
illuminated aquarium. When they had had their fill of looking, the brokers would call it quits and pour the young
woman some champagne, and she would sit on the table
and drink toasts with them, and they would call her by
her first name, and she could help herself to anything she
wanted from the table. The older men made jokes and were
courteous to her, while from the other chambers you could
hear raucous laughter, sometimes suddenly silenced, and I
often felt the urge to barge in there, certain I'd find a dead
body or a dying broker lying on the floor. Then my old
men would dress the young woman, like running a movie
backward, and dress her just the way they had undressed
her, with none of the apathy that comes afterward, none
of the indifference, but with the same courtesy they had
shown her from the start. When they left, one of them
would always pay the whole bill, they would tip the headwaiter, and I always got a hundred crowns, and they would
leave, glowing and at peace with themselves, full of beautiful images that would last them a week. By next Monday
they would be looking forward to examining a different
woman on Thursday, because they never had the same
woman twice, perhaps in order to spread their reputation
among the Prague prostitutes. At the end of each session,
the young woman they had just examined would hang
around the private chamber, waiting, breathing heavily,

eyeing me greedily as if I was a movie actor, because she was so aroused she couldn't bring herself to leave. So after I finished clearing the table and put away the last piece of cutlery, I'd have to finish what the old men began. The women would throw themselves on me with such passion and eagerness, it was as if they were doing it for the first time, and for those few minutes I felt tall and handsome and curly-haired, and I knew that I was king for those beautiful young women, though it was only because their bodies had been so tickled by eyes, hands, and tongues that they could scarcely walk. Not until I felt them climaxing once, twice, would they come to life again, their eyes would return, the glassy absent stare of passion would disappear, and they would see things normally again. Once more I became a tiny waiter, standing in for someone strong and handsome, performing on command every Thursday with increasing appetite and skill. This had been the specialty of Karel my predecessor, who had the aptitude and the capacity and the love for it, though I had that too. And I must have been good in other ways as well, because all the young women would greet me when they met me, in the hotel or on the street, and if they were a long way off they'd bob or wave their hankies or their purses, and if they had nothing in their hands, they'd at least give me a friendly wave, and I'd bow or acknowledge them with a wide sweep of my hat, then stand straight again and raise my chin, feeling taller than my double-soled shoes could make me.

And so I started setting more store by myself than I should have. When I had time off, I would dress up, and I fell in love with neckties, the kind of ties that really make the clothes, which in turn make the man. I bought myself the same kind of ties our guests had, but that wasn't enough for me, because in my mind I kept opening the door to the hotel closet hung with clothes and things that guests had left behind. I had never seen anything, anywhere, like the ties in that closet, ties with small name tags attached to them by thin thread, one belonging to Alfred Karniol, a wholesaler from Damascus, another to Salamon Pihovaty, the director of a company from Los Angeles, a third to Jonathan Shapliner, who owned spinning mills in Lvov, and a fourth and a fifth, and there were dozens of ties, and I longed to have one of that class and wear it someday, and it was all I could think of. I had it narrowed down to two, a metallic blue one and a dark red one made of the same kind of material as the blue one. They both shimmered like the wings of rare beetles or butterflies, and with a summer jacket, one or two buttons undone, one hand in my pocket and a fine tie hanging from my neck to my waist, I would be admired by everyone. When I tried the red tie on in front of a mirror, I could see myself walking down Wenceslaus Square and along Národní, and the other pedestrians, most of them elegantly dressed, stopped in their tracks, startled by my beautiful tie, and I strolled by with my jacket unbuttoned so all the connoisseurs could see it. So I was standing before the mirror in the attic of the Hotel Paris, slowly undoing the shiny red Bordeaux necktie, when another one caught my eye, one I'd never noticed before. There was my tie! It was white and seemed to be made of an unusual rough fabric covered with small blue dots, light blue, like forget-me-nots, and though those dots were part of the weave, they looked as if they'd been stuck on and glittered like sparks struck from an anvil. A tiny tag hung from the thread, which said the tie had been left behind by Prince Hohenlohe. When I put it on and saw myself in the mirror, I felt some of Prince Hohenlohe flow from his tie to me, and I put a little powder on my nose and on my freshly shaved chin, walked out of the restaurant, and paraded up and down Příkopy, looking into the shopwindows. And it turned out just the way I'd seen it in the attic mirror. But it wasn't the money, because almost everyone who wore a special tie and beautifully tailored clothes and suede shoes and carried an umbrella like an English lord had money, but no one had a tie like mine. I entered a men's haberdashery, and the minute I walked in the door I was the center of attention, or rather the tie was. I asked to see several pairs of muslin shirts, which I examined carefully, and then to add some polish to my appearance I asked the saleswoman to choose for me one out of their dozen white handkerchiefs and arrange it in my breast pocket the way it was supposed to be worn those days. She laughed and said, You can't be serious, you tie your necktie so beautifully. And she took a handkerchief— and I finally saw how it was done, because I had never been able to get it right—and spread it on the table and picked it up lightly in the middle with three fingers as if taking a pinch of salt from a saltcellar, and she shook it gently to make beautiful pleats, then drew the pleats through her other hand, folded the bottom under, tucked it into my breast pocket, and teased the corners into place. I thanked her, paid the bill, and was given two parcels, a beautiful shirt and five handkerchiefs, both tied with golden cord. Next I went into a shop selling men's suit fabrics, and my white necktie with its blue dots and my white handkerchief with its cone-shaped folds and corners as sharp as the points of a curled linden leaf drew the attention not only of the salesmen but also of two well-dressed gentlemen, who were staggered when they saw me, because their confidence in their own ties and handkerchiefs was shaken. Then I looked at some material for a suit, though I didn't have the money for it with me, and I chose an Esterházy, an English cloth, and asked them to take it outside so I could examine it in sunlight. They saw at once that I was a customer who knew his fabrics, and the salesman carried the whole bolt outside for me and flipped back the corner so I could judge for myself how my future suit would look in the city streets. I thanked him and then hesitated awkwardly, but the salesman reassured me that it was quite all right to take my time deciding, tomorrow was another day, I could buy this material any time, and the firm of Heinrich Pisko was assured of my business since it was the only one in Prague that carried this material. I thanked them and walked out and crossed the street, cocking my head slightly and furrowing my brow to make myself look distinguished and thoughtful. Then something happened that convinced me the necktie had changed me a lot, because along came Věra, who'd been in the Department of Internal Medicine only last Thursday. She saw me, and I could tell she was about to give me a friendly wave with her purse and white gloves, but suddenly she stopped, as if she wasn't quite sure now that it was me, the one who'd had to give himself to her so she could leave the hotel and go home after the old men had got her so excited. So I pretended I was someone else, and she turned to look back at me and then walked on, certain she'd made a mistake, and it was all because of the necktie and handkerchief. At Prašná Brána I crossed the street again, so I could walk back along Příkopy, and just as I was congratulating myself on my outfit, who should I see coming toward me, his hair like a white lambskin cap, but the headwaiter Mr. Skřivánek, but he wasn't looking at me though I knew he'd seen me. As he walked past, I stopped as if he'd greeted me, and turned to look after him, and Mr. Skřivánek stopped too, turned around, and walked back to me. When he looked into my eyes, I realized that all he had seen of me was a white tie walking down Příkopy, and the headwaiter, who knew everything, looked at me as if to say he knew where I'd got the tie, that I'd borrowed it without permission. And as he looked at me, I said silently to myself, How did you know all this? And he laughed and replied out loud, How do I know? I served the King of England. And he went on walking down Příkopy. The sun was shining, but now it seemed to turn dark, and I felt like a lamp whose wick the headwaiter had turned down, or an inflated tire whose valve he had loosened. I could hear the air hissing out of me as I walked along, and I felt that I was no longer lighting my own way, and that the tie and the handkerchief had wilted like me and were limp, as if I had just run through the rain.

A glorious event, the greatest honor that could ever have been bestowed on a single hotel and restaurant, took place at the Hotel Paris, and I was lucky enough to be there. A delegation had come to Prague on an official state visit, and the word was that they liked gold. But it was discovered that there was no gold cutlery at the official residence in the Prague Castle, so the President's head chamberlain and the Chancellor himself began to make arrangements to borrow a set from private sources, perhaps from Prince Schwartzenberg or Prince Lobkowitz. As it turned out, these aristocrats had the cutlery, but not enough of it, and what they did own, every knife and spoon, had their initials and their archducal coats of arms engraved or stamped on the handles. The only one who might have been able to lend the President a gold service was Prince Thurn Taxis, but he would have had to send to Regensburg to get it, because it had been used there a year before at the wedding of a family member who owned not only his own hotels and his own street, but also a whole district of the city, including a bank. At last, after all the contenders had dropped out, the Chancellor came to our hotel in person, and when he left the boss's office he was in a rage, which was good news for us, because Mr. Skřivánek, who had served the King of England, had read everything in the Chancellor's face without his knowing it, and then from the face of Mr. Brandejs, who owned the Hotel Paris, and what he learned was that the boss had refused to lend the President his gold service unless the banquet was held here in the hotel. That was how I learned—it practically knocked me down—that our hotel had gold flatware for three hundred and twenty-five people. And so it was decided that the luncheon in honor of the esteemed guest from Africa and his suite would be held here, in our hotel. Then the cleaning began. Brigades of women arrived with buckets and rags and washed not just the floor but the walls and the ceilings too, even the chandeliers, until the hotel was bright and sparkling. When the day came for the Emperor of Ethiopia and his entourage to arrive and take up residence, a truck went around to all the Prague flower shops and bought up all the roses and asparagus ferns and orchids. But at the last minute the Chancellor came in person again and canceled the suite reservations, though he confirmed the gala luncheon. The boss didn't mind, he simply added all the expenses of getting ready to put the Emperor up, including the cleaning, onto the bill. So we began preparing a banquet for three hundred people. We borrowed the maître d' and the waiters from the Hotel Steiner, and Mr. Šroubek closed his hotel for the day and lent us his waiters. Detectives from the Castle—the same ones who had taken the *Bambino di Praga* to the cathedral with me—showed up with three chef's outfits and two waiter's uniforms, which they changed into at once so they could rehearse and sniff about the kitchen to make sure no one was trying to poison the Emperor, and they checked the restaurant to pick out the best places to keep an eye on the Emperor. When the chief cook and the Chancellor and Mr. Brandejs sat down to draw up a menu for three hundred guests, it took them six straight hours, and afterward Mr. Brandejs had fifty legs of veal brought to his icebox, six cows for soup, three foals for tenderloin, one dray horse for sauce, sixty swine, none heavier than sixty kilograms, ten suckling pigs, and three hundred chickens, not to mention a doe and two bucks. For the first time I went down into our cellars, with the headwaiter Mr. Skřivánek, and under his watchful eye the cellar manager counted again the supplies of wine, cognac, and other liquors, and it was like being at Oplt's, the wine and liquor wholesaler. For the first time in my life I saw an entire wall bristling with bottles of Heinkel Trocken and sparkling champagnes, from Veuve Cliquot to Weinhardt's of Koblenz, walls of Martell and Hennessey cognac, hundreds of bottles of Scotch whiskies of all kinds. I also saw rare Mosel and Rhine wines, and our own Bzenecka wine from Moravia, and Czech wines from Mělník and Žernoseky. As he walked from cellar to cellar Mr. Skřivánek would caress the bottle necks fondly, like an alcoholic, though as a matter of fact he didn't drink, at least I'd never seen him drink, and I suddenly realized I'd never seen him sit down either, he was always standing. As he looked at me in the cellar he read my thoughts or at least guessed them, because suddenly he said, Just remember, if you want to be a good headwaiter, never sit down. If you do, your legs will start hurting and the rest of your shift will be pure hell. Then the cellar manager turned the lights off behind us and we came back up. The very same day, news came that the Emperor of Ethiopia had brought his own cooks with him, and that they were going to prepare an Ethiopian specialty right here in our hotel, because we had the gold cutlery just like the Emperor had in Ethiopia. The day before the banquet the cooks and their interpreter arrived, shiny and black, complaining of the cold. Our cooks were to be their assistants, but our chief cook felt insulted and took off his apron and left in a huff. The Ethiopian cooks began by making several hundred hard-boiled eggs. Laughing and grinning, they then brought in twenty turkeys and put them in our ovens to roast, then mixed dressing in enormous bowls, using thirty baskets of rolls and fistfuls of spices, and they brought a cartload of parsley, which our cooks chopped up for them. We were all dying to see what these black fellows would concoct. When they got thirsty, we brought them Pilsner beer. They took a great liking to it and in exchange offered us shots of their own liquor, which was made from grasses of some sort, and we drank toasts with it, and it was terribly intoxicating and smelled of pepper and freshly ground allspice. We were shocked when they had two antelopes brought in from the zoo, already gutted, and they quickly skinned them and roasted them in the biggest roasting pans we had, with huge chunks of butter and a bagful of their spices, and we had to open all the windows because of the fumes. Then they put the stuffing in the half-roasted turkeys, and the turkeys into the antelopes, and hundreds of hard-boiled eggs to fill in the empty spaces, and they roasted everything together. But no one, not even the boss, was prepared for what happened next. The Ethiopian cooks had a live camel brought to the hotel and they wanted to slaughter it on the spot, but we were afraid to let them. The interpreter pleaded with Mr. Brandejs, and then newspaper reporters showed up and our hotel became the center of attention. They tied up the camel, who was bleating, Noooo, noooo, as if to say, Don't cut my throat, but one of the cooks cut his throat anyway, with a kosher knife, and there was blood all over the courtyard, and then they hauled the camel up by his hind legs with a block and tackle and took out his heart and lungs and liver and things. Then they had three wagonloads of wood delivered, and while the fire department stood by with their hoses ready the cooks quickly made a huge fire, let it burn down until only the glowing coals remained, then barbecued the camel on a spit supported by tripods. When the camel was almost done, they put into it the two antelopes with the stuffed turkeys inside them, and fish as well, and lined the cavity with hard-boiled eggs, and kept pouring on spices, and because it was still too cold for them, even by the fire, they went on drinking beer, the way brewery wagon drivers drink beer in the winter to keep warm. Now when the guests began to arrive and the doormen were holding open the doors of the limousines, the black cooks were still barbecuing suckling pigs and lambs in the courtyard and making huge cauldrons of soup that used so much meat the boss was glad he'd laid in all those supplies. Then Haile Selassie himself arrived, accompanied by the Prime Minister, all our generals, and all the potentates of the Ethiopian army, every one of them covered with medals. The Emperor won us all over. He was dressed almost casually, in a kind of white uniform with no medals, while the members of his government or the atamans of his tribes wore colorful robes and some of them carried big swords, but as they took their places it was obvious that they were well behaved and natural. Tables for three hundred guests were set in the dining rooms of the Hotel Paris, and at each place was a set of sparkling gold forks and knives and spoons. Haile Selassie was given a warm welcome by the Prime Minister, and he responded in a barking voice, saying through his interpreter that he had the pleasure of welcoming his guests to an Ethiopian meal. Then a fat man draped in ten meters of cretonne clapped, and we began carrying around the hors d'oeuvres the black cooks had made in our kitchen—cold veal with a black sauce so strong it made me gag when I licked a drop of the stuff off my finger. When the waiters elegantly slipped the small plates in front of the guests, I had my first sight of three hundred golden forks and knives raised and glittering through the dining rooms. The headwaiter signaled us to begin pouring the Mosel, and my moment came when I saw they'd forgotten to serve the Emperor his wine. I wrapped a napkin around a bottle, approached the Emperor, and without really knowing how it happened, I went down on one knee like an acolyte and bowed, and when I stood up, everyone was looking at me while the Emperor made the sign of the cross on my forehead and blessed me. Then I poured his wine. The headwaiter from the Hotel Šroubek was standing right behind me. It was he who had forgotten to pour the Emperor's wine, and I was nervous about what I'd done, so I searched for our headwaiter Mr. Skřivánek with my eyes and saw him nod to say he was glad I'd been so observant. I set the bottle aside and watched how slowly the Emperor ate, how he dipped a piece of cold meat in the sauce and appeared merely to taste it, how he'd nod and then chew very slowly. Then he laid the fork across his plate as a sign that he'd had enough, sipped a little wine, and carefully dabbed his whiskers with a napkin. Next they brought in the soup. Meanwhile the black cooks were so animated, perhaps because they were still cold and drinking beer, that they had their snapshots taken with the detectives disguised as cooks while our own cooks were out in the courtyard slowly turning the stuffed camel over the glowing coals and basting it with bundles of mint leaves dipped in beer, which was something new the black cooks thought up. When the soup was over with, all the cooks and maids and maître d's and busboys and waiters relaxed, because the black fellows had everything under control, though they were constantly pouring beer down their throats. I was singled out by the Emperor himself, so the interpreter said, for the honor of continuing to serve him food and drink. Each time, I would first kneel on one knee in my tuxedo, then serve him, then retire and wait to top up his glass or remove his plate when he gave the sign. But the Emperor ate very little, he'd only wet his mouth, savoring the aroma like the chief taster, taking a smidgen of food and a sip of wine, and then continue his conversation with the Prime Minister. The further the guests were in rank and order from the host, the more voraciously they ate and drank. The guests at the tables in the back of the room, and in the alcoves and the adjoining rooms, ate as if they were insatiable. They devoured all the bread rolls, and one guest even sprinkled salt and pepper on the flowers of three potted cyclamen plants and ate them. Meanwhile the detectives stood in the corners and recesses of the rooms looking like waiters in their black tuxedos, with napkins folded over their arms, watching to see that no one stole any of our golden cutlery. When the high point of the meal drew near, the black cooks sharpened long sabers, two black fellows lifted the spit onto their shoulders while a third basted the camel's stomach with clusters of peppermint, and they carried it into the restaurant. The Emperor stood up and pointed to the barbecued camel and with the interpreter translating said that it was an African and Arabian specialty, a modest gift from the Emperor of Ethiopia. Two assistants brought two huge cutting boards into the middle of the dining room, fastened them together with clamps, set the camel down on this enormous table, and brought in the knives and sliced the camel in half with broad strokes, then cut each half in half again. A stupendous aroma spread through the room. In every slice there was a piece of camel and antelope, and inside the antelope a slice of turkey, and inside the turkey some fish and stuffing and little circles of hard-boiled eggs. The waiters held out the plates and then, starting with the Emperor, we served the roast camel. I knelt down, the Emperor gave me a sign with his eyes, and I served him his national dish. It must have been wonderful, because all the guests fell silent and the only sound came from the clinking of all those golden knives and forks. Then something happened that neither I nor anyone else, perhaps not even Mr. Skřivánek, had ever seen before. First, a government counselor, a well-known epicure, was so enraptured with the barbecued camel that he stood up and yelled with an expression of bliss on his face. But it tasted so delicious that not even that yell was enough, so he did what looked like a gymnastics routine, then started pounding his chest, then ate another piece of meat dipped in the sauce. The black cooks stood there, their knives in their hands and their eyes on the Emperor, but the Emperor must have seen this kind of thing before because he just smiled, so the black cooks smiled, and the chieftains—wrapped in those rare and wonderful fabrics with patterns of the kind my grandmother used to have on her aprons—smiled too, nodding their heads. Finally the counselor couldn't contain himself any longer and ran out of the hotel shouting and dancing and cheering and beating his chest, and then he ran back in again and there was a song in his voice and a dance of thanksgiving in his legs. Suddenly he bowed deeply to the three cooks, first bending to the waist in the Russian style, and then right to the floor. A second epicure, a retired general, stared at the ceiling and let out a long ecstatic moan that rose in cadences with each mouthful, and after he took a drink of Zernoseky Riesling he rose and whimpered so that even the black cooks understood, and they cried out happily, Yes, yes, samba, yes! The mood became so exalted that the Prime Minister shook hands with the Emperor and the photographers ran up and took pictures of everything, their bright flashguns popping, and in the light of that fireworks the representatives of our country and Ethiopia shook hands.

When Haile Selassie left, bowing, all the guests bowed too, the generals of both armies exchanged medals, and the government counselors pinned on the stars they'd been given by the Emperor and they draped the sashes across their chests. And I, the smallest one there, was suddenly taken by the hand and led to the Ethiopian Chancellor, who pressed my hand and pinned a medal with a blue sash on me—the lowest in degree, of course, but the largest in size—for exemplary service rendered to the throne of the Emperor of Ethiopia. When the medal had been pinned to the lapel of my tuxedo, and the blue sash draped across my breast, I lowered my eyes. Everyone envied me, most of all the headwaiter of the Hotel Šroubek, who was supposed to have got the medal. I saw in his eyes that I should let him have it: he had only a couple of years to go before he retired, and had probably been waiting for something like this to come along, because with a medal like that he could open a hotel somewhere in the foothills of the Krkonoše Mountains of the Bohemian Paradise district and call it the Hotel of the Order of the Ethiopian Empire. But the journalists and reporters had already taken down my name and snapped my picture, so I walked around with the medal and the blue sash as we cleared the tables and took the plates and the cutlery into the kitchen and worked far into the night. When the women, supervised by the detectives disguised as cooks and waiters, had washed and dried three hundred sets of gold cutlery, our headwaiter Mr. Skřivánek counted them, assisted by the headwaiter from the Hotel Sroubek. They counted them a second time and a third time, and then the boss counted the small coffee spoons himself. When he was done, he turned pale—one spoon was missing—and they counted again, and talked it over, and I saw the headwaiter from the Hotel Šroubek whispering something to the boss, and they looked surprised. The waiters who were on loan cleaned up, and then they all went into the serving room, because there was so much food left over. The cooks and the waitresses all came too —not to finish the food, but to taste it at their leisure, and watch our cooks, who were analyzing it and guessing what spices went into which sauces and what methods were used to produce dishes so exquisite that the government counselor Konopásek, who used to be the official taster at the Prague Castle, had been moved to yell in ecstasy. But I'd lost my appetite, because the boss wouldn't look at me, and I could see that he took no joy in my unfortunate decoration. The headwaiter from the Hotel Šroubek was still talking quietly with our headwaiter, Mr. Skřivánek, and suddenly I realized they were talking about the missing gold spoon and were thinking that I had stolen it. So I poured myself a glass of the cognac that was reserved for us and took a drink, then poured another and walked up to my headwaiter, the one who had served the King of England, to see if he was angry with me. I told him that I thought I'd been given the medal in error, and that the headwaiter from the Hotel Šroubek should have got it, or he himself, or our boss. But no one paid any attention to me, and I could see that even Mr. Skřivánek was staring at my bow tie with the same intense look he'd given me a few days before when he stared at the white tie with the blue dots, as blue as the spots on a swallowtail butterfly's wings—the tie I had borrowed without permission. I could see in his eyes that he was thinking that if I'd taken the tie without permission I could have taken the gold spoon too. And in fact it was the last thing I'd cleared from the Emperor's table, I'd taken it and put it right in the sink. I felt covered with shame as I stood there, my glass held out, waiting to drink a toast with a headwaiter I thought the world of, more than the Emperor himself or the President, and he raised his glass too, but hesitated, and I was desperate for him to toast that miserable medal with me, but though he always knew everything, this time he did not know, and he clinked his glass with the headwaiter from the Hotel Šroubek, who was the same age as he, then turned away from me.

I walked away with my outstretched glass and drank it. Everything began to burn, I was on fire, I poured myself another cognac and ran out, just as I was, into the night in front of our hotel, my former hotel, because I didn't want to be in this world any longer. I caught a cab, and the driver asked me, Where to? I told him to take me out to some woods, because I needed the fresh air. As we drove along, everything swept by me to the rear—first lights, a lot of lights, then just a streetlamp here and there, then nothing. The driver stopped by an honest-to-goodness woods. As I paid the fare, he looked at my decoration and the blue sash and said he wasn't surprised I was so excited, that lots of headwaiters had themselves driven to Stromovka Park or wherever to stretch their legs. I just laughed and told him I wasn't going to stretch my legs, I was going to hang myself. Seriously? the cab driver said, laughing. With what? He was right, I had nothing to do it with, so I said, My handkerchief. The driver got out of his cab, opened the trunk, rummaged around with a flashlight, then handed me a piece of rope. Still laughing, he made an eye in one end and ran the other end through it to make a noose and showed me the proper way to hang myself. He got back in his cab, rolled down the window, and yelled, Good luck! With that he pulled away, blinking his lights in farewell, and as he drove out of the woods he honked his horn. I walked down a footpath through the woods and sat on a bench. When I'd gone through the whole thing again in my head and come to the conclusion that the headwaiter didn't like me anymore, I decided I couldn't go on living. If it had been over a girl I'd have said, There's more than one flower under the sun, but this was a head-waiter who had served the King of England and who be-lieved I could have stolen the little spoon. True, the spoon was missing, but someone else could have stolen it. I stood up and felt the rope in my fingers, then it got so dark I had to grope my way forward, touching the trees with my hands, thin little trees, and then I came to a clearing, and by the sky I could see that I was walking through a stand of young spruce. Then there were woods again, but all the trees were birch now, tall birch, and I'd have needed a ladder to reach one of the branches. I saw it wasn't going to be easy. Then I came to a patch of older pines, with branches so close to the ground that I had to crawl under them on my hands and knees, and my medal kept bumping my chin and face, reminding me over and over of the missing gold spoon. I stopped, still on all fours, and turned everything over in my mind again. But I kept coming to the same painful place in my brain and I couldn't get past it: Mr. Skřivánek wouldn't be training me anymore, we wouldn't be laying any more bets about what the different guests would or should order or what nationality they were, and I began to moan like the chief government counselor Konopásek after several bites of that wonderful stuffed camel, and I made up my mind to hang myself. As I knelt there, I felt something touch my head, so I reached up and touched the toes of a pair of boots, and then I groped higher and felt two ankles, then socks covering a pair of cold legs. When I stood up, my nose was right up against the stomach of a hanged man. I was so terrified I started to run, pushing through rough old branches that tore my face and ears, but I made it back to the path, where I collapsed on the ground, and right there with the rope still in my hands I fainted. I was roused by lanterns and human voices, and when I opened my eyes I saw that I was lying in the arms of Mr. Skřivánek, and I kept saying, Over there, over there. And they found the hanged man who had saved my life, because I had been all set to hang myself a little way from him or alongside him. The headwaiter stroked my hair and wiped away the blood, and I cried out, The gold spoon! The headwaiter whispered,

Don't worry, they found it. I said, Where? Very quietly he said, The water wasn't draining out of the sink, so they took the drain apart and the spoon was right there in the elbow. Forgive me. Everything will be all right, just as before. I said, How did you know where I was? And the headwaiter said, The taxi driver came back to the hotel and asked the waiters if they knew of anyone who might want to hang himself, and just then the plumber brought in the missing spoon. The headwaiter, who had once served the King of England, knew at once that it was me and set out to look for me.

And that's how I came to be back in the Hotel Paris, as snug as a pea in a pod, and how Mr. Skřivánek began to trust me with the key to the wine cellars and the liqueurs and cognacs, as if trying to make up for that incident with the gold spoon. But the boss never forgave me for getting the medal and the sash, and he treated me as if I didn't exist, even though I made enough money to cover my entire floor, and every three months I took a whole floor's worth of hundred-crown notes to the bank, because I was determined to be a millionaire, to be the equal of everyone else. Then I'd rent or buy a small hotel, a nice cozy little place somewhere in the Bohemian Paradise district, and marry a rich woman, and when we put our money together I would be as respectable as the other hotel owners, and if they didn't acknowledge me as a man, they would have to acknowledge me as a millionaire, a hotel owner, and a man of property. But then another unpleasant thing happened to me. I went before the recruiting board three times and was turned down three times because I wasn't tall enough, and even when I tried to bribe the military authorities they wouldn't take me as a soldier. Everyone in the hotel laughed at me, and Mr. Brandejs himself asked me about it and made fun of my size again. I knew now that I would be small till the day I died, because I had finished my growing. The only way to change that now was to do what I'd been doing all along, wear double-soled shoes and hold my head high, as though the collar of my suit was too small. Something else happened too: I started taking German lessons, going to German movies, and reading German newspapers, and it didn't bother me that German students began walking about the streets of Prague in white socks and brown shirts. I was practically the only one left in the hotel who would serve German guests, because all the other waiters started pretending they didn't understand German, and even Mr. Skřivánek would speak only English or French or Czech with Germans. Once, at a movie, I stepped on a woman's foot and she started speaking German. I apologized to her in German, and I ended up seeing her home. She was attractively dressed, and to get on the good side of her and show her how grateful I was that she spoke German with me I said it was awful what the Czechs were doing to those poor German students, that I'd seen with my own eyes on Národní how they pulled the white socks and brown shirts off two German students. And she told me that I spoke the truth, that Prague was part of the old German Empire and the Germans had an inalienable right to walk about the city dressed according to their own customs. The rest of the world cared nothing for this right, but the hour and the day would come when the Führer would come and liberate all the Germans, from the forests of Šumava to the Carpathian Mountains. When she said this, I was looking straight into her eyes and I noticed that I didn't have to look up at her the way I did at other women, because it was my bad luck that all the women I'd had in my life were not just bigger than me but giants among women, and whenever we were together I would be looking at their necks or their bosoms, but this woman was as short as I was and her green eyes sparkled, and she was as spattered with freckles as I was, and the brown freckles in her face went so well with her green eyes that she suddenly seemed beautiful to me. I also noticed that she was looking at me in the same way. I was wearing that beautiful white tie with the blue dots again, but it was my hair she was looking at, as blond as straw, and my big blue eyes. Then she told me that Germans from the Reich yearn for Slavic blood, for those vast plains and the Slavic nature, that they've tried for a thousand years through good and evil to wed themselves to that blood. She told me confidentially that many Prussian noblemen had Slavic blood in them and that this blood made them more worthy in the eyes of the rest of the nobility, and I agreed. I was surprised at how well she understood my German, because this was not the same as taking a guest's order for lunch or dinner, I actually had to carry on a real conversation with the young lady whose black shoes I had stepped on, so I spoke a little German and a lot of Czech, but I felt as though I were speaking German all the time, because what I said seemed to me in the German spirit. The young lady told me her name was Lise, that she was from Cheb, that she taught physical education there, that she was a regional swimming champion, and when she opened her coat I saw she was wearing a pin with four F's arranged in a circle like a four-leaf clover. She smiled at me and kept staring at my hair, which made me uneasy, but my confidence was restored when she said I had the most beautiful hair in the world, and the way she said it made my head spin. I said I was a headwaiter at the Hotel Paris, and I told her this expecting the worst, but she put her hand on my sleeve, and when she touched me her eyes flashed so intensely I was alarmed, and she said her father had a restaurant in Cheb called the City of Amsterdam. So we made a date to see the movie *Love in Three-Quarter Time*, and she came wearing a Tyrolean hat and something I've loved since childhood, a jacket that looked green but was really gray and had a green collar with oak fronds embroidered on it. It was just before Christmas and snow was falling. She came to see me several times in the Hotel Paris, to have lunch or supper, and the first time she came Mr. Skřivánek looked at her and then at me and just like the old times we went into the alcove and I laughed and said, Shall we put a twenty on what the young lady orders? I saw that she was wearing that jacket again and those white socks. I pulled out a twenty and set it down on the sideboard, but Mr. Skřivánek gave me a queer look, like the time I'd tried to drink a toast with him the evening I'd served the Emperor of Ethiopia and the gold teaspoon got lost. My fingers were resting on the twenty-crown note, and he pulled out twenty crowns too and slowly laid it down, as if everything was all right, but then he snatched it away and stuck it back in his wallet, took another look at Lise, waved his hand dismissively, and never said another word. After the shift he took back the keys to the cellars and looked at me as though I wasn't there, as though he had never served the King of England and I had never served the Emperor of Ethiopia. But I didn't care now, because I could see that the Czechs were being unjust to the Germans, and I even began to feel ashamed for being a dues-paying member of Sokol, because Mr. Skřivánek was a great supporter of the Sokol movement, and so was Mr. Brandejs. All of them were prejudiced against the Germans and particularly against Lise, who came to the hotel only because of me, but they wouldn't let me wait on her, since her table belonged to another waiter's station. I watched how miserably they treated her, how they would give her cold soup and the waiter would put his thumb in it. Once I caught the waiter spitting into her stuffed veal just before he went through the swinging door. I jumped to grab the plate away from him, but he pushed it into my face and then spit at me, and when I wiped the thick gravy out of my eyes he spit into my face again, so I'd see how much he hated me. That was a kind of signal, because everyone from the kitchen ran out, and all the other waiters gathered around and everyone spat in my face. They kept it up until Mr. Brandejs himself came and, as head Sokol for Prague One, he spat on me too and told me I was fired. Covered with spittle and roast-veal sauce, I ran into the restaurant to Lise's table and pointed to myself with both hands, to show her what these Sokolites, these Czechs, had done to me because of her. She looked at me, wiped my face with a napkin, and said, You can't, you mustn't expect anything else from those Czech jingoes, and she said she was fond of me because of what I had put up with on her account. We left the hotel after I changed my clothes so that I could walk Lise home, but right outside the Prašná Brána some Czech roughnecks ran up and gave her such a slap in the face that her Tyrolean hat went flying into the street. I tried to defend her by shouting in Czech, What do you think you're doing! Is that any way for Czechs to behave? But one of the gang pushed me away while two others grabbed Lise and shoved her to the ground. As two of them held her arms, another pushed up her skirt and ripped her white socks from her suntanned legs. I was still shouting as they were beating me—What the hell do you think you're doing, you Czech jingoes?—until they finally let us go and carried off Lise's socks like a white scalp, a white trophy. We went through a passageway to a small square, and Lise was weeping and hissing, You'll get yours, you pack of Bolsheviks, we'll teach you not to shame a German schoolteacher from Cheb. I felt like a big man as she held me tight. I was so livid, I looked for my Sokol membership card so I could tear it up, but I couldn't find it. Suddenly she looked at me, her eyes full of tears, and right there on the street she burst out crying again, put her cheek against my face, and pressed herself against me. I knew then that I had to defend her against any Czechs who tried to harm a hair on this sweet little Egerlander's head, this daughter of the owner of the City of Amsterdam hotel and restaurant in Cheb, which the Germans had annexed as imperial territory last fall, along with the rest of the Sudetenland, taking it back to be a part of the Reich as it had once been many years before. And now, here in the Prague of the Sokols, I could see with my own eyes what was happening to the poor Germans, and it confirmed everything they said about why the Sudetenland had to be taken back and why Prague might end up the same way if the lives and honor of German people were threatened and trodden in the mud. And that's just what happened.

Not only was I fired from the Hotel Paris, but I couldn't get a job anywhere, not even as a busboy, because every time I was hired, the management was informed the following day that I was a German sympathizer and, what was worse, a Sokol who was going out with a German gym teacher. So I was unemployed for some time, until the German army finally came and occupied not just Prague but the whole country. About that time, Lise disappeared on me for two months. I wrote her and her father too, but got no reply. The second day after the occupation of Prague, I was out for a walk. On the Old Town Square the German army was cooking tasty soup in big kettles and passing it out in mess cans to the population. As I stood there watching, who did I see, in a striped dress with a red badge on her breast and a ladle in her hand, but Lise. I didn't say a word to her, just watched for a while as she ladled out the soup and handed people their mess cans with a smile, until I finally got a grip on myself and joined the line. When my turn came, she handed me a cup of warm soup. She wasn't shocked to see me, but excited and pleased and proud of her military dress of the front-line Sisters of Mercy or whatever uniform it was. When I told her I'd been out of work ever since I defended her honor at the Prašná Brána over those white socks, she got someone else to take her place, put her arm through mine, and laughed and bubbled over with excitement. I felt, and she did too, that the German army had occupied Prague because of her white socks and because they had spit on me in the hotel. As we walked along Příkopy, soldiers in uniform greeted Lise, and I would bow to them each time, and just past the Prašná Brána we turned and walked by the place where she was down on the sidewalk while they tore off her white socks three months before, and when we entered the Hotel Paris I pretended to be a customer looking for a table. The place was full of German officers now, and I stood there with Lise in her Sister of Mercy uniform, and the waiters and Mr. Skřivánek were pale as they waited on the German guests. I sat down by the window and I ordered coffee in German, a white Viennese coffee with a small glass of rum on the side, the way we used to serve it, á la Hotel Sacher, *Wiener Kaffe mit bespritzer Nazi.* It was a beautiful feeling when even Mr. Brandejs came out and bowed, kowtowing with particular politeness to me, and all of a sudden he began talking about the embarrassing incident that had happened back then and he apologized for it, but I told him I wouldn't accept his apology and that we would have to see. And when I paid the headwaiter, Mr. Skřivánek, I told him, You may have served the King of England but it hasn't done you any good. And I got up and walked among the tables, while the German officers greeted Lise, and I bowed too, as though they'd included me in their greetings. That night Lise took me home, but first we went to a military casino of some kind on Příkopy, in a brown building, where we drank champagne in honor of the occupation of Prague. The officers drank toasts with Lise and even with me, and she told everyone how courageously I'd behaved in defending her German honor against the Czech jingoes, and they acknowledged me with raised glasses, and I bowed and thanked them. But I didn't know that their greetings were meant for Lise alone and that they were actually ignoring me, barely tolerating me as someone who went along with Lise. She was a commanding officer in the nurses' corps, as I learned during the toasts, because they addressed one another by rank. It felt wonderful to be a part of this occasion, to be among captains and colonels and young people with eyes as blue and hair as blond as mine, and though my German wasn't up to much, I felt German. As we were coming back from celebrating Lise asked me to look up my family tree, because she was sure I must have some German ancestry. I could only tell her that my grandfather's name was spelled Johan Ditie on his tombstone, that he had been a groom on a large estate, something I'd always been ashamed of, but when Lise heard that, I seemed to gain stature in her eyes, more than if I'd been a Czech count, and with this name Ditie, all the fortifications and walls, thick and thin, that had separated us seemed to collapse, and she was silent all the way home. She unlocked the big main door to an old tenement house and we walked up the stairs, and on each landing she gave me a long kiss and fondled the crotch of my trousers, and when we went into her little room and she turned on the table lamp, she was all moist, her eyes and her mouth, and a whitish film seemed to have fallen across her eyes. She pushed me back on the couch and kissed me again, for a long time, running her tongue over all my teeth, counting them and whimpering and moaning like an ungreased gate opening and closing in the wind. What came next was bound to happen, and I'd expected it, but this time it didn't come from me, as it always had at such times before, but from her, because it was she who needed me. Slowly she undressed and watched me as I undressed, and I thought that since she was in the army even her underclothes, her panties and her slip, would be part of her uniform, that the nurses from the military hospital had some kind of government-issue underwear. But what she had on was like what the young ladies wore in the Hotel Paris when they came for their Thursday sessions with the stockbrokers, or like what the women at Paradise's wore. And then our naked bodies twined together and everything seemed liquid, as though we were snails, our moist bodies oozing out of our shells and into each other's embrace, and Lise shuddered and trembled violently, and I knew for the first time that I was both in love and loved in return, and it was so different from anything before. She didn't ask me to watch out or be careful, everything that happened was just right, the movements and the merging and the journey uphill and the dawning, and the gush of light with the muffled panting and moaning. She wasn't afraid of me afterward either, not for a minute, and her belly lifted toward my face and she wrapped her legs around my head and squeezed me tight without being ashamed. No, it all belonged, and she raised herself up and let herself be lapped and licked with my tongue until she arched her back and let me taste and feel with my tongue everything that was going on in her body. Then, when she lay on her back with her arms folded and her legs spread apart with that muff of pale hair blazing, brushed up into a crest, my eyes fell on a table that held a bouquet of spring tulips, a bunch of pussy willows, and several sprigs of spruce. As in a dream, without thinking, I took the sprigs and pulled them to pieces and lay them around her vagina, and it was beautiful, her lap strewn with spruce. She cast furtive glances at me, and when I bent over and kissed her through the branches I felt their sharp needles pricking my mouth, and she took my head tenderly in her hands and arched her back and pushed her lap into my face so hard that I groaned in pain, and with several powerful thrusts of her belly she reached such a pitch of passion that she shrieked, collapsed on one side, gasping so violently that I thought she was dying, but she wasn't. She leaned over me and spread her fingers and said she would scratch my eyes out and scratch my face and my whole body in gratitude and satisfaction, and again she spread her nails above me like claws and then closed them in a spasm, only to collapse in tears a few moments later. Gradually her silent weeping turned to faint laughter. Calm and quiet, lying there wilted, I watched her tear off the rest of those spruce boughs with nimble fingers, the way hunters do when they've killed an animal, and she covered my belly, my wilted penis, and my whole lap with tiny branches. Then she raised me up slightly and with her hands she caressed me and kissed my thighs, till slowly I got an erection and the branches began to rise and my penis pushed its way through, growing larger all the time, pushing the sprigs aside. But Lise rearranged them around it with her tongue, then raised her head and plunged my penis into her mouth, all of it, right down into her throat. I tried to move her off, but she pushed me back down and shoved my hands out of the way, so I looked up at the ceiling and let her do what she wanted with me. I hadn't expected her to be so wanton and rough, and so crude in the way she sucked me to the marrow, thrashing her head about violently without even pushing the sprigs aside, so they tore her mouth till she bled, and I thought this must be the way the Teutons did it. I was almost afraid of Lise then. Afterward, when she had crawled her tongue up my belly, leaving a trail of saliva behind her like a snail, she kissed me, and her mouth was full of semen and spruce needles, and she didn't think of it as unclean but rather as a consummation, as part of the Mass: This is my body and this is my blood and this is my saliva and these are your fluids and my fluids and this has joined us and will join us forever.

And I Never
Found the Head

My new job as a waiter, and then as headwaiter, was in the mountains above Děčín. When I first arrived at the hotel, I nearly jumped out of my skin. It wasn't a small hotel, as I'd been expecting, but a small town or a large village surrounded by woods, with hot springs in the forest and air so fresh you could have put it in a cup. All you had to do was turn and face the pleasant breeze and drink it in freely, as fish breathe through their gills, and you could hear the oxygen mixed with ozone flowing through your gills, and your lungs and vital parts would gradually pump up, as though earlier, somewhere down in the valley, long before, you'd got a flat tire, and it was only now, in this air, that you'd got it automatically pumped back up to a pressure that was safer and nicer to drive on.

Lise, who brought me here in an army truck, walked

around the place as though she owned it, smiling constantly as she led me down the main colonnade, a long double line of statues of German kings and emperors wearing helmets with horns on them, all made of fresh marble or white limestone that glistened like sugar. The other administrative buildings were the same, built off the main colonnade like the leaves of a locust tree. Everywhere you went there were more of these colonnades, and before you entered any building you had to walk past columns of horn-helmeted statues. All the walls were covered with reliefs showing scenes from the glorious German past, when they still ran around with hatchets and dressed in animal skins, like something right out of Jirásek's *Old Czech Legends*, except that the outfits they wore were German. When Lise explained what was going on here, I remembered the porter at the Hotel Tichota who loved to talk about how the unbelievable came true. Lise told me proudly that this place had the healthiest air in Central Europe and that the only other place like it was near Prague, above Ouholičký and Podmořání. She said this was the first breeding station in Europe for a refined race of humans, that the National Socialist Party had been the first to cross noble-blooded young German women with pure-blooded soldiers, both from the Heereswaffe and the SS, all scientifically. And so National Socialist intercourse was taking place here every day, no-nonsense intercourse, as the old Teutons used to do it. But even more important, the future mothers, who were carrying the new people of Europe in their bellies, dropped their litters here too, and a year later the children would be shipped to the Tyrol and Bavaria and the Black Forest, or to the sea, and the education of the New Man would begin in the first creches and nursery schools—not with the mothers, of course, but supervised by experts. Lise showed me beautiful little houses built to look like country cottages, with flowers spilling out over the windowsills, terraces, and wooden balconies. The future mothers and those who were already mothers were all robust, blonde young women who looked as though they were living in the wrong century, like the peasant girls you find in places such as Humpolec or Haná, or in villages that are so out of the way you still see women in striped petticoats and the same sort of blouses the Sokol women wear in our part of the country, or like the kind Božena wears in the famous painting where she's doing the wash and Oldřich rides by on horseback and finds her to his liking. And they all had nice breasts, and whenever they went for walks—and these young women were always wandering about—they would stroll up and down the colonnades, staring closely at the statues of the horned warriors as though this was part of their job, or they would stand in front of the handsome German kings and emperors, trying to etch in their minds those famous historical faces and personalities and their life stories. Later, outside a classroom window, I heard these women listening to lectures about those legendary heroes and then being tested to see if they knew it all by heart. The women were taught, Lise said, that the images of those heroes in their heads gradually percolated down through their bodies, reaching the thing that was just a blob at first, then something like a pollywog or a tree frog, then a tiny person, a homunculus, a dwarf that grew month by month until the ninth month, when it became a human being, and all the teaching and all the staring at the statues and pictures left an imprint on the new creature. Lise took me around and showed me everything, and she clung to me, and I noticed that whenever she glanced at my blond hair it seemed to put joy in her step, and when she introduced me to her section chief she introduced me as Ditie, the name inscribed on my grandfather's grave in Cvikov. I knew that Lise longed to spend those nine months here and more, so that she could donate a pure-blooded offspring to the Reich. But when I thought about it, it seemed to me that everything to do with that future child would happen the way it did when we put the cow in with the bull, or our nanny goat in with the village billy goat. When I stared down that row of columns and statues, I saw nothing but a tiny cloud of an enormous horror swirling around and enveloping me. And then I thought—and this was what saved me—about how I was so small that they wouldn't let me onto a Sokol gymnastics team, though I was as agile on the parallel bars and the rings as any big fellow, and I remembered the incident with the gold teaspoon in the Hotel Paris, and finally how they'd all spit in my face just because I'd fallen in love with a German gym teacher, and now here was the commander of the socialist breeding camp himself shaking my hand, admiring my straw-colored hair, and laughing pleasantly, as if he'd just seen a pretty girl or had a drink of some sweet liqueur or his favorite schnapps, and I stood straight and tall. I didn't wear a stiff collar anymore, but I think I felt for the first time in my life that you didn't actually have to be big, you just had to feel big. I looked about me with an easy mind and stopped being a little table boy, a busboy, a small waiter who was condemned to be small for the rest of his life and to put up with being called Pipsqueak and Squirt and Shorty and hear jokes insulting his family name, Dítě, which means child. Now I was Herr Ditie, and for the Germans there was no child in my name, and I bet the word reminded them of something completely different, or maybe they couldn't connect it to anything at all in German. So I began to get some respect here, because, as Lise told me, even the Prussian and Pomeranian nobility would envy a name like Ditie because their names all have Slavic roots, as mine does, von Ditie, so I became a waiter in section five, and I had to cover five tables at noon and at supper and serve five pregnant German girls whenever they rang for milk or cups of cold mountain water or Tyrolean cakes or plates of cold cuts—anything that was on the menu, in fact.

It was here that I first felt myself really blossoming. Though I was good at waiting on tables at Tichota's or the Hotel Paris, here I became the darling of the pregnant German girls. True, I had been the darling of the bar girls at the Hotel Paris every Thursday, when the stockbrokers came to the private chambers, but these German women, like Lise, all looked fondly at my hair, my tuxedo, and my blue sash with the medal, which Lise arranged for me to wear when I served meals on Sundays or holidays—a splash of gold radiating from a red stone in the middle, with the inscription Viribus Unibus. In this small mountain town, evening after evening soldiers from all the forces fortified themselves with good meals and fired their spirits with special Rhine and Mosel wines while the girls drank only cups of milk, and night after night the men were let in to them and were under strict scientific supervision right up to the very last moment. I was known as the waiter who had served the Emperor of Ethiopia, and I enjoyed the same standing as the headwaiter at the Hotel Paris, Mr. Skřivánek, who had served the King of England. I had a younger table boy under me and I taught him, just as Mr. Skřivánek had taught me, how to recognize what region a soldier came from and what he was likely to order. We'd ante up ten marks each and put them on a sideboard, and I'd almost always win. I learned that feeling victorious makes you victorious, and that once you lose heart or let yourself be discouraged the feeling of defeat will stay with you for the rest of your life, and you'll never get back on your feet again, especially in your own country and your own surroundings, where you're considered a runt, an eternal busboy. That's what would have happened if I'd stayed at home, but here the Germans treated me with respect. Every afternoon when the sun was out, I took cups of milk or ice cream or sometimes cups of warm milk or tea to the blue swimming pools where the beautiful pregnant German girls would swim naked with their hair down. They treated me as if I was one of the doctors, and I could watch their bright bodies ripple in the water as they spread their arms and legs, and after each swinging, rhythmic stroke their bodies would stretch out and glide, and their arms and legs would go on making those beautiful swimming motions. But it wasn't the bodies that attracted me so much now, because I fell in love—and this was a shock to me—I fell in love with that floating hair, the hair that swayed and flowed behind those bodies like pale smoke from burning straw, hair that went straight to full length with each powerful thrust of their arms and legs and then seemed to hang still for a moment, rippling slightly at the ends, like the corrugated metal in a shopfront shutter. And there would be the wonderful sunshine, and the background of blue or green tiles shimmering with broken reflections of sun and waves on the undulating water, syrupy drops of light and shadow, and the movement of bodies along the walls and the blue floor of the pool. When they were done swimming they pulled their legs under them and stood up, their breasts and bellies shedding rivulets of water like water nymphs, and I would hand them the cups, and they would drink from them slowly, then slip back into the water, clasping their hands in front of them as if praying, pushing the water aside with their first kicks, and swimming off again, not for themselves but for those future children. Several months later, in the indoor pools now, there were little babies in the water swimming along with the mothers, three-month-old tads who were already swimming with the women like cubs with female bears, or seals who can swim the day they're born, or ducklings who swim almost as soon as they hatch. But already I saw that these women thought of me as a flunky, as less than a flunky, in fact, despite my tuxedo. It was as if I wasn't there at all, as if I meant no more to them than a clothes horse. They felt no shame in front of me, because I was someone who served them, the way queens used to have jesters or midgets. Whenever they stepped out of the water they were always making sure no one was looking at them through the board fence, and once they were surprised by a drunken SS man, and they all shrieked, clapped their towels over their laps, covered their breasts with their arms, and ran into the changing booths. But when I brought them their cups on a tray, they would just stand there nonchalantly, naked, chatting to each other, leaning with one arm against the towel rack and casually drying their golden-haired laps with the other in unhurried, careful movements, wiping their crotches thoroughly and then each half of their backsides. And I would stand there while they took their cups from the tray, drank a little, and put them back, as if I was a serving table, and they would go on wiping their crotches with their towels, and then they would lift their arms and wipe dry each fold and crease of their breasts. Once an airplane swooped in low over the pool, and they ran into their changing booths for cover, shrieking with laughter, and returned a few moments later and took up the same positions as before, and all the while I was standing there holding the tray with the cooling cups.

In my free time I wrote long letters to Lise. She had an address somewhere near Warsaw, which they'd conquered by now. Then it was letters to Paris. And then, perhaps because of those victories, things became more relaxed, and they built a cyclorama just outside the town, and a shooting gallery and a merry-go-round and swings and everything, just like the Carnival of Saint Matthias in Prague, full of attractions of all sorts. Just as the gables of our cottages in the countryside used to be covered with murals of nymphs and sirens and allegorical women and animals, here regiments of German warriors wearing horned helmets filled the shooting galleries and the canopy on the merry-go-round and the panels on the sides of the swings, and I learned German national history from those pictures. All year long, whenever I had some free time, I would wander around looking at them and I'd ask the cultural instructor about them. He was delighted to explain it all to me, and he addressed me as *Mein lieber Herr Ditie*, pronouncing the Ditie so nicely that I asked him again and again to teach me about the glorious German past from those pictures and reliefs, so that I too might one day father a German child, just as Lise and I had agreed. When she came back all full of the victory over France, she told me she wanted to marry me but I would have to ask permission from her father, who owned the City of Amsterdam restaurant in Cheb. And so the unbelievable came true, because in Cheb I had to undergo an examination by a Supreme Court judge and I submitted a written request in which I listed my entire family, going back beyond that cemetery in Cvikov where Grandpa Johan Ditie lay, and with reference to his Aryan and Teutonic origins I respectfully requested permission to marry Elisabeth Papánek. According to the laws of the Reich, I also had to request a physical examination by an SS doctor to determine whether I, being of a different nationality, was eligible under the Nuremberg Laws not merely to have sex with someone of Aryan Teutonic blood but actually to impregnate her. And so while execution squads in Prague and Brno and other jurisdictions were carrying out the death sentence, I had to stand naked in front of a doctor who lifted my penis with a cane and then made me turn around while he used the cane to look into my anus, and then he hefted my scrotum and dictated in a loud voice. Next he asked me to masturbate and bring him a little semen so they could examine it scientifically because, as the doctor said in his atrocious Egerlander German—which I couldn't understand, though I got the gist well enough—when some stupid Czech turd wants to marry a German woman his jism had better be at least twice as good as the jism of the lowliest stoker in the lowliest hotel in the city of Cheb. He added that the gob of phlegm a German woman would spit between my eyes would be as much a disgrace to her as an honor to me. And I knew from reading the papers that on the very same day that I was standing here with my penis in my hand to prove myself worthy to marry a German, Germans were executing Czechs, and so I couldn't get an erection and offer the doctor a few drops of my sperm. Then the door opened and the doctor came in with my papers in his hand, and he'd probably just read them and realized who I was, because he said to me affably, *Herr Ditie, was ist den los?* And he patted me on the shoulder, handed me some photographs, and turned on the light. I found myself looking at pornographic snapshots of naked people, and whenever I'd had this kind of picture in my hands before I'd always turn stiff right away, but now the more I looked at them the more I saw those headlines and the stories in the papers announcing that so-and-so and four others had been sentenced to death and shot, and there were more of them every day, new ones, innocent ones. And here I was standing with my penis in my hand and pornographic snapshots in the other, so I put them down on the table, because I still couldn't manage to do what I was asked. Finally a young nurse had to come in and after a few deft strokes of her hand, during which I didn't have to think about anything anymore, she carried off two beads of my sperm on a piece of paper, and half an hour later they were pronounced first-class and worthy of inseminating an Aryan vagina with dignity. And so the Bureau for the Defense of German Honor and Blood could find no objection to my marrying an Aryan of German blood. With a mighty thumping of rubber stamps I was given a marriage license, while Czech patriots, with the same thumping of the same rubber stamps, were sentenced to death.

The marriage took place in Cheb, in a hall painted red, with red swastika flags everywhere and officials in brown uniforms with red straps over their shoulders and swastikas on the straps. I wore a morning suit and the blue sash across my chest bearing the Emperor of Ethiopia's medal, and Lise, the bride, wore her gamekeeper's outfit, a jacket embroidered with oak leaves and a swastika on a red background in her lapel. It was more like a state military ceremony than a wedding because all they talked about was blood and honor and duty. Finally the mayor of the city, who was also wearing a uniform, riding boots and a brown shirt, asked us, the betrothed, to approach a makeshift altar. Hanging behind the altar was a long flag with a swastika, and on the altar was a bust of Adolf Hitler scowling as the light from below cast shadows across his face. The mayor took my hand and the bride's hand and wrapped them in the flag and held our hands through the cloth, looking solemn. Now came the moment of betrothal. The mayor told us that from now on we belonged to each other and it was our duty to think only of the National Socialist Party and to conceive children who must also be raised in the spirit of that Party. Then, with tears welling up in his eyes, the mayor told us not to fret that we couldn't both die in the struggle for the New Europe, because they, the soldiers and Party members, would keep up the struggle for us until the final victory. And then they played a gramophone record of "Die Fahne hoch, die Reihen dicht geschlossen," and everyone sang along with the record, including Lise, and I remembered how I used to sing patriotic songs like "On the Strahov Ramparts" and "Where Is My Homeland," and that memory made me sing under my breath, until Lise nudged me gently with her elbow and gave me a nasty look, so I sang along with the others, and I found myself singing with feeling, as though I were a real German. When I looked around to see who was there, I saw army colonels and all the top Party brass from Cheb, and I knew that if I'd been married back home, it would have been as though nothing had happened, but here in Cheb it was practically a historical event, because Lise was well known here. When the ceremony was over, I stood with my hand ready, waiting to be congratulated, but then I began to sweat, because the Wehrmacht and SS officers didn't shake it. I was still just a runty little busboy as far as they were concerned, a Czech pipsqueak, a pygmy. But they practically flung themselves on Lise and congratulated her, while I stood there alone. When the mayor tapped me on the shoulder, I held out my hand, but he didn't take it either. So there I stood, my whole body stiff from holding my hand out, until the mayor put his arm around my shoulder and led me into his office to sign the register and pay the fee. Here I tried again and put an extra hundred marks on the table, but one of the clerks told me in a broken Czech that tips were not given here because this wasn't a restaurant or a canteen or a bar or a pub, but a bureau of the creators of the New Europe, where blood and honor were the deciding factors, not—as in Prague—

terror and bribery and other capitalist and Bolshevik practices. The wedding supper was held in the City of Amsterdam restaurant, and again I saw that although everyone seemed to be including me in the toasts, Lise was the center of attention, and that they put up with me as an Aryan but still considered me a dumb Bohemian despite my bright-yellow hair, the blue sash across my chest, and on the hip of my suit the medal shaped like a sunburst of gold. But I didn't let on how I felt or that I saw what was going on. Instead, I smiled and even managed to enjoy being the husband of a woman so famous that all the officers, who must have been single, would have loved to try for her hand, but not one of them had succeeded, because it was I who had enchanted her. These officers had their heads full of notions of defending honor and blood, and were probably incapable of doing anything more than jumping on a woman in bed with their riding boots on, not realizing that in bed you needed love and playfulness. That was my way of doing it, a way I had discovered a long time before, at Paradise's, when I'd spread ox-eye daisies and cyclamen petals over the laps of naked girls and finally, two years ago, on the lap of this political-minded young German, this commander in the nursing corps, this high-ranking Party member. While she was being congratulated, no one could have imagined her the way I had seen her, naked on her back as I garnished her lap with green spruce, which perhaps for her was even a greater honor than when the mayor pressed both our hands through the red flag and said how sorry he was that we couldn't both fall in the struggle for the New Europe and the new National Socialist man. When she saw my smile and realized that I'd decided to play the game I'd been condemned to play by the Bureau for Racial Purity, Lise picked up her glass and looked at me, and everyone fell silent, expecting a ceremony. I stood up, making myself taller, and we faced each other, holding our glasses in our fingers, and the officers watched us carefully, as if this was some kind of interrogation, and Lise laughed the way she laughed when we were in bed together, when I'd be gallant in the French manner. We looked at each other as though we were both naked, and again that white film came over her eyes, the kind of look women get when they are ready to cast aside the last shred of inhibition and let themselves be treated any way that seems right at the moment, when a different world opens up, a world of love games and wantonness. She gave me a long, slow kiss in front of everyone, and I closed my eyes, and as we kissed, our champagne glasses tilted in our fingers and the wine slowly spilled onto the tablecloth, and all the guests were silent. After that, everyone seemed abashed and looked at me with respect and curiosity, realizing that German blood has a lot more fun with Slavic blood than it does with other German blood. So though I was still an alien, I became an alien everyone respected with a touch of envy or maybe even hatred. The women looked at me as if they were trying to imagine what sorts of things I might do in bed. They must have thought I was up to some rather special games, and maybe even rough behavior, because they sighed sweetly, looked up at the ceiling, and talked with me, even though I mixed up *der*, *die*, and *das* when I spoke. These women talked to me slowly in their atrocious German, articulating the way you would in a nursery school, and they loved my answers and found the mistakes I made in conversational German charming and funny, and besides it gave them a taste of the magic of the Slavic plains and birch trees and meadows. But all the soldiers from the Heereswaffe and the SS glared at me because they could see only too well that I had won the affections of the beautiful, blonde Lise, that she had chosen a beautiful, animal love over German honor and blood, and that there was nothing they could do about it, even though their chests were plastered with medals and decorations from the campaigns against Poland and France.

When we came back from our honeymoon to that small town above Děčín where I was a waiter, Lise wanted us to have children. But like any true Slav, I was a creature of moods. I could do anything in the emotion of the moment, but when Lise told me to get ready because that night she was set to conceive the New Man, the founder of the New Europe, I felt exactly the way I had when the *Reichsdoktor*, acting on the Nuremberg Laws, asked me to bring him a bit of my sperm on a piece of white paper. For a week she'd been playing Wagner on the record player, *Lohengrin* and *Siegfried*, and she'd already decided that if it was a boy she'd call it Siegfried Ditie, and all week long she'd walked around gazing at those scenes in relief along the covered walkways and colonnades. She would stand there in the late afternoons with German kings and emperors and Teutonic heroes and demigods rising against the blue sky, while my only thought was how I would strew her lap with flowers and how we'd start by playing like little children, especially since our name was Ditie. That evening Lise appeared in a long gown, her eyes full of duty and blood and honor, and she put her hand in mine, babbled something in German, and rolled her eyes upward, as though all the denizens of the Teutonic heaven were gazing down on us from the ceiling, through the ceiling—all the Nibelungs, and even Wagner himself, whom Lise invoked for help in becoming pregnant the way she wished, in harmony with the new Teutonic sense of honor, so that her womb would be graced by the New Man, who would establish and live in the New Order of the New Blood and the New Thinking and the New Honor. When I heard all this, I felt everything that makes a man a man drain out of me, and I just lay there staring at the ceiling, dreaming about a lost paradise, about how wonderful everything had been before we were married, about how I had slept with all women the way a mongrel dog would, whereas now I had a job to do, like a purebred sire with a purebred bitch. I'd seen the trouble and bother dog breeders went to, waiting for days on end for the right moment, and one breeder brought a bitch to our town from the far end of the republic and had to turn around and go all the way back because a prize-winning fox terrier wouldn't have anything to do with her. The next time they came, they put the bitch over a wooden bucket in the stable and, wearing a glove on her hand, the lady guided the dog's sex organ to its place, and the dog impregnated the bitch with a whip over his head. But the bitch would have surrendered herself just as happily to any old mongrel. Or there was the major who had a Saint Bernard and spent the whole afternoon with a bitch all the way from Šumava, but couldn't get them together because the bitch was bigger, and finally Engineer Marzin took them to a slope in the garden where he dug out a kind of depression. They spent an hour landscaping the terrain, getting ready for that Saint Bernardian wedding, and by evening they were all worn out, but at last the slope was ready, and they stood the bitch under the step in the hillside so that the male was now the same height as she was, and union took place, but by compulsion, while left to their own devices a German shepherd will eagerly join with a dachshund bitch, or an Irish setter bitch with a stable-bred terrier. And I was in exactly the same position. So the unbelievable came true, because a month later I had to go for some potency injections, and each time needles as blunt as nails were poked into my buttock to strengthen my vigor, and one night, after I'd been through the routine ten times, I managed to impregnate Lise in the regulation manner. Now that she had conceived, it was she who had to go for the injections, because the doctors were afraid she might not carry the New Man to term. And so of all our love nothing remained, and all that was left was an act of National Socialist intercourse, and Lise wouldn't even touch my penis, and I was only admitted to her bed according to regulations and the order of the New European, which did me no good. Both our behinds were so punctured by those dull needles that we spent most of our time tending the wounds, mine especially, which kept running. And all this so I could beget a beautiful New Child.

About the same time, an unpleasant thing happened to me. Several times I noticed that you could hear lessons in Russian coming from the classrooms where they usually gave lectures on the glorious past of the old Teutons. Now that the soldiers had fulfilled their duties as studs and impregnated the beautiful blonde girls, they were learning basic Russian as well. Once, when I was listening to these Russian courses under the window, a captain asked me what I thought of it. I said it looked as if there was going to be a war with Russia. At this he started yelling at me, accusing me of inciting the public, and I replied that there was no public here, just the two of us, and he yelled back that we had a pact with Russia and what I'd said was sedition and the spreading of a false rumor. It was then I realized that he was the same captain who had been Lise's witness at the wedding, who not only had refused to shake hands and congratulate me but had been trying to win Lise's favor before me, and I had beat him to it. Now he was trying to get back at me, and so he lodged a complaint, and I found myself before the commandant of the town that served as a breeding station for the New Europe. Just as the commandant yelled that I was a Czech chauvinist and they would have me court-martialed, the alert was sounded in the camp, and when the commandant picked up the telephone he turned pale, because it was war, just as I had predicted. In the corridor all the commandant said to me was, How did you guess? And I replied modestly, I served the Emperor of Ethiopia. The next day, a son was born to us, and Lise had him christened Siegfried, because the walls of those covered walkways and Wagner's music had inspired her to have a son. But I was fired all the same and given a new position in a restaurant called Košíček in the Bohemian Paradise district. The restaurant and hotel were at the very bottom of a rocky canyon, in a kind of natural basket submerged in the morning mists below the clear air. It was a small hotel for people in love, couples who would go on dreamy walks along the cliffs and lookouts and return hand in hand to their lunches and their suppers. Every movement they made was relaxed and unhurried, because although Košíček was also meant for the Heereswaffe and the SS-Waffe the officers would meet their wives and mistresses here for the last time before going off to the Eastern front. Just about everything in Košíček was poles apart from the small town that was incubating the New Race, where the soldiers were stud horses or purebred boars who were expected, the same day they arrived or at least within a couple of days, to impregnate German females scientifically with Teutonic sperm. But here it was different and more to my taste. There was not much gaiety, there was instead a melancholy sadness, a kind of dreaminess I had never expected to see in soldiers. Almost all our guests were like poets before they begin writing a poem—not because they were that kind of person, no, they were just as crude and vulgar and arrogant as other Germans, always drunk with their victory over France, even though a third of the officers from the Grossdeutschland division had fallen in the Gallician campaign. It was because these officers were preparing for a different journey altogether, a different mission, a different battle: they were going to the Russian front, which was quite another kettle of fish. By November, the Germans had driven a wedge right up to the outskirts of Moscow but no farther, so the armies coming up from the rear just kept spreading to Voronezh and on to the Caucasus. And then there was the vast distance, and the bad news from the front—that is, from this side of it—that partisans were harassing the troops so badly that the front had become a rear guard, as Lise told me when she came back from there herself, very upset about how the Russian campaign was going. Lise also brought me a tiny suitcase. At first I didn't realize how valuable the contents were because it was full of postage stamps, and I wondered how Lise had come by them. It turned out that while she was in Poland she had ransacked Jewish apartments for stamps, and when they were searching deported Jews in Warsaw she had confiscated these stamps. She told me that after the war they would be worth a fortune, enough to buy us any hotel we wanted.

My little son, who stayed with me, was a strange child. I couldn't see any of my own features in him, not a single sign that he took after either me or Lise, certainly nothing of what was promised by those Valhalla surroundings, and not a trace in him of Wagner's music. He was a nervous little child who suffered from convulsions in the third month of his life. Meanwhile, I served guests from all the regions of Germany, and I could now guess correctly whether a German soldier was from Pomerania, Bavaria, or the Rhineland. I could also tell the difference between a soldier from the coast and one from inland, and whether he had been a worker or a farmer, and that was my only entertainment as I waited on tables with no break or free time from morning till evening and into the night. I waited not just on men but also on women, who were here on a secret mission, but that mission was sadness and a kind of ceremonial anxiety. I never again, as long I lived, saw married couples and lovers who were so gentle, kind, and considerate to each other, or who had so much wistfulness in their eyes and tenderness, like the girls back home who used to sing "Dark Eyes" or "The Mountains Resounded." In the countryside around Košíček, no matter what the weather, there would always be couples out for walks, always a young officer in uniform and a young woman, quiet and absorbed in each other. I who had served the Emperor of Ethiopia had never experienced this and couldn't put myself in their place. Only now have I got to the core of it, that what made these people beautiful was knowing that they might never see each other again. The New Man was not the victor, loud-mouthed and vain, but the man who was humble and solemn, with the beautiful eyes of a terrified animal. And so through the eyes of these lovers—because even married couples became lovers again with the danger of the front hanging over them—I learned to see the countryside, the flowers on the tables, the children at play, and to see that every hour is a sacrament. The day and the night before the departure for the front, the lovers didn't sleep, but they weren't necessarily in bed either, because there was something more here than bed: there were eyes and a special feeling, like seeing a sad, romantic play or movie in a large theater or movie house. I also learned that the closest that one person can be to another is through silence, an hour, then a quarter-hour, then the last few minutes of silence when the carriage has arrived, or sometimes a military *britzska*, or a car. Two silent people rise to their feet, gazing long at each other, a sigh, then the final kiss, then the man standing in the *britzska*, then the man sitting down and the vehicle driving off up the hill, the final bend in the road, the waving handkerchief. And then the carriage gradually slipping like the sun behind the hill, until there is nothing more to be seen, only a figure standing in front of the hotel, a woman, a German, a person in tears, still waving, moving her fingers, while a tiny handkerchief flutters to the ground. Then she turns and in a fit of weeping rushes up the stairs to her room, where like a Barnabite nun who has seen a man in the cloister she falls on her face in the eiderdown and sinks into the bed for a long, invigorating cry. The next day, their eyes still red, these mistresses would drive off to the station, and the same carriage or *britzska* or automobile would bring other lovers from all directions, from all the garrisons in all the towns and villages, for a final rendezvous before the men went to the front. Despite the armies' rapid advance, the news from the front was so bad that Lise became increasingly worried, worried about the blitzkrieg, worried that she wouldn't be able to stand it here. So she decided to take Siegfried to Cheb, to the City of Amsterdam restaurant, and go to the front herself, where she would feel less tense.

I kept the rare stamps in an ordinary-looking little suitcase made of cardboard, inside an old vulcanite trunk, because when I checked on the value of some of the stamps in Zumstein's catalogue I knew right away that I wouldn't have to tile my room with green hundred-crown bills anymore, because even if I covered the walls with them and glued them on the ceiling and in the hallway and the toilet and the kitchen, this could never equal the sum of money I would one day rake in, since according to Zumstein four of the stamps alone would make me a millionaire. And then I thought about coming back one day after the war, because the Germans were losing and the war would be over before we knew it. Whenever I saw a high-ranking officer I could read the whole situation in his face. Faces were my newspapers and my dispatches from the front, and even if they wore flashing monocles or dark glasses or pulled their helmets down like black masks, I could still see how things stood on the battlefield from the way people walked and held themselves and behaved. And once more the unbelievable came true. By this time I had left Košíček, and like those soldiers I too said my farewells, waved until the carriage slipped over the hill, wept, and then took the train to my new place of work. As I walked up and down the railroad platform it occurred to me to look at myself in a mirror that was fastened to the station wall, and when I did I suddenly saw myself as a stranger, like those Germans from all the regions and districts with their different professions and interests and states of health that I'd been able to guess correctly because I had served the Emperor of Ethiopia, because I'd been schooled by the headwaiter Mr. Skřivánek, who in his turn had served the King of England. So I took a penetrating look at myself from that angle and saw myself as I never had before, as a member of Sokol who when the Germans were executing Czech patriots had allowed Nazi doctors to examine him to determine if he could have sexual intercourse with a German gym teacher, and while the Germans were provoking a war with Russia he was gettng married and singing "Die Reihen dicht geschlossen," and while people at home were suffering, he was sitting pretty in German hotels and inns, serving the German army and the SS-Waffe. With the war coming to an end, I knew I could never go back to Prague, and I could see myself, not being lynched exactly, but hanging myself on the first lamppost, or at the very least sentencing myself to ten years and maybe more. So I stood there in the early morning at the railroad station, which was empty, looking at myself as a guest who was coming toward me, and I who had served the Emperor of Ethiopia was condemned to face the truth, because just as I had been curious about the suffering and indiscretions of other people, so now, using exactly the same method, I looked at myself, and the sight made me sick, especially since I had a dream of becoming a millionaire and showing Prague and all those hotel owners that I was one of them, and perhaps even better than they were. It was entirely up to me now what I would do, go back home and buy the biggest hotel and be equal to Mr. Šroubek and Mr. Brandejs and all those Sokol people who looked down their noses at me, people you could only talk to from a position of strength, and use my little suitcase containing those four stamps that Lise had plundered in Warsaw or somewhere in Lemberg to buy me a hotel, the Hotel Ditie—or instead should I buy something in Austria or Switzerland? And as I deliberated like this with my own image in the mirror, behind me, silently, a train pulled into the station, an express train, a military-hospital train from the front, in fact, and when it stopped I could see in the mirror that the blinds on all the windows were down. Then one blind went up, the hand holding the cord let go, and I saw a woman in a nightgown lying on the berth. She yawned so widely she almost put her jaw out of joint, then rubbed her eyes and when she had finished rubbing them she looked out the window to see where the train had stopped. I looked at her and she looked at me and it was Lise my wife. I saw her jump up and before I knew it she was out of the train just as she was and hanging around my neck and kissing me the way she did before we were married, and I who had served the

Emperor of Ethiopia saw that she had changed, just as all the officers who had gone to the front after a pleasant week at Košíček with their wives or their mistresses had changed. Lise, like them, must have seen and lived through unbelievable things that had come true. She was escorting a military transport of crippled men to the place where I was going, to Chomutov, to a military hospital by a lake. So I simply got on the train with my little suitcase, and when the train pulled out of the station I went into the compartment with Lise and drew the curtains and locked the door, and when I took off her nightgown she trembled the way she used to before we were married, because the war must have made her free and humble again. And then she undressed me and we lay naked in each other's arms and she let me kiss her lap and do everything to her in the rhythm of the ride, moving and touching like the bumpers between the cars.

At the station in Chomutov, ambulances, cars, and buses, mobile hospitals on six wheels, were already waiting. I didn't obey Lise but stood at the end of the platform, which had been cleared of people, and they let me stay there only because I'd got off the train with Lise, who reported to the stationmaster, and then they unloaded a fresh batch of transportable cripples from the front, all those who couldn't walk, who had one or both legs amputated—a platform full of cripples—and loaded them all into the cars and buses. Though I didn't recognize anyone in particular, I knew these were the same ones who'd been on stud duty in that little town above Děčín and who'd said their last farewells at Košíček. And this was the final scene in their comedy, their play, their movie. I went off with the first busload to the place I'd been assigned to, a canteen in the military hospital, and I kept my little suitcase on my lap and tossed my leather suitcase on the roof rack among the military duffel and kit bags. That day I walked through the countryside and the camp, which was laid out along the edge of a hill, in an orchard of sweet and sour cherry trees that went right down to the bank of a small lake in a quarry. The lake resembled the Sea of Galilee or the sacred River Ganges, because attendants would bring out the cripples with gangrenous amputation wounds and carry them down long wooden jetties branching into the lake. There wasn't a single insect or a single fish in the water, because everything had died and nothing would grow as long as water flowed into the lake from the stone quarry. The cripples whose wounds were already slightly healed would lie in the water or paddle gently about. Some were missing one leg or both legs below the knees, and others had no legs at all, just stumps. They moved their arms in the water like frogs, with their heads poking out of the blue lake, and they were handsome young men again, but when they swam to the edge, they would pull themselves out with their arms and crawl up the bank like turtles to lie on the shore, waiting for the attendants to wrap them in bathrobes and warm blankets and carry them, hundreds of them, back across the jetties and to the main patio in front of the restaurant, where an all-woman orchestra was playing and meals were being served. I was most moved by the ward for men with severed spinal cords, who dragged their whole lower bodies after them on dry land, and in the water they looked like mermaids. Then there were the legless ones who loved playing ping-pong, and some had small chrome-plated folding carts that allowed them to move about quickly enough to play soccer, except that they would use their hands instead of their feet. As soon as they'd recovered a little—the one-legged and armless ones, and those with badly burned heads—they developed a tremendous appetite for life, and they would play soccer and ping-pong and handball until dark, and I would call them to supper by playing a tattoo on a trumpet. When they approached in their carts or hobbled up on crutches, they radiated health. I was working in the rehabilitation department, but in the three other departments the doctors were still putting the wounded back together with operations and then electrical and iontophoresis treatments. And sometimes I'd have an opposite vision of those cripples and see only the arms and legs they'd lost, the missing arms and legs and not the real ones that were there. I'd put my finger to my forehead and ask myself, Why are you seeing things that way? Because you served the Emperor of Ethiopia, because you were trained by one who served the King of England.

Once a week, Lise and I went to see our son in Cheb, at the City of Amsterdam Hotel. Lise had now gone back to her swimming and she was in her element, always splashing about in the lake. The swimming had made her so taut and beautiful, like a bronze statue, that I could hardly wait until we were together again. She'd bought a book by some imperial German athlete named Fouré or Fuké or something, about the cult of the naked body, and because Lise had a beautiful body she became a nudist, though without actually joining a club. In the morning she'd serve me coffee wearing nothing but a skirt, or sometimes we'd pull the

curtains and she'd walk around the house completely naked, and when she looked at me, she would nod contentedly and smile, because she could see in my eyes that she
pleased me and was beautiful. But our little son Siegfried
caused us a lot of worry. Everything he picked up he threw
down again, until one day, when he was crawling around
the floor of the City of Amsterdam, he picked up a hammer.
His old grandfather gave him a nail, just for fun, and the
boy set the nail up and drove it into the floor with one
blow. From then on, while other little boys were playing
with rattles and teddy bears and running around, Siegfried
would lie on the floor and throw a tantrum until he got
his hammer and nails, which you could only get for cou-
pons or on the black market. He didn't talk, he didn't even
recognize his mother or me, and as long as he was awake
the City of Amsterdam would tremble with the blows from
his hammer, and the floor was full of the nails he'd driven
into it. I found our weekly visits unbearable, and each blow
would drive me to distraction, because I could see right
away that this child, this guest who was my own son, was
a cretin and would always be a cretin. When other children
his age were going to school, Siegfried would just be starting to walk, and when others were graduating, Siegfried
would barely be learning how to read, and when others
were getting married, Siegfried would still be learning how
to tell the time and fetch the newspaper. But there was
more to it than a little boy obsessed with pounding nails
into the floor. Whenever the air-raid siren went off and
everyone else rushed into the shelter, Siegfried got excited
and glowed with pleasure. And while other kids were mess-
ing their pants out of fear, Siegfried would clap his little

hands, laugh, and pound nail after nail into the board they'd brought into the cellar for him, and suddenly he was beautiful, as though the convulsions he had suffered as a baby and the defect in his cerebral cortex had vanished. And I, who had served the Emperor of Ethiopia, was pleased that my son, though he was feeble-minded, could prophesy the future of all the German cities, because I knew that most of them would end up exactly like the floors of the City of Amsterdam hotel. I bought three kilos of nails, and in a single morning Siegfried drove them all into the kitchen floor. In the afternoon, as he was driving nails into the rooms upstairs, I would carefully pull the nails out of the kitchen floor, rejoicing secretly as the carpet bombing of Marshal Tedder drove bombs into the earth in exactly the same way, precisely according to plan, because my boy would drive nails in along straight lines and at right angles. Slavic blood had triumphed once again, and I was proud of the boy, because although he hadn't spoken a word yet, he was already like Bivoj, a hammer in his strong right hand.

Now I began to see pictures, images from long ago that I'd forgotten about, and suddenly they were right before me, so fresh and clear that I would stand there by the quarry with my tray of mineral water, thunderstruck. I saw Zdeněk, the headwaiter at the Hotel Tichota, who enjoyed having a good time so much when he was off work that to get it he'd spend all the money he had with him, which was always several thousand. Then I saw his uncle, a military bandmaster now retired, who split wood on his little plot of land in the forest where he had a cottage overgrown with flowers and wild vines. This uncle had been a bandmaster at the time of the Austro-Hungarian Empire and still wore his uniform when he split wood, because he had written two polkas and several waltzes that still got played all the time, although no one remembered who the composer was and everyone thought he'd died a long time ago. Zdeněk and I, as we were riding along in a rented buggy on one of our days off, heard the sound of a military brass band playing one of his uncle's waltzes, and Zdeněk stood up and signaled the driver to stop, then went over to the band and had a little talk with the bandmaster. He offered to give him all the money he had, four thousand crowns, for the soldiers to buy themselves beer, if they would do what he asked. Buses were waiting, and the whole band was getting ready to climb aboard to go to a band tattoo, so we left the buggy there and got on the first bus with them. After an hour's drive we stopped in a forest, and soon a hundred and twenty uniformed musicians with their shiny instruments were advancing slowly down a road through the woods. Then they turned onto a footpath lined with thick bushes and pine trees that towered overhead, and Zdeněk signaled them to stop and slipped through some loose planks in a fence, disappeared into the bushes for a few moments, then came back and told them his plan. When he gave the sign, the soldiers climbed one by one through the hole in the fence into the bushes while Zdeněk, like a soldier at the front, directed them to take positions around the tiny house. They could hear the sound of an ax striking wood, and the entire band silently surrounded the chopping block and an old man in an ancient Austrian bandleader's uniform. When Zdeněk gave the signal, the bandmaster flung his golden ceremonial baton in the air, gave a loud command, and out of the bushes rose a glistening array of brass instruments and the band began to play a clamorous polka by Zdeněk's uncle. The old bandleader stood transfixed over the piece of wood he had just split, while the band moved forward a couple of steps, still up to their waists in pine and oak shrubs. Only the bandmaster stood in the greenery up to his knees, swinging his golden baton while the band played the polka and their instruments flashed in the sunlight. The old bandleader slowly looked around with a heavenly expression on his face, and when they finished the polka the band started right in on one of his concert waltzes, and the old bandleader sat down, put his ax across his knees, and began to cry. The bandmaster came up and touched his shoulder, the old man looked up, and the bandmaster handed him the golden baton. Now the old man got to his feet and, as he told us afterward, he thought he'd died and gone to heaven with a military band all around him, and he thought they must play military music in heaven and that God Himself was conducting the band and was now turning His own baton over to him. So the old man conducted his own pieces, and when he'd finished, Zdeněk stepped out of the bushes, shook hands with his uncle, and wished him good health. Half an hour later the band climbed back into their buses and as they were driving away they played Zdeněk a farewell ceremonial fanfare. Zdeněk stood there filled with emotion and bowed and thanked them, and finally the buses, and with them the fanfares, faded down the road through the woods, lashed by beech branches and shrubs.

As a matter of fact, there was something of the angel in

Zdeněk. Once he financed a wedding for a stonecutter's daughter, and another time we went to a clothing store and bought some white sailor's uniforms for all the boys at an orphanage. During a fair he would pay the expenses of all the merry-go-round and swing operators so everyone could ride for nothing all day. On one of our days off we bought jars of jelly and the most beautiful bouquets we could find in Prague and went from one public toilet to another, congratulating all the old women attendants on name days they didn't have and birthdays that had come and gone, though Zdeněk always managed to strike it lucky with at least one of them. One day I decided to go to Prague, take a taxi out to the Hotel Tichota, and ask if Zdeněk was still there and if not where I could find him, and I also planned to visit the mill by the Charles Baths where I once lived with Grandma, to see if the little room was still there where the shirts and underwear flew past the window. While I was standing at the station in Prague I pulled my sleeve back to see what time it was, and when I looked up I saw Zdeněk over by a newsstand, and I stiffened, because here it was again: the unbelievable was coming true. I stood frozen in that position, with one hand holding up the other sleeve, and I saw Zdeněk looking around as though he had been waiting a long time for someone, then he raised his arm and was just about to look at his watch too when three men in long leather coats stepped up and grabbed me by the arm. I saw Zdeněk staring at me as though he couldn't believe his eyes. He was pale and just stood staring as the Germans bundled me into a car and drove off, and I wondered where on earth they were taking me and why. They drove to Pankrác prison, the gates opened, and they led me in like a criminal and threw me into a cell. I was dazzled by what had happened to me, I rejoiced, hoping against hope they wouldn't let me out right away. What I really wanted, since the war was coming to an end anyway, was to be arrested and sent to a concentration camp, and now it seemed my lucky star was shining. The cell door opened and I was led off to interrogation, and after I had given them all my particulars and my reason for coming to Prague, the investigating officer grew serious and asked me who I had been waiting for. I said, Nobody. The door opened and two men in civilian clothes rushed in, punched me in the nose, knocked two of my teeth out, and I fell back to the floor. They leaned over me and asked me again who I was waiting for and who I was supposed to pass the message to, and when I said I'd just come to Prague for a visit, one of them brought his face down close to mine, lifted my head up, grabbed me by the hair, and pounded my head on the floor while the interrogating officer screamed that glancing at my watch had been a prearranged signal and that I was connected with the underground Bolshevik movement. When they tossed me back in the cell the SS men shouted, You Bolshevik swine! And the words were sweet and tender music to my ears, because I was beginning to see that this could be my return ticket to Prague, an eraser that would wipe away what I'd got myself into when I married a German and had to stand before the Nazi doctor in Cheb, who examined my penis to see if I was worthy of having sexual intercourse with a Teutonic Aryan, and I laughed and laughed, because some-how I hadn't felt the beating or the wounds, and because now my battered face was a passport that would allow me one day to return to Prague as an anti-Nazi fighter. The main thing was that I'd be able to show all those Šroubeks and Brandejses and all the hotel owners that I was one of them, because if I survived this I would buy a big hotel, not in Prague perhaps, but certainly somewhere else, because with the stamps in that little suitcase, as Lise had intended, I'd be able to buy two hotels and have my choice of Austria or Switzerland. In the eyes of those Austrian and Swiss hotelkeepers I'd be a complete stranger, with no need to prove to them that there was nothing in my past. If I had a hotel in Prague, on the other hand, and was a member of the Association of Prague Hotelkeepers, and worked my way up to executive secretary for all the Prague hotels, they'd have to respect me—not love me, perhaps, but at least respect me, and that was really all I wanted.

I was in Pankrác prison fourteen days in all, and after further interrogation they realized it had been a mistake, that they had been waiting for someone else who was supposed to look at his watch, and they'd already caught the contact man and got everything they wanted out of him, except the other person's identity, and I remembered that Zdeněk had been standing there and that he was just about to look at his watch too. Zdeněk had seen me get arrested for him, and that could be very important to me, because if no one from the cells vouched for me later, certainly Zdeněk would. So when I came back from the interrogations and just before they pushed me into the cells, I started my nose bleeding again and I laughed and laughed while the blood flowed. When they let me go, the interrogator apologized but reminded me that in the interests of the Reich it was better to punish ninety-nine just men by mistake than to let a single guilty person slip through their fingers. Toward evening, I stood outside the gates of the Pankrác penitentiary, and another man was let out just after me, and when he came out he broke down and sank to the sidewalk. The streetcars were going by in the purple twilight of the blackout, crowds flowed up and down the street, young people walked hand in hand and children played in the dusk as if there was no war going on at all, only flowers and embraces and loving glances. The girls wore their blouses and skirts in the warm twilight just so, and I too looked at them hungrily, because everything seemed prepared for men's eyes, deliberately put into an erotic frame. It's so beautiful, said the man when I came over to offer my help. How long? I asked. He said he'd just finished a ten-year stretch. Then he tried to stand up, but couldn't, and I had to help. He asked me if I was in a hurry, and I said no, and when he asked me what I'd been in for, I said illegal activity. So we walked to a Number 11 trolley, and I had to help him on, and everywhere, in the trolley and on the streets, were crowds of people who all seemed to be on their way home or going to a dance, and that was when I noticed for the first time that Prague girls were prettier than German girls, with better taste, because the German girls wore their clothes as if they were uniforms, all those dresses and dirndls, those green suits and hunter's hats. I sat down beside the man, who had gray hair though he couldn't have been much over thirty, and I told him he looked too young for his gray hair, and then I asked him out of the blue, Who did you kill? He hesitated a moment, then stared at the prominent breasts of a girl who was hanging on to a strap with one hand,

and finally asked me, How did you know? And I told him I had served the Emperor of Ethiopia. We went right to the end of the line, and the murderer asked me to come with him to his mother's, to be with him in case he fell on the way. We smoked as we waited for the bus, which wasn't long in coming, then went three stops and got out at Koníčkový Mlýn, and the murderer told me that he'd rather go the back way, through the village of Makotřasy, to surprise his mother and ask her forgiveness. I said that I'd go with him to the edge of the village, to the gate of his house, and then return to the main road and hitchhike home. I was doing this not out of any kindness but to give myself as many alibis as possible once the war was over, and it would be over before we knew it.

We walked together through the starry night, and the dusty road took us through a blacked-out village and then back into damp countryside as blue as carbon paper, with a narrow little moon that cast an orange light and made a thin, barely visible shadow behind us or in front of us or in the ditches beside us. Then we walked up to the top of a small rise, not much more than a sigh in the earth, and he said that from here we should be able to see his native village. But when we got to the top of the rise, not a single building was visible. The murderer hesitated, seemed almost alarmed, and stammered that it was impossible, or could he have made a mistake? Perhaps over the next rise. But after we'd gone a hundred meters or so, fear came over us both and the murderer began trembling more violently than he had when he first walked through the gates of the Pankrác penitentiary. He sat down and wiped his forehead, which glistened as if sprinkled with water. What's the matter? I asked. There was a village here once, and there's not a trace of it now, babbled the murderer. Am I losing my mind, have I gone crazy, or what? What was the name of the village? I asked. Lidice, he said. That explains it, I said, the village is gone. The Germans blew it up and shot the men and took everyone else off to a concentration camp. Why? the murderer asked. Because the *Reichsprotektor* was assassinated and the assassins' trail led them here, I said. The murderer sat down, his hands hanging over his knees like two flippers, then stood up again and stumbled through that moonlit landscape like a drunk. He stopped by what looked like a post in the ground, fell down, and embraced it. It wasn't a post at all, it was what was left of a tree trunk with the stump of a single branch on it, as though it had been used as a gallows. This, said the murderer, used to be our walnut tree, this is where our garden was, and here—and he walked slowly around—somewhere here. And he knelt down and felt around with his hands for the crumbled foundations of the house and the farm buildings. He felt with certainty now, as if he was reading Braille reinforced by memory, and when he had felt out the whole foundation of his family home on his hands and knees, he sat down under the tree trunk and yelled, You murderers! Then he stood up and clenched his fist until the blue veins stood out on his neck in the light of the sickle moon. After he had cursed the murderers, the murderer sat down on the ground, bent forward with his hands under his knees, rocked back and forth as in a rocking chair, and stared at the branch outlined against the moon, then he spoke as if he was making a confession: I had a handsome father who was better-looking than me, and I'm a failure compared with him, and Dad was crazy about women and women were even crazier about him. He had a fling with the neighbor's wife, and I was jealous of her, and my mother suffered, and I saw it all. See this branch right here? He'd grab it and swing himself over the fence to visit the neighbor's pretty wife. Once I waited for him, and when he swung back over the fence we had an argument and I killed him with an ax. It wasn't that I wanted to kill him, but I loved my mother and my mother was suffering. Now all that's left is the trunk of the walnut tree, and my mother, I'll bet she's dead too.

I said, Maybe she's in a concentration camp, and she'll be coming back soon. So the murderer got up and said, Will you come with me to ask? And I said, Why not? I can speak German. So we set out for Kladno. Just before midnight we got to Kročehlavy and asked a German patrol where the Gestapo headquarters was. The patrol told us how to get there, and soon we were standing in front of the main door. There was some kind of party on the second floor—we could hear the hum of talk, the clinking of glasses, and piercing female laughter. Then the patrol arrived and the sentry changed. It was already an hour past midnight, and I asked the commander of the guard if we could talk to the head of the Gestapo, and he roared, *Was?* and told us to come back in the morning. Just then the door opened and a crowd of SS men in high spirits came pouring out, gaily saying their farewells as though they'd been at some kind of celebration or birthday or name-day party, just the way our exhilarated guests used to leave the Hotel Paris every day when it was time for them to leave.

And on the very top step stood a soldier holding a candelabra with burning candles in it. He was drunk, his uniform was a mess, his hair fell over his forehead as he held the candelabra up in a gesture of farewell. When he saw us, he came down the stairs to the threshold and asked the sentry, who saluted him respectfully, who we were. The sentry replied that we wanted to talk to him. The murderer told him, and I translated it, that he'd been in prison for ten years and had come home to Lidice and hadn't been able to find a single house or his mother, and he wanted to know what had happened to her. The commander laughed, and little tears of hot wax dripped to the ground from the tilted candelabra. He turned and started walking back up the stairs, but then he roared out, *Halt!* And the guards opened the door and the commander came back down the stairs and asked the murderer what he'd got the ten years for. The murderer said he'd killed his father. Now the commander held the candelabra, with the candles still dripping wax, up to the murderer's face, and somehow he became sober, as though he was delighted that fate had sent him a man that night who was looking for his mother after he'd killed his own father, and who now was standing where the commander himself often stood as a murderer, whether he murdered on orders or of his own free will. And I, who had served an emperor and had often seen the unbelievable come true, I saw this imperial German state murderer, this wholesale murderer with decorations clanking on his chest, climb the stairs followed by a simple murderer, a patricide. I wanted to leave now, but the sentry took me by the shoulder and roughly turned me back toward the stairs. So I sat at a large table covered with the leftovers from the banquet, and it looked just the way tables look after a wedding or a large graduation party, with scraps of cake and bottles empty and half empty, and the drunken SS man sat down on the table and made the murderer tell him the story all over again, while I translated—everything that had happened ten years ago by the walnut tree—but what the commander got the biggest kick out of was how efficient the organization in Pankrác was, so efficient that the prisoner never learned about the people and the town of Lidice. And something even more unbelievable came true that evening. Hidden behind the mask of a translator with a battered and healing face, unrecognized, I recognized in this Gestapo commander one of the guests at my wedding, the military gentleman who hadn't even congratulated me or offered his hand, though I raised my glass and clicked the heels of my polished shoes and stood there with my arm and my glass extended, offering to drink to my own happiness, only to find the gesture not repeated. I had felt terribly humiliated, so I blushed to the roots of my hair, just as I'd done when Mr. Šroubek refused to drink to my health, and Mr. Skřivánek too, who had served the King of England. And now fate was offering me another one, another of those who had ignored my offer of friendship in the glass. Here he was, sitting right in front of me, making a big thing out of getting up from his chair to wake up the archivist and have him bring out the registry book, and then flipping through the pages on the banquet table, getting them all smeared with sauce and liquor, turning the pages until he found the right page, so he could read what had happened and announce that the murderer's mother was in a concentration camp and that so far there was no date and no cross after her name to indicate her death.

The next day, when I got back to Chomutov, I found myself fired: they'd heard the news of my arrest, and mere suspicion was enough to have me packing my bags. I also found a letter saying that Lise had gone to see Siegfried at his grandfather's in Cheb, in the City of Amsterdam hotel. She asked me to come too and said she'd taken the little suitcase with her. I got a ride by car right to the edge of Cheb, where I had to wait because an air-raid warning was in effect for Cheb and Aš. As I lay in the ditch with the soldiers, I heard a pounding like the regular and rhythmic working of a machine, and it came closer and closer, and my son appeared to me, and I saw how every day—today too, because I'd bought him five kilos of eight-inch nails— he would crawl along and regularly and rhythmically pound nails into the floor with powerful blows from his hammer, one beside another, with a single energetic blow for each, as if he were planting radishes or a thick row of spinach. When the air raid was over, I got back into the military automobile. Driving into Cheb, we saw people, old Germans, walking out of the city and singing songs. But they were happy songs, and I wondered if what they'd seen had driven them mad or confused them, or was it a custom of theirs to sing a happy song in the face of adversity? Then we ran into clouds of dust and yellow smoke, and there were dead bodies in the ditches, and then streets with houses ablaze, and ambulance crews pulling people out of the rubble, and nurses kneeling and wrapping bandages around heads and arms. You could hear moans and wailing on all sides. I remembered how we'd driven past this place in carriages and cars on the way to my wedding, when everyone was drunk with the victory over France and Poland. And I saw red swastika flags with the flames licking at them, the banners burning and crackling as though the fire was devouring them with a special relish, and the fire advanced up the red cloth, followed by the blackening end, which curled up behind it like the tail of a sea horse. Then I found myself standing in front of the collapsed and burning front wall of the City of Amsterdam hotel, and a slight breeze came up and drew aside a curtain of beige smoke and dust, and on the top floor I saw my little son still sitting, picking up nails and pounding them into the floor with powerful blows. Even from that distance I could see how strong his right arm was, and how that was all he really had, just a strong fist and a rippling bicep that could drive a nail right into the floor with a single blow, as if no bombs had fallen, as if nothing in the world had happened. And the next day, when people came out of their bomb shelters, Lise, my wife, had still not shown up. I asked about a small, scuffed suitcase, and they told me Lise kept it with her all the time. So I took a pick and dug around in the courtyard all day long. The next day I gave my little boy five kilos of nails, and he gaily pounded them into the floor while I went on looking for my wife, his mother. It wasn't until the third day that I came across her shoes. Slowly—while Siegfried was having a tantrum because he'd run out of nails—I freed my Lise from the pile of rubble and dust, and when I uncovered half her body I saw that she was curled into a ball to protect the little suitcase. First I carefully hid it, then I dug out the rest of her, all but her head. The blast had taken her head off, and we spent two more days looking for it while my son went on pounding nails into the floor and into my brain. On the fourth day I took the little suitcase and without saying good-bye to anyone walked away, and behind me the blows of the hammer grew fainter, blows I would hear for the rest of my life. That evening a society for mentally handicapped children was supposed to come for Siegfried. And Lise was buried in a common grave with a scarf wrapped around the stump of her neck so people wouldn't get strange ideas, because though I had dug up the whole courtyard, I never found the head.

How I Became
a Millionaire

◆◆◆◆◆◆◆◆◆◆◆◆◆

The little suitcase with the rare stamps brought me good luck, though not right away. When the war was over, I was served with a warrant for collaboration under the small decree, even though I'd turned over the address of the Gestapo commander, the one who had murdered so many people and then gone into hiding in the Tyrolean Mountains. I'd pried his whereabouts out of my father-in-law in Cheb, and Zdeněk got permission from the American officials, and they set off with a car and two soldiers to arrest him. They found him cutting grass in a meadow, disguised in Tyrolean lederhosen and a beard he'd let grow. But even if I had arrested him single-handed, the Prague Sokolites would still have wanted me in jail, not because I married a German woman but because when thousands of Czech patriots were being executed I had stood before the Nazi Bureau for the Defense of German Honor and Blood and let them examine me, a dues-paying member of the Sokol organization, to see whether I was worthy of having sexual intercourse with a Teutonic Aryan woman. For that I was sentenced to half a year in prison.

When I got out I sold those stamps for so much money that I was able to cover the floor of my room ten times over, and when I got enough to cover it forty times over I bought myself a hotel on the outskirts of Prague, a hotel with forty rooms. But the very first night, I had the feeling that in the highest room, right under the mansard roof, someone was pounding nails into the floor, a nail a minute, with heavy blows from a carpenter's ax. Each day the sound spread to another room, a second and then a third and then a tenth, until at last it reached the fortieth room, and it was happening in all of them at once. Everywhere, in every one of those rooms my little son was crawling around the floor, forty sons, each one pounding nails into the floor with powerful blows from his hammer. On the fortieth day, deafened by the blows, I asked whether anyone else heard them, but no one did, only me, so I traded the hotel for another one, and this time I purposely chose a place with only thirty rooms, but it started up all over again. So I decided that the money from the stamps was cursed, that it was money taken by force from someone who might have been killed in the process, or maybe the stamps had belonged to a rabbi with miraculous powers, because those nails were really being pounded into my head, and with each blow of the hammer I felt the nail puncturing my skull, and the next blow would drive the nail halfway in, and then all the way in, and I'd end up not being able to swallow, because those long spikes would go right into my throat. But I didn't lose my mind, because I'd set myself the goal of owning a hotel and being on equal terms with all the other hotel owners, and I couldn't give up on that, it was the only thing that kept me going, the fact that one day I would make it as far as Mr. Brandejs had. Not that I wanted four hundred sets of gold cutlery like him, a hundred sets would do, as long as there were famous foreigners coming to stay at my place. So I began to build a hotel of my own, one that would be very different from all the other hotels. I bought a huge abandoned quarry near Prague and started adding things to it and sprucing up what was already there, as the Hotel Tichota had done. The basis for the hotel was a large blacksmith's shop with a dirt floor and two chimneys. I left the four anvils just the way they were, with all the hammers and tongs hanging on the black walls, and I bought leather armchairs and tables. All this was at the suggestion of a mad architect who did things for me that he had been dreaming about, and he was as enthusiastic as I was. Here, in these chimneys and on these forges, the shashlik and the roast pork à la Živaň would be grilled right in front of the guests. The same day the conversions in the blacksmith's shop were finished, I slept there, and the first night I heard hammer blows, but they were faint, because the nails went into the dirt floor like butter, and the feeling inside my head was muffled as well, so I threw myself with more excitement than ever into building the guest rooms inside a long building that looked like a concentration camp barracks, where the workers used to have their cloakrooms and dormitories. I converted these into small rooms, thirty of them, and as an experiment I had the floors made of those rough tiles, the kind they have in Italy and Spain and other places where the weather is hot. The first day I listened carefully, but the tiles were so hard that all I could hear were nails glancing off my head, showering sparks, and then the blows let up altogether and I recovered and began to sleep again the way I used to. Construction proceeded so rapidly that the hotel opened in two months, and I called it the Hotel in the Quarry, because something inside me had been broken and crushed and carted away. It was a first-class hotel, and you could stay overnight only if you had a reservation. It was in the woods, and the rooms were set out in a semicircle above a blue pond at the bottom of the quarry. In the rock, forty meters of granite straight up, I had rock climbers plant alpine flowers and shrubs that grow in places like that. A steel cable was stretched above the pond, with one end anchored at the top of the cliff and the other at the bottom, so the cable went down over the water, and every evening I provided entertainment, I hired an acrobat who had a small, grooved steel wheel with a short grip underneath it, and he'd wait for the right moment, kick off, and come swooping down from the top of the cliff, and when he was right over the pond, with a spotlight on his phosphorescent costume, he'd let go of the wheel, hang for a moment in midair, and then do a jackknife, straighten, and with his hands stretched out in front of him slip into the deep water. Then slowly, easily, in his skintight phosphorescent suit, he would swim to the edge of the pond where the tables and chairs were. I'd had everything painted white, because white was my color now—something like the terrace restaurant at Barrandov, except that this was original, and now I could compete with anyone. The idea of the wheel came from a busboy who was standing on the top of the hill one afternoon, grabbed the wheel, and slid down the cable. When he was halfway down, he let go, and all the guests screamed and stood up or shrank back in their armchairs, which were all in the Ludwigian style, but the busboy straightened and did a flip in midair and then, in his waiter's tuxedo, slipped headfirst into the water, as though the pond had swallowed him up. I realized at once that this sort of thing had to go on every day, and that in the evening he would have to wear a phosphorescent costume. I couldn't possibly lose money on it, and even if I did, it wouldn't matter, because no one else had anything like it, not in Prague, not in all of Bohemia, and maybe not even anywhere in Europe or the rest of the world. One day they told me a writer had come to stay whose name was Steinbeck. He looked like an old sea captain or a highwayman, and he loved it here, loved the blacksmith's shop turned into a restaurant and the cooks working right in front of the guests, cooking on the open forges so that by the time the shashlik and roast pork à la Živaň were done the guests were as famished as little children. But what the writer liked most were all those granite crushers, the dusty old milling machines with their insides laid bare so you could see how they worked, like an exhibition where cars are sliced in half so you can see inside the motor. The writer was enchanted with these machines. They were in an open field above the quarry, from which you could see out across the countryside, and there the machines stood, abandoned stonecutting machines and lathes, looking as if they'd been invented by mad sculptors. This writer had them bring up his white table and a white lounge chair, and every afternoon he'd drink a bottle of French cognac and every evening he'd have another. Sitting among those machines with the mill down below, he'd gaze off into the countryside, and it was just the dull, ordinary countryside near Velké Popovice, but with the writer there it seemed beautiful and the machines seemed like works of art. The writer told me he'd never seen anything like it before, had never actually stayed in a hotel like this before. In America—this is what he said—only a famous actor like Gary Cooper or Spencer Tracy could have such a place, and the only writer who could afford a hotel like this would be Hemingway. By the way, what did I say I wanted for it? I said two million, so he did some figuring on the table, then called me over, pulled out a checkbook, and said he'd take it and write me a check then and there for fifty thousand dollars. I questioned his figures several times, and he went to sixty, then seventy, then eighty thousand dollars, but I realized that I couldn't sell my hotel even for a million dollars, because the Hotel in the Quarry represented the height of my powers, the pinnacle of my efforts, and I had become the first among hotelkeepers. There were hundreds and thousands of hotels like Mr. Brandejs's or Mr. Šroubek's, but I knew that no one else in the world had a hotel like mine.

One day the biggest Prague hotel owners, including Mr. Brandejs and Mr. Šroubek, came and ordered supper. The maître d' and the waiters set their table with the utmost care and taste, and just for them I turned on ten spotlights that were hidden under the rhododendrons and aimed so they would light up the whole face of the rock from below, bringing out the highlights, the sharp edges, the fantastic shadows, and the flowers and shrubs. I decided that if these hotel owners were inclined to make peace, to take me among themselves and offer me a membership in the Association of Hotelkeepers, I would let bygones be bygones. But they pretended not to see me, and not only that, they deliberately sat with their backs to all the beauties of my establishment. But I felt I was the winner, because they had turned their backs on the unique features of my enterprise only because they saw and they knew that I had outdone them. And it wasn't just Steinbeck who stayed here, but Maurice Chevalier too, and a lot of women came to see him, and they stayed near the quarry. Chevalier would receive them in the morning in his pajamas, and they would throw themselves at him, these admirers, and undress him and tear his pajamas to shreds so they'd each have a piece as a souvenir, and if they'd been able to they would have torn Chevalier himself apart and carried away pieces of his body, depending on how their tastes ran. Looking at them, you'd think that most of them would tear out the famous singer's heart first, and then his penis. Chevalier attracted such a swarm of reporters that pictures of my quarry were carried not only in all the local magazines, but in foreign ones as well, and I had clippings from the *Frankfurter Allgemeine* and the *Zürcher Zeitung* and *Die Zeit*, and in the *Herald Tribune*, of all places, there was my hotel and Chevalier surrounded by those crazy women in the middle of the field with the machine sculptures, machines surrounded by white tables and chairs with stylized grapevines wound into their backrests. And that was the real reason these hotelkeepers had come, not to bury the hatchet but because they'd heard I'd bought this quarry and everything in it for a song, and when they saw it, what they saw was far stronger and far more beautiful than they'd ever imagined. And they were jealous of me, because I left everything just the way I found it, building the hotel from the inside, so to speak, and anyone who understood anything could see that and give me credit, as though I were an artist. That was the height of my career, that was what made me a man who had not lived in vain. I began to look at my hotel as a work of art, as my own creation, because that was how others saw it, and they opened my eyes, and I understood that those machines were really sculptures, beautiful sculptures that I wouldn't have given up for anything. One day I began to see that my Hotel in the Quarry was something like the things Holub or Naprstek brought back with them from their travels abroad, and I knew the time would come when every one of those machines, every stone, everything would become a historical site. But those hotel owners could still make me feel humiliated, because I wasn't one of them, I wasn't of equal rank, though I was actually above them, and often at night I would regret that the old Austrian Empire was gone, because if there were military maneuvers, say, and if, not the Emperor perhaps, but one of his archdukes were to stay here, I would serve him and prepare his meals so well and make his visit so pleasant that he would give me a title, not a high title, but he'd make me a baronet at least. And so I dreamed on, and when a great heat wave came and the crops dried up in the fields and cracks opened up in the ground and children threw letters into the cracks in the earth, I dreamed of winter, of the snow falling and everything freezing, and I dreamed of sweeping off the surface of the pond and putting two small tables there, with two old Victrolas on them, one horn painted blue and the other pink like two big flowers, and I would buy old gramophone records and play old-fashioned waltzes, and fires would be flickering in the blacksmith's shop, logs blazing in steel baskets around the edge of the pond, and the guests would go skating on the ice, and I would buy old-fashioned skates or have them made, the kind you fasten on with a key, and the men would get down on their knees and put them on for the ladies, and hot punch would be served. And while I dreamed, the newspapers and the political parties argued about who was going to pay for the drought that had inspired in me such wonderful dreams of winter revels in the quarry. When Parliament and the Cabinet discussed the drought and decided that the millionaires should pay for it, I accepted their verdict with satisfaction, because I was a millionaire now too, and as a millionaire I wanted to see my name in the papers alongside Šroubek's and Brandejs's and the others, so I understood that the drought was in fact sent by my lucky star, and that the bad luck would be my good luck and put me right up there where I dreamed of being when I imagined the archduke making me a baronet. Although I was still no taller than when I'd been a busboy, I was big now, I was a millionaire, but months passed and nobody sent me any notification, nobody demanded that I pay the millionaire's portion. By this time I had bought the two gramophones, and I had a magnificent orchestrion brought in too, along with an old merry-go-round with huge horses, deer, and elk on it. It had once been a German merry-go-round, belonging to some wealthy amusement-park and shooting-gallery owner, and I had the merry-go-round taken apart and the horses and the deer mounted on their original springs on a stone curb around the pond. I put the deer and the horses in twos, side by side, and the guests and their wives would sit on them and talk, as though they were out on a Sunday ride, and the idea really caught on. The horses and the deer were always occupied, and the orchestrion played while the guests rocked back and forth on the wooden animals with their magnificent saddles, bridles, and trappings, and with their beautiful eyes, and everything about them was wonderful.

Then one day, out of the blue, Zdeněk came to see me. By now he was a big man in the district, maybe even in the region, and he'd changed a lot. He rocked back and forth on one of the horses and looked around, and when I sat down on the horse beside him, he talked to me quietly and then took a folded document out of his pocket and before I could stop him slowly tore it up. This was the document that named me a millionaire and ordered me to pay my millionaire's share. Zdeněk then jumped down and tossed it in the fire. For me it would have been a wonderful document to have, almost like a letter of appointment. He smiled at me sadly and drank the rest of his mineral water—this was Zdeněk, who never had drunk anything but hard liquor—and walked away with a sad smile on his face. There was a big, fancy black car waiting to take him back where he came from, back to the politics he was busy with and I suppose he believed in, because it kept him going, and it must have been wonderful if it could take the place of those grand, generous gestures of his, the kind he used to spend all his money on, as if the money was too hot for him to hang on to and he had to give it back to the people he thought it properly belonged to. Events began to move very fast now, and just as I had dreamed I would, I gave sensational evenings and afternoons in the quarry with gramophone music, ice skating, and bonfires, in the blacksmith's shop and around the pond. But the guests who came now were sad, or if they were gay it was not the kind of gaiety I was used to, but a forced gaiety, the kind the Germans had displayed when they celebrated at Košíček, knowing that they were there with their wives or lovers for the last time because afterward they would go straight to the front. And that's exactly how my guests would leave, they'd shake my hand and wave from their cars as though this were it, as though they'd never be coming back again. If they did come back, it was the same thing all over again, they were melancholy and gloomy. Normally events outside were not felt here, but now everything in politics had turned upside down, it was February 1948 and all my guests knew they were doomed. They'd spent what they could but the joy and the spontaneity had gone out of it. I felt their sadness too and stopped locking myself up every night and pulling the curtains so I could lay the hundred-crown notes from the daily take out on the floor—like playing solitaire or reading my own fortune in the cards— before taking them to the bank the next morning, where I now had a million crowns on deposit. Spring came, and many of my guests, my regulars, stopped coming, and I learned that they had fallen, that they had been arrested and locked up, or that some of them had escaped across the border. Now a different kind of customer started coming, and the daily take was even bigger, but I wondered what had happened to the ones who used to come here every week. One day two of them came and told me that they were millionaires and that they had to be ready tomorrow, with a pair of heavy boots, a blanket, and extra socks and food, because they were going to be taken away to a holding camp somewhere because they were millionaires. I was delighted, because I was a millionaire too, and I brought them my bankbook and showed it to them. One said he was a factory owner who made gym equipment, and the other said he manufactured false teeth. So I went and got my rucksack, heavy lace-up boots, an extra pair of socks, and canned food, because the false-teeth manufacturer told me that all the Prague hotel owners had been sent summonses too. In the morning they drove off, weeping, because they didn't have the courage to make a run for it across the border. That was too risky, they thought, and anyway America and the United Nations wouldn't leave things like this, and the millionaires would get everything back and return to their villas and their families. I waited a day, then another, then a week, then I got news from Prague that all the millionaires were already in the camp at a Catholic seminary in Svatý Jan pod Skalou, an enormous monastery and boarding school for future priests who had been moved out. So I made up my mind, and that was on the day they came from the district Party headquarters and broke it to me very gently that the National Committee was going to confiscate the quarry, that I could stay on as a caretaker for the time being, but all the property rights had devolved to the people. I was outraged, and I guessed that Zdeněk had had a hand in this,

so I went straight to his office in the district Party headquarters. But he said nothing, he just smiled at me sadly,
took a piece of paper off his desk, and tore it up in front
of me, then told me that he was tearing up my summons
on his own account, because I had once taken his punish-
ment for him, the time when I'd looked at my watch outside
the station. I told Zdeněk that this was the last thing I
expected of him, that I had thought he was my friend but
he was really against me, because I never wanted anything else and never worked for anything else all my life
except having my own hotel and being a millionaire. And
I walked out.

That night I stood outside the gate of the seminary. The
lights were on, and a militiaman with an army rifle stood
at the gate, and I told him that I was a millionaire, the
owner of the Hotel in the Quarry, and that I wanted to
speak to the commanding officer about an important matter. The militiaman picked up a telephone, and pretty soon
I was let through the gate and shown to an office where
another militiaman, this time without a rifle, was sitting
at a desk covered with lists and papers. He kept drinking
from a bottle of beer, and when he'd emptied it he'd reach
under the table and pull another bottle out of a case, open
it, and drink thirstily, as though it were his first. I asked
him if he wasn't short a millionaire and told him I hadn't
got a summons even though I was a millionaire too. He
ran down a list with his pen, name by name, and then told
me I wasn't a millionaire and could go right back home if
I wanted. I said, There must be some mistake, because I
am a millionaire. He took me by the shoulder and walked
me to the gate, then started pushing me and shouting,

You're not on my list so you're not a millionaire! I pulled out my bankbook and showed him I had one million one hundred crowns and ten hellers in the bank. What do you call that? I said triumphantly. He looked at the bankbook. Surely you're not going to throw me out? I said. And he took pity on me, pulled me back into the seminary, declared me officially interned, and took down all my particulars. This boarding school for theological students actually looked like a jail, or a military barracks, or a residence for poor university students, except that in every bend in the corridors and between the windows there were crucifixes along with scenes from the lives of the saints. Almost every picture showed some kind of torture, horrible scenes rendered by the painter with such loving detail that the idea of four hundred millionaires living in the seminary, four and sometimes six to a cell, seemed like a joke. I'd been expecting a reign of terror and malice here, like the half-year I'd spent in jail after the war, but life in the seminary of Svatý Jan was more like a movie comedy. They set up a court of sorts in the refectory, and the militiamen appeared with army rifles on red slings over their shoulders, but the slings kept slipping off. The uniforms weren't made to measure and seemed deliberately too big for the small men, and too small for the big men, so they all went around with their buttons undone. The way they ran the trial, every millionaire got a year for each million he had, so I got two years because I had over a million, and the gym equipment manufacturer got four years because he had four million, and Šroubek the hotelkeeper got the heaviest sentence, ten years, because he had ten million. The biggest problem the militiamen had was finding the right column to enter the sentences and our particulars. Roll call every evening was a terrible problem too, because someone was always missing. The reason was that we would take watering cans and go to the nearest village for beer, and another reason was that our guards, who were always drinking, had a hard time counting us, even if they started in the afternoon. So they tried counting us by tens instead, and one of the guards would clap, and another guard would drop a pebble, and after they'd counted the last man they would tally up the pebbles, add a zero to the result, and then tack on the remainder, the ones that didn't go into ten. Some days there'd be more of us, some days fewer, even though we were all there. Every once in a while the sum of interned millionaires would actually come out right and be duly entered into the record, and everyone would be relieved, but just then four millionaires would walk in carrying cases and jugs of beer, and so to keep the books straight the guards would enter them as new arrivals and give each of them another sentence on top of his original one, depending on how many millions he had. It may have been a seminary, but there was no fence around it. The militiamen would sit at the gate, and the millionaires would go out for walks and come back through the garden, but then they had to walk around and come through the gate, because the militiamen would unlock it each time and then lock it again, even though there was no fence and no wall around the place. The militiamen themselves would take shortcuts through the garden, but then their consciences would bother them and they'd go back to the gate, take the key from the inside, go around and unlock the gate from the outside, walk through it, lock it again, and go into the seminary. The worst thing was the food, but even that problem was solved because the commander and the militiamen started eating with the millionaires, and they would give the food they brought with them from the militia barracks to the pigs that one of the millionaires, the false-teeth manufacturer, had bought. First there were ten pigs, then twenty, and everyone looked forward to the slaughter, because there were some wholesale butchers among us who promised culinary delights that had the militiamen licking their lips. Then the militiamen started suggesting pork specialties of their own, and after that the cuisine here was not the kind you'd normally find in a seminary, but more the way they used to cook in the rich monasteries—the way the Crusaders cooked, for instance. Whenever a millionaire ran out of money, the commander would send him home for more, and at first a militiaman disguised as a civilian would go with him, but later a promise to come back was enough. The internee would drive to Prague for the money and take it out of the million or millions in his account, because the commander had given him an authorization saying the money was to be spent in the public interest. And so they cooked their own meals in the seminary, drew up their own menu, then gave it to the militia commander for approval, asking him to kindly pass along any suggestions, because the millionaires thought of the militiamen as their guests, and we would all eat together in the dining hall.

Once, one of the millionaires, Tejnora, got permission to drive into Prague to hire a Schrammel-quartet that played dinner music. When he brought the musicians back in a taxi—taking a taxi to Prague became part of the fun—

they walked around the locked gate into the millionaires' camp and woke up the guards, since it was already past midnight, then they went back out and around to the front of the gate and waited. But the guards were so groggy they couldn't get the gate open, so Tejnora walked through the garden, took the key from the guards, went around again, and unlocked the gate from the front. But there was something wrong with the key and he couldn't lock the gate again, so he went around to the other side and locked it from there, then handed over the key. I kept thinking it was too bad Zdeněk wasn't a millionaire, he'd be right in his element here, because besides his own money he could spend money for the ones who didn't have the imagination to do anything interesting with it. Within a month, all the millionaires were tanned, because we would sunbathe on the hillsides, while the militiamen stayed pale, because all they ever did was stand outside the gate or make out reports and sit around in the cells. They couldn't even put together a proper list of prisoners: some names, like Novák and Nový, came up three times. They had to carry their weapons at all times, and they were forever dropping their rifles and cartridge pouches, and rubbing things out and rewriting their reports, so the millionaire hotelkeepers ended up doing it for them, because it was no more difficult than drawing up a menu. There was a farm attached to the Catholic seminary with ten cows, but the milk from those udders was not enough for our morning coffee, which was café au lait made from real ground coffee and spiked with a shot of rum, a touch introduced by Mr. Šroubek, just the way they used to do it in the Café Sacher in Vienna. So the poster-paint manufacturer bought five more cows, and then there was enough milk, but since some of the prisoners couldn't stand café au lait, they had only a glass of rum for breakfast, drinking it straight from the coffee cup. The monthly family visits were wonderful too. The commander bought some white clothesline and hung it up to make an imaginary wall, and when the rope ran out he scraped a line in the ground with his heel to separate the internees from the world outside. The wives and children would show up with rucksacks and bags full of food—Hungarian salami and foreign canned goods. Although we tried to look careworn, the fact is we were suntanned and well fed, and a passerby who didn't know the real situation could easily have taken the visitors for the prisoners, because the internment of the millionaires was obviously far harder on their families than it was on the millionaires themselves. There was no way we could eat everything the wives brought us, so we shared what we had with the militiamen, who enjoyed the food so much they got the commander to agree to two visits a month, a visit every other week. And whenever cash was needed, thirty or fifty thousand crowns, the commander would let the experts go through the monastery library and pick out rare books, to be taken to Prague by car and sold in the secondhand bookstores. Then the militiamen discovered they could sell the sheets, pillowcases, nightwear, and vestments belonging to the future priests at Svatý Jan pod Skalou, where we sunned ourselves on the slopes and took naps after lunch. But by that time it was almost too late, because the millionaires had figured this out long ago and taken the best of the sheets and the long nightshirts made of cloth handwoven on mountain looms, and beautiful towels by the gross, and they'd carried them all off in suitcases. Later the millionaires started taking holidays, which showed how much the militiamen trusted us, because they knew we wouldn't run away. Even when we did, and this happened twice, we brought another millionaire back with us, a good friend who wanted a vacation from his family. Eventually the militiamen started taking their uniforms off and wearing civilian clothes, and we would put on their uniforms and guard ourselves, and when we got Sunday duty or the watch from Saturday to Sunday, we all looked forward to it, because it was real comedy, beyond Chaplin's wildest imagination. All afternoon we would pretend we were going to close down the millionaires' camp, and the commander of the gate, who was the millionaire Tejnora in a militiaman's uniform, declared the camp officially closed and told the millionaires they could go home, but the millionaires would go back to their cells. Then millionaires dressed up as militiamen would try to persuade them to change their minds, telling them how wonderful it was outside in the world of freedom, how they'd no longer have to suffer under the scourge of the militia, how they'd live the life of a millionaire again. But the millionaires wouldn't have any of it, and so Tejnora, in militia uniform and commanding the other millionaires in militia uniforms on guard duty at the gate, ordered the camp to be closed by force. We dragged the millionaires out of their cells, those who had eight and ten million and therefore eight and ten years ahead of them. At first the militia-millionaires couldn't find the key to the gate, and when they found it they couldn't get the lock to work, so they ran around and unlocked it from outside, then ran around it again, and we all watched and roared with laughter as the millionaires were dragged outside by the militia-millionaires and the gate was locked behind them. The millionaires walked up to the top of the hill, took one look around, changed their minds, and came back down, pounded on the jailhouse door, got down on their knees, and begged the militia-millionaires to take them in again. I laughed too, but I wasn't really laughing at all, because although I was with the millionaires, I hadn't really become one of them, even though I slept in the same cell as Mr. Šroubek. He was so cold to me, he wouldn't even let me hand him back a spoon when it fell on the floor in the refectory, though I picked it up and stood there holding the spoon out, just as I'd done years before when I held up my glass and no one wanted to drink a toast with me. The hotelkeeper would get another spoon and eat with that one, squeamishly taking a napkin and pushing away the one I'd put down beside his plate, until it fell back on the floor and he kicked it under the table where the vestments were kept. So I laughed, but my heart wasn't in it. Whenever I'd start talking about my million crowns and my Hotel in the Quarry, all the millionaires would clam up and turn away, refusing to recognize my million, my two million, and I saw that they thought I wasn't worthy of them, because they had got their millions a long time ago, long before the war, whereas I was a war profiteer. They couldn't bring themselves to accept me, because I wasn't of their rank, and it probably would have been the same in my dream if the Archduke had made me a baronet, because I still wouldn't have been a real baronet, the rest of the nobility wouldn't have accepted me, just as the millionaires now were not accepting me. A year before, when I was still free, I dreamt that they might accept me one day, and was convinced that as owner of the Hotel in the Quarry I was as good as they were, because some of them shook hands with me and talked nicely to me, but it was all for show, the way every rich man tries to be on good terms with the maître d' in a hotel or restaurant, and he'll even ask the maître d' to bring an extra glass and drink a toast with him, but if the rich man meets the maître d' on the street, he won't stop and pass the time of day with him. I also saw how their millions got accumulated, how Mr. Brandejs had always served potato croquettes to his help and saved on small details, and here too he had been the first to see those beautiful sheets and towels and figure a way to get his hands on them, sneak them through the gate in a suitcase, and smuggle them home—not because he needed them, but because his millionaire's spirit wouldn't let him pass up an opportunity to acquire, gratis, those beautiful things from the wardrobes of future priests.

It was my job to look after the pigeons, two hundred pairs of carrier pigeons that had stayed behind after the priests left. The commander assigned me to clean the dovecote and give them water and scraps from the kitchen. Every day after lunch I took them a little cart full of leftovers. The commander got so tired of eating meat that he began longing for potato pancakes and blini filled with plum jam and grated cheese and drenched in sour cream. The millionaire couturier Barta was having a visit from his family, and he mentioned to the commander that his wife was from good peasant stock, so why not try her out as a pastry cook? That was how the first woman appeared in camp. Since we were all tired of eating meat, three more wives came into the prison, three millionairesses, with Mrs. Bartová the chief pastry cook. When the millionaires who could prove they had Austrian or French citizenship were released and there were ten empty cells, the millionaires came up with the idea of renting those cells to their wives, who might come to visit them once a week, because it was inhuman for a married man to be denied access to his lawful spouse. And so beautiful women began showing up, ten at a time, and I discovered later that they weren't wives at all, because I recognized two women, getting on in years but still beautiful, who used to come to the Hotel Paris for the Department of Internal Medicine on Thursdays when the stockbrokers showed up. But I was growing fond of my pigeons, all two hundred pairs of them. They were so punctual that exactly at two o'clock they would perch on the crest of the monastery roof, where they could see right into the kitchen, and I would come out of the kitchen with my little cart loaded with two bags of scraps—leftover vegetables and things like that—and I who had served the Emperor of Ethiopia would feed the pigeons, something no one else wanted to do, because it was no work for the delicate hands of a millionaire. I had to come out of the kitchen on the stroke of two, and if for some reason the clock didn't strike but the sun was out, I would go by the sundial on the wall of the church, and when I emerged, all four hundred pigeons would swoop down from the roof and fly straight at me, and a shadow flew with them, and the rustling of feathers and wings was like flour or salt being poured out of a bag. The pigeons would land on the cart, and if they couldn't find a place they would sit on my shoulders and fly around my head and beat their wings against my ears, blotting out the world, as though I were tangled up in a huge bridal train stretching in front of me and behind me, a veil of moving wings and eight hundred beautiful blueberry eyes. The millionaires almost died laughing when they saw me covered with pigeons as I pulled the cart to the courtyard, where the pigeons started devouring the food, pecking away until the two sacks were empty and the pots looked as though they'd been scoured clean. Once I was late, because the commander was busy tasting the minestrone soup with Parmesan cheese and I was waiting for the pot. I heard the clock strike two, and before I knew it the pigeons flew through an open window and into the kitchen, all four hundred of them, and they swirled around everyone, knocking the spoon out of the camp commander's hand. I rushed out of the kitchen, and on the doorstep the pigeons flocked around me and pecked me with their gentle beaks, and I covered my face and head with my hands and ran across the yard with pigeons swirling around me and swarming over me, because for them I was a god of life. And I looked back on my life and saw myself now, surrounded by these divine messengers, these pigeons, as though I were a saint, and meanwhile I could hear the laughter and the shouts and snide remarks of the millionaires, and suddenly the message of the pigeons hit me, and the unbelievable came true again, because even if I'd had ten million crowns and three hotels it wouldn't have mattered, no, this kissing of tiny beaks was sent by heaven itself, just as I'd seen on the altar panels and the stations of the cross that we walked past to get to our cells. And even though I had seen nothing and heard nothing, wanting to be what I had never been able to be, a million-aire, despite my two million, I became a millionaire, a multi-millionaire, only now, when I saw for the first time that these pigeons were my friends, that they were the parable of a mission I had yet to accomplish, and that what was happening to me now was what happened to Saul when he fell off his horse and God appeared to him. I swept aside the beating of eight hundred wings and stepped out of the surging mass of feathers, as if stepping out from under the branches of a weeping willow, and pulled the cart with two sacks of scraps and the pots with the leftover vegetables from the kitchen, and the pigeons perched on me again, and surrounded by a cloud of pigeons beating their wings I had another vision, in which I saw Zdeněk.

He was not a political functionary but a headwaiter back in the Hotel Tichota. On our day off we'd gone for a walk, and in a grove of birches we saw a small man darting among the trees, blowing his whistle, pointing, holding the trees at arm's length, and shouting, You've done it again, Mr. Říha. One more time and you're out of the game. Then he ran back and forth among the trees again. Zdeněk found this amusing, but I couldn't figure out what was going on. That evening Zdeněk told me the man was Mr. Šíba, the soccer referee. At the time, no one wanted to referee a Sparta-Slavia match, because the crowd then always in-sulted the referee, so Mr. Šíba said that if no one else wanted the job he'd referee the game himself. He went into training for it in this birch grove, running about sowing confusion among the birches, reprimanding and threat-ening Burger and Braine with expulsion, but mostly yelling at Mr. Říha, One more time and you're out of the game.

That afternoon Zdeněk took a bus full of inmates from an asylum for the mildly lunatic who had permission to go into the village because it was fair time, and they could ride on the merry-go-round and swing on the swings in their striped clothes and bowler hats. Zdeněk went into a pub and bought them a barrel of beer and a spigot, borrowed some half-liter glasses, and took them to the birch grove, where they broached the barrel and drank while Mr. Šíba ran among the birch trees blowing his whistle. The lunatics watched him for a while, then, figuring out what he was doing, they began to shout, cheer, and yell out the names of all the famous players for Sparta and Slavia. They even saw Braine kick Pláníček in the head, and they jeered until Mr. Šíba threw Braine out of the game. Finally, after the referee had warned Říha three times, there was nothing he could do but toss him out of the game for fouling Jezbera. The lunatics cheered, and by the time we'd polished off the barrel of beer they weren't the only ones shouting, because I too saw the striped uniforms and the red-and-white uniforms instead of birch trees as the tiny referee Mr. Šíba blew his whistle. When it was over, the lunatics carried him off the playing field on their shoulders for doing such a beautiful job of refereeing. A month later Zdeněk showed me an article in the paper about Mr. Šíba, who had thrown Braine and Říha out of a game and thus saved the match with his energetic whistle.

And so the circle began to close and I started going back to my childhood and youth, and I was a busboy again, and at the same time I stood face to face with myself, forced to look at my life. I remembered how I had waited with my grandmother in her little room by the open window below the toilets of the Charles Baths, where every Thursday and Friday the traveling salesmen would toss out their dirty underwear, which would sometimes spread out against the black of the evening sky—crucified white shirts—and drift down onto the enormous mill wheel, from which my grandmother would fish them in with a gaff so she could launder them, mend them, and sell them to construction workers. Then the news came through that we'd only be interned in the millionaires' camp another week and then be sent to work somewhere else, and the oldest ones would be able to go home. So we decided to have a last supper, and because we needed as much money as possible, I was given leave to go with the false-teeth manufacturer to his cottage, where he had money stashed away, and that was another unbelievable experience. We didn't arrive at his cottage until after dark, and by flashlight we put up a ladder and went through a trapdoor in the ceiling. But the manufacturer had forgotten which trunk he'd left his hundred thousand crowns in, so I started opening up the trunks one by one, and when I got to the last one and shone the flashlight inside, I was horrified, though I should have expected as much from a manufacturer of dentures, because the trunk was full of false teeth and gums. The sheer numbers made it terrifying, all those pink palates with white teeth, hundreds of them. There I stood on the ladder, terrified, because the teeth looked like flesh-eating flowers, some clenched tight, others half open, and still others wide open, yawning as though their hinges were out of joint. I began falling backward, and the trunk spilled over me, and I felt the cold kiss of teeth on my arms and face, and as I fell backward I dropped the flashlight, and

I ended up on my back on the floor with the teeth spilling over me, but I managed to turn over on my stomach and scuttle out from under them on all fours, like an animal or an insect. At the very bottom of the trunk was all the money, thousands of crowns, and the manufacturer very carefully swept the dentures into a dustpan and put them back in the trunk, tied a rope around it, and hoisted it back up where it had come from. Then we locked the attic and walked back to the station in silence. The millionaires' last supper was like the wedding banquets we used to have in the Hotel Paris. I stopped at my room in Prague for a new tuxedo, and especially for the medal presented to me by the Emperor of Ethiopia and the sash to go across my chest. We bought flowers and several bunches of asparagus fern, and all afternoon Mr. Šroubek and Mr. Brandejs decorated the tables in the priests' refectory, and Mr. Brandejs said he was sorry he couldn't provide us with his gold cutlery, and we invited all the militiamen, including the commander of the camp. We'd run into him the evening before in the village and he asked us where we were going, and Mr. Brandejs said, Come along with us, Commander, we're going to a dance. But the commander merely shook his head and walked off with his gun, which he carried as though it were a fishing rod. He hated that army rifle, and he was already dreaming about getting back to the mines just as soon as he handed over the millionaires' camp for liquidation. And I became a waiter once more and put on my tuxedo, but it was different from the other times I had put it on—it felt more like a costume now—and I pinned the star to the side of my jacket and stretched the blue sash across my chest, but I didn't bother standing straight or holding my head high to add a couple of centimeters to my height, because I had no desire anymore to be the equal of the other hotelkeeper millionaires. I saw this banquet from the other side, and I served the food without enthusiasm, even though Mr. Šroubek and Mr. Brandejs were with me serving the tables in their tuxedos, and when I thought about my Hotel in the Quarry, I felt no regret that it was no longer mine. All things considered, it was a pretty gloomy meal. Everyone was sad and dignified, as though it was the real Last Supper, which I had seen in pictures, and here in the refectory too there was a picture like that, filling an entire wall, and gradually, as we ate our salpicon and drank South Moravian white wine with it, we raised our eyes to look at the picture of the Last Supper, and we began to resemble those disciples more and more. While we ate our beef Stroganoff we began to feel melancholy, and our banquet turned into something like the wedding in Cana of Galilee, and the more the millionaires drank, the more sober they became. During coffee and cognac there was silence, and even the militiamen, who had their own table—the table where the teachers and the professors at the seminary had eaten—began to be sad too, because they knew that at midnight we'd see each other for the last time. It had been a wonderful time for them too, and some of them were wishing we could have gone on that way until the end of time. Suddenly, from the monastery, where a single lame priest had been allowed to remain out of the original thirty monks, the bell sounded Midnight Mass, which the priest was serving to the Catholic millionaires. There were only a few of them in the chapel, and their suitcases and duffel bags were already packed, but now the limping priest, as he was blessing the believers with the chalice, lay the chalice aside and raised his hand, and the organ thundered and the priest began to sing, Saint Wenceslas, Prince of Bohemia. His voice and the thundering of the organ carried all the way to the refectory, where we were gazing at the painting of the Last Supper of our Lord, and for us, Catholic or not, it all seemed so in tune with the sad and gloomy mood that we stood up, singly at first and then in clusters, and hurried across the courtyard and through the open door and into the chapel, into the golden light of the candles. We didn't genuflect, we fell to our knees, that is, we were forced to our knees by something stronger than we millionaires were, something stronger than money, something that had been hovering above us, waiting for a thousand years. We sang, kneeling, Lord, may we live, and those that come hereafter. And some of us fell on our faces. As I knelt there, I saw that the millionaires were different, I wouldn't have recognized them— there was not a sign of money on a single face. All those faces seemed to have been kindled by something higher, something more beautiful, perhaps the most beautiful thing a person has. The priest didn't seem to be limping either, his limping seemed to come from carrying heavy wings, because in his white gown he looked like a angel. When we knelt and threw ourselves on our faces, the priest raised the chalice and blessed us. Then he walked between the kneeling men and the golden chalice and strode across the courtyard, and in the darkness his frock shone like the phosphorescent costume of the acrobat who had once slid down the wire and jackknifed into the quarry pond, where the water swallowed him up just as the priest swallowed the Host after first blessing it for us. Twelve o'clock began to strike, and we said our farewells and walked through the open gate, where the militiamen and their commander—they were all miners from the Kladno region—shook hands warmly with everyone. Then we vanished into the darkness and walked to the station, because the camp was now officially closed, and we were urged to go to our homes, regardless of whether we'd been sentenced to ten years or only two, or whether we had ten million or only two.

All the way I thought of those two hundred pairs of pigeons and how they'd be waiting next day at two o'clock and I wouldn't come out of the kitchen. So with my head full of pigeons I went home, not to Prague but to the quarry, and I climbed the path, and on the other side of the woods I should have seen the illuminated hotel, but everything was in darkness. When I came to the sculptures and stone-crushers, I saw why. The quarry was closed, the entrance gate shut, and there was a new gate cobbled together from boards and locked with an enormous padlock. I walked around the fence and over a knoll of blooming heather and descended into the heart of the quarry. The place was a mess, the chairs were smeared with dirt and knocked over, and when I grasped the door handle of the blacksmith's shop, it was open. There was nothing to show that this had ever been a restaurant, everything had been removed, and the only sign of life was a fire smoldering in the forge. All that was left of the cooking utensils were a couple of ordinary coffee cups. With every step I took, I remembered, almost with pleasure, that Steinbeck himself had offered a check for fifty, then sixty, then eighty thousand dollars for this beautiful quarry, but I'd refused, and it was a good thing I had, because if I couldn't be the hotelkeeper anymore then the hotel should go down with me. They seemed to have turned the hotel into a public swimming pool, because instead of tea towels there were hand towels, and bathing suits hung on a wire stretched from corner to corner. The only thing that hadn't been here before that I found pretty was a naked female mannequin from a clothing-store window, hanging from the ceiling in a horizontal position. I walked through the corridors, and the carpet was gone, and the small glass lamps that had stood outside every door were gone too. I turned the door handle of one of the little rooms and found it open. I looked in and switched on the light, but the room was empty, and I was relieved to find that it wasn't just as I'd left it. So it was right that the entire quarry had vanished along with me, because no one would ever have the strength to do it the way I had done it, and all those who had been here, whenever they felt like it or on the whim of a moment, could recall what it used to be like and find a place for my quarry in their daydreams. They could do whatever they wanted in my hotel, meet the most beautiful young women or slide down the cable from seventy meters up and halfway down, right over the pond, let go, hang suspended in the air for a moment, and then plunge headfirst into the water. Or— since anything goes in a daydream—they could hover in the air above the pond and look around like a bird on fluttering wings, the way a skylark does, holding itself aloft on nothing more than a breeze.

When I arrived in Prague, I was given a choice: either report to Pankrác and begin serving a sentence or join a forest labor brigade, whichever I preferred, on condition that the brigade be in the border regions, what used to be the Sudetenland. That afternoon I went to the labor office and accepted the first job they offered me, and I was happy, and my happiness grew when I found I'd lost the heel of my shoe and the piece of leather I'd hidden the last two stamps under had worn away. So the rest of my fortune was gone, the fortune my wife Lise left me after bringing those stamps from Lemberg, from Lvov, when the ghetto was burned to the ground and the Jews were murdered. When I walked through Prague now, I didn't wear a tie, I didn't want to be a bit taller than I was, I no longer tried to decide which of the hotels I walked by on Příkopy or Wenceslas Square I would buy. I was happy with myself in a gloating sort of way, glad that I'd ended up as I had, that the way forward was now my own way, that I wouldn't have to bow and scrape anymore or be careful to say my good-mornings and good-afternoons and good-evenings and de-lighted-to-see-yous or keep an eye on the staff or, if I was one of the staff myself, make sure that the boss didn't catch me sitting down or smoking or filching a piece of meat. Tomorrow I would leave for somewhere far away, far from people, though of course I knew there'd be people there too, and I'd always believed, like everyone who works in artificial light, that one day I would get out of the city and into nature, that when I retired I would see what a forest really looked like, what the sun really looked like, the sun that had shone into my face every day of my life, making me shield my eyes with a hat or a shadow. When I was a waiter I used to love it when at least once a day all those doormen and superintendents and stokers would come out of their buildings, turn their faces upward, and from the abyss of the Prague streets gaze at the strip of sky overhead, at the clouds, to see what time it really was, according to nature and not by the clock. And the unbelievable that came true stayed with me, and I believed in the unbelievable, in the star that had followed me through life, and with its gleam constantly before my eyes I began to believe in it more and more, because it had made me a millionaire, and now that I had been brought to my knees I realized that my star was brighter than ever, that only now would I be able to see its true brightness, because my eyes had been weakened by everything I had lived through, weakened so that they could see more and know more.

When I arrived at Kraslice I had to walk another ten kilometers through the woods, and just as I was about to give up I came to a dilapidated gamekeeper's lodge, and when I saw it I thought I'd go mad with delight. The lodge had belonged to Germans, and it looked exactly the way someone who's grown up in a city imagines a gamekeeper's lodge. I sat down on a bench underneath wild tendrils and vines and leaned back against the wooden wall, and inside I could hear the ticking of a genuine Black Forest cuckoo clock, which I'd never seen in my life before, and I could hear its wooden works and cogwheels and the rattling of its chains and weights, and I looked out at a vista between two hills opening into the countryside beyond, but I couldn't see any crops. I tried to guess where they grew their potatoes, oats, and rye, but here all the fields were overgrown, reminding me of the villages I had walked through, when I felt as if I was in another world, because everywhere enormous unpruned branches and bushes of ripening black currants were poking out of the crumbling buildings and stone walls, and I was determined to go into some of the buildings, but I couldn't bring myself to do it. All I could do was to stand there in solemn terror, not crossing the threshold of houses where everything had been chopped to pieces, where the furniture was scattered about, the chairs lying as if wrestled to the floor. In one village I came across some cows grazing—it was noon—and the cows seemed to be on their way home, so I followed them as they ambled up a hill between two rows of old lime trees. The tower of a baroque château poked above the trees, then the rows parted, and there stood a beautiful château with large oblong designs scraped with nails into the plaster, probably done back in the Renaissance, and the cows walked through a broken gate into the château and I followed them inside. I thought they might just have been wandering around aimlessly and ended up here, but this was where they had their shed. It was a great knights' hall that you entered up a wide, gently rising staircase, and the cows were living on the second floor, underneath a crystal chandelier and beautiful frescoes of pastoral scenes, but painted as though the shepherds were living in Greece or farther away than that, in the Promised Land, because everyone was wearing clothes like those worn by Jesus Christ and the people who lived with Him back then, and there were huge mirrors between the windows, and the cows would stand there gazing at themselves, obviously enjoying it. When I left and tiptoed down the stairs, I realized that this was probably going to be another case of where the unbelievable comes true. I also began to think of myself as someone who'd been chosen, because I knew that if anyone except me had been here, he wouldn't have seen a thing, but I enjoyed what I saw, and was fascinated to see a wasteland that could terrify me, the way people are terrified of crime and shun misfortune, but when a misfortune actually strikes, everyone who can gathers around for a look, and stares at the ax lodged in the skull, at the old woman pinned underneath the streetcar. So I walked along and did not try to run from the place of great misfortune, but was glad of it, and I even found that this misfortune and this suffering and these atrocities were not enough for me, and that I could do with more—not only me but the world as well.

As I was sitting in front of the gamekeeper's lodge, two people arrived, and I could see that they lived here and that I'd be spending the whole year with them, maybe more. When I told them who I was and why I'd been sent, the man, who had a gray beard and one good eye, said or rather gumbled that he was a professor of French literature. Then he pointed to the other person, a pretty girl, who I could tell had once been to reform school, or else she was one of those who used to hang around the Prašná Brána in Prague and would come into the hotel after the stock market had closed. As a matter of fact, from the way she moved I could imagine what she looked like naked and what the hair under her arms and in her lap was like, and I found that I could imagine this redhead awakening in me the desire, after all these years, to take her clothes off slowly, and I regarded that as a good sign. She told me she had been sent here for being too fond of dancing at night, that her name was Marcela and that she'd apprenticed in the Maršner Orion chocolate factory. She was wearing men's trousers covered with pine pitch and pine needles, and she had pine needles in her hair. The professor wore rubber boots, as she did, with crude work socks sticking out of them, and he too was covered with pine and spruce gum. Both of them smelled like a meadow or a stick of firewood. I followed them into the gamekeeper's lodge, and never in my life had I seen such a mess, not even in those broken buildings the Germans left behind, where people had been looting for valuables with axes and prying open locks on cupboard doors and trunks. The table was littered with cigarette butts and matches, and the floor was the same. The professor told me I'd be sleeping upstairs, and he showed me to the room right away. He opened the door handle with his foot, with the sole of his rubber boot, and I found myself in a beautiful wood-paneled room that had two little windows framed with branches and grape-vines. I opened another door and stepped out onto a bal-cony, also made of wood, which ran all the way around the house, so I had a view in all four directions, while the wild grapevines tickled my face. I sat down on a box and folded my hands in my lap, and I felt like shouting for joy. To celebrate what I'd seen and what was to come, I opened my suitcase and put on the blue sash, pinned the gilded star to the side of my jacket, and went down into the living room. The professor was sitting there with his feet on the table, smoking, and the girl was combing her hair and listening to what he was telling her. He called her Miss, repeating it constantly, until he was trembling all over from the hidden strength of the word or as if he was trying to persuade her of something. Because nothing mattered now, everything was precious, and so I walked into the room theatrically, my arms raised as though I were parading a costume at a fashion show, and I showed myself off from all sides. Then I sat down and asked if I was supposed to join them at work that afternoon. The professor laughed— he had beautiful eyes—and said, You evil, stupid, criminal son of man. Then, pretending not to notice my medal, he said we'd be going to work in an hour, and started talking to the girl again. I wasn't surprised to hear him speaking French words to her, *la table*, *une chaise*, *la maison*, and she would repeat the words and pronounce them all wrong. With enormous tenderness he said to her, You poor stupid Nana, I'll have to take off my belt and slap your face, not with the leather part but with the buckle. He repeated the French words very tenderly, patiently, as though caressing her with his eyes and voice, this girl from the Maršner Orion chocolate factory. Marcela must have pronounced the words badly again—she seemed to be sulking and un- willing to learn, knowing the right answer but pretending not to—so the professor scolded her gently: You evil, stu- pid, criminal daughter of man. As I was closing the door behind me, the professor said, Thank you! I stuck my head back through the doorway and said, I served the Emperor of Ethiopia, and I ran my hand over the blue sash.

They had to lend me an extra pair of boots, because the country was extremely damp. In the morning the dew was so thick it tore like a curtain when you walked through it, and it fell in a kind of rosary on every blade of grass and every leaf, and if you just brushed against a branch the dew dropped off like pearls from a broken necklace. My job the very first day was wonderful. We went to a spruce tree, a beautiful spruce surrounded by cut boughs piled halfway up the trunk, and we cut down more boughs and piled them even higher. Finally two workers came with a cross-cut saw, and the professor told me this was not just an ordinary spruce tree, but a resonating spruce. As proof, he pulled a tuning fork out of his briefcase, struck it on the tree, then held it against the trunk and made me put my ear against the tree and listen. It sounded wonderful, giving off a very light, luminous, heavenly sound. So we stood there embracing the spruce while the girl sat on a stump smoking and wearing an expression not of indifference but of boredom and exasperation. Her eyes turned accusingly to heaven, as if heaven itself were to blame for her boredom here on earth, while I slid down to my knees and put my arms around the trunk, which was reverberating louder than a telegraph pole. When the workers knelt to cut it, I climbed up on the mound of boughs piled up around the tree and listened, and as the saw bit into the wood a loud wail rose through the spruce, and the graceful sound that I'd been hearing was overwhelmed by the sound of the saw as the trunk complained that they were slicing into its body. The professor hollered at me to come down, so I did, and in a while the spruce tilted, hesitated for a moment, and then with a cry that came from its very roots began to fall. Its fall was cushioned by the boughs, as though it were falling into outstretched arms that prevented it, as the professor explained, from breaking and losing its music. Spruces like this one were rare, and it was up to us now to trim the branches and then, according to a plan he had with him, carefully saw the tree into lengths and carry it gently on a feathery bed of boughs to the factory. There it would be sawed into planks, then into boards, then into thin sheets to be used in making violins and cellos. But the main thing was to find the sheets of wood that still had the music inside them. A month went by, then two, and we would prepare the bed of branches like a mother making a bed for her baby so that we could bring down the resonant spruce without destroying the music imprisoned in its trunk. And every evening I listened to the professor swearing at us, calling us all sorts of filthy names, me and the girl—idiots and morons and spotted hyenas and squalling skunks—and then he would teach us French words. While I was cooking supper at a tiled stove and lighting the kerosene lamps, I would listen to those beautiful badly pronounced words coming out of the mouth of the girl who'd been sent here from the chocolate factory because she liked a good time, liked sleeping with a different fellow each time, she told us. Her confession wasn't much different from what I'd heard from other girls like her, girls of the street, except that this girl liked doing it for nothing, for love, for the pleasure of having someone love her for a moment, maybe for a whole night, and that was enough to make her happy. But here she had to work, and on top of that spend her evenings learning French words, not because she wanted to, but because she was bored and because she didn't know how else to kill the long evenings. The second month, the professor began giving us lectures on the French literature of the twentieth century, and at this point there was a change that delighted both him and me. Marcela began to show an interest, and the professor would spend the whole evening telling her about the Surrealists and Robert Desnos and Alfred Jarry and Ribemont-Dessaignes, about all the beautiful men and women of

Paris, and once he brought out an original edition of something called *La rose publique*, and every evening he would read and translate a different poem, and when we were out working we'd analyze it image by image. At first everything was vague, but when we analyzed it we somehow managed to get through to the idea. I would listen, and then I too began to read books and difficult poems, which I'd never really liked before, and sometimes I understood them well enough to suggest an interpretation, and the professor would say, You jackass, you idiot, how did you know that? And I would feel like a tomcat when someone scratches him under the chin, because when the professor insulted you, it felt like a compliment. I suppose he'd begun to like me, because he would insult me as much as he insulted Marcela, and by now he'd speak only French with her at work. Once I drove a load of the musical wood to the factory, and when I delivered it, they gave me our wages to take back, and I bought food and fuel and a bottle of cognac and a bouquet of carnations as well. Just as I left the factory it started to rain, so I waited under a tree, then ran into an old wooden outhouse to get out of the pouring rain. The water drummed on the sheets of wood that served as the roof of the outhouse, which wasn't really an outhouse at all but probably some kind of sentry box. There were holes in the sides of the sentry box that were covered with sheets of wood as well, to keep the wind out, and as I waited for the rain to stop, I tapped on those sheets. When it stopped raining, I ran back into the musical instrument factory, and they threw me out twice before they finally let me see the manager, and I took him behind the factory, behind the ramshackle warehouse, and—just as I thought—there were ten rare pieces of resonant wood, several decades old, that someone had used to patch the sentry box. How did you know what they were? asked the astonished manager. I served the Emperor of Ethiopia, I said. The manager laughed, slapped me on the back, choked with laughter, and said, That's a good one. I smiled too, because I had obviously changed so much that no one could tell by looking at me that I really had served the Emperor of Ethiopia.

But it meant something quite different to me now. When I mentioned serving the Emperor of Ethiopia, it was a way of making fun of myself, because I was independent now and beginning to find the presence of other people irksome, and I felt that in the end I would have to speak only with myself, that my own best friend and companion would be that other self of mine, that teacher inside me with whom I was beginning to talk more and more. It may also have been because of everything I learned from the professor, who outdid himself in insults, because no coachman cursed his horses the way this professor of French literature and aesthetics cursed us. But he would lecture us on all the things he was interested in, every evening he would start lecturing, start while I was still opening the door, and he'd continue right up until he fell asleep, until we fell asleep, and he would tell us all about aesthetics and ethics and philosophy and philosophers. He'd say that all philosophers, Jesus Christ not excepted, were nothing but a bunch of con men, sons of bitches, murderers, and good-for-nothings, and if they'd never existed mankind would have been better off, but mankind was an evil, stupid, criminal lot. So perhaps the professor confirmed my feelings that it was best to be alone, that although the stars were visible at night, at noon you could see them only from the bottom of a deep well. So I made up my mind, and one day I got up and shook hands with everyone, thanked them for everything, and went back to Prague, because I'd already extended my stay in the forest by half a year. By now the professor and his girl spoke only French together, and they always had something to talk about, and wherever they went, the professor would think up fresh ways to browbeat the girl, who by now was really beautiful, and fresh ways to surprise her with facts, because I could see that he was in love with her in this wilderness, in love with her for life and for death. And because once upon a time I had served the Emperor of Ethiopia, I could see that the girl would be his fate, that one day she'd walk out on him, when she knew everything he knew, learning against her will though it had sanctified her and made her beautiful. One time, she repeated something that the professor had told her, a quotation from Aristotle: when Aristotle was criticized for plagiarizing Plato, he replied that after a colt has sucked his mother dry, he gives her a kick. And I was right, because when I had settled the last formalities for my last job, or what I thought would be my last job—and I expect it will be my last job, because I have served the Emperor of Ethiopia and I know myself—I was walking past the railroad station one day and there coming toward me was Marcela. She had a thoughtful expression on her face and her hair was pulled back in a braid, a pigtail tied with a violet ribbon, and she was walking along absorbed in her own thoughts. I looked at her, but she walked absently right past me, and other passersby stopped to look at her too, and she had a book under her arm, the girl who had once worked at the Maršner Orion chocolate factory. Even with my head twisted around, I could read the title of the book she was carrying, *L'Histoire de la surréalisme*, and as she walked past I laughed and cheerfully went on my way, because I had seen that rebellious and vulgar girl who talked to the professor just the way she had talked in Košíře, and the good professor had taught her everything a well-educated young lady should know, and now she walked past me as if I were a barbarian. I knew for certain that this girl could never be happy, but that her life would be sadly beautiful, and that life with her would be both an agony and a fulfillment for a man. Afterward, many times, I thought about that book under her arm and wondered what had spilled over from its pages into her thoughtful and rebellious head, and what I saw was just the head with those beautiful eyes, eyes that had not been beautiful a year before, and it was all the professor's doing, he had turned this girl into a beauty with a book. I could see her fingers piously opening the covers and turning the pages, one after another, like the Eucharist, because I saw that before these hands picked up a book, they would wash themselves first, and the way she carried the book was striking in its devoutness. I adorned the memory of my chocolate girl with peony petals and flowers, crowned her head with fronds of spruce and pine and mistletoe—I who had looked at women only from the waist down, their legs and their laps, but with this girl I turned my gaze and my longing upward, to her beautiful forehead and her beautiful hands opening the book, to her eyes radiating everything wonderful that she'd gained through her transformation.

This transformation filled her young face, it was in the way she narrowed her eyes, in her easy smile and how she rubbed her nose from left to right with a charming index finger. Her face was a face humanized by French words, French sentences, French conversation, and finally by difficult but beautiful verses written by beautiful young men, poets who had discovered the miraculous in the human.

On the train I thought about the girl, I smiled, I became her, and I posted her portrait in every station and on all the moving sides of trains passing or standing on adjacent tracks. I would even hold my own hand, take myself under the arm, and put my arm around myself, as though it was her I was holding. I looked at the faces of my fellow travelers, and no one could see what I was doing with myself and in myself, no one could see from my face what I was carrying inside. When I got out at the last station, I continued by bus through a beautiful countryside that resembled the countryside where I had felled the resonant spruce after first surrounding their trunks with feathery pine boughs neatly stacked to a good height. I went on thinking and completed my portrait of the girl from the Maršner Orion chocolate factory, and I pictured her as her boyfriends were making a fuss over her, welcoming her back, behaving the way they had before she'd been sent away to work, and how they would try to lure her into talking with them the way she used to, talking with her belly and her legs, with the lower half of her marked off by the elastic band in her underwear, and no one would understand that she was now favoring the half above the elastic. I got off the bus at Srní, asked where the roads department was, and reported to them, telling them I was the one who would be mending the roads all year round, somewhere far away, practically in the mountains, sections of road where no one wanted to be. That afternoon I was issued a small horse and a wagon, and they suggested I buy a goat too, which I did, and they made me a present of a German shepherd, so I set off with the horse, my baggage on the cart, and the goat tethered behind the cart. The German shepherd took to me right away, and I bought him some salami, then we drove along a road that gradually led upward as the country opened out into a region of stately spruce and tall pines. Every once in a while we came to a patch of young trees and aftergrowth surrounded by lattice fences that were crumbling like gingerbread, gradually rotting and changing back into humus from which wild raspberries and ravenous blackberries grew like seaweed, and I walked beside the little horse's nodding head. It was the kind of horse they have in mines—he must have worked underground somewhere because his eyes were so beautiful, the kind I would see in stokers and people who worked in artificial light all day or in the light of safety lamps and emerged from the pit or the furnace room to look up at the beautiful sky, because to such eyes all skies are beautiful. As the countryside became bleaker and more forlorn, I drove past little cottages in the woods that used to belong to German forest workers who had left the country, and at each cottage I would stop and stand on the doorstep, up to my chest in nettles and wild raspberries, and look through the vines into kitchens that were filling up with grass, and into tiny living rooms. Almost every one of these dwellings had electricity, and I would follow the wires down to a brook where I would find the remnants of a small generating plant driven by a miniature turbine put there by the hands of workers who had cleared the woods but then had to leave when the war was over, were forced to leave, transported from the country. They had been treated no differently from the rich Germans who had been political leaders and who carried out the policies I had come to know so well, the arrogant, loutish, vain, crude Germans full of pride, which in the end had brought them down. That I understood, but I didn't understand why these workers' hands had to go away, leaving no one to continue their work. It was a terrible loss—these people who had had nothing but hard work in the forest and on the meadows and hillsides, workers who had had no time for arrogance or pride, who must have been humble because they were taught humility by the kind of life I'd had a glimpse of and was now approaching myself. Then I got an idea, and I opened my trunk and I pulled out the case with the golden star in it, slung the pale-blue sash across my corduroy coat, and set out once again with the star sparkling at my side. I walked to the rhythm of the nodding head of the little horse, who kept turning around to look at my sash and whinnying, while the goat bleated and the German shepherd barked happily at me and tried to catch my sash. I stopped again and after untying the goat went to look at another building, which had been a kind of inn in the woods. It had an enormous hall, which was dry, oddly enough, and tiny windows. Everything was just as the people had left it, right down to the dusty beer mugs on the shelves and a keg with a spigot and a mallet to broach it with. As I was leaving, I felt a pair of eyes on me—it was a cat, and I called to her and she meowed, and

I went to get some salami and bent down and tried to coax her to come to me. I could tell she wanted me to pat her, but she was so lonely and so unaccustomed to the human smell that she kept scooting away, so I put the salami down and she ate it hungrily. I held out my hand, but she jumped away again, bristling and hissing at me, so I went back out into the light and found the goat drinking from the brook, and I took a bucket and filled it with water for the little horse. When he'd drunk his fill, we set off again, and at a bend in the road, where I turned back to see what the landscape looked like from the other direction—as though I'd let a beautiful woman go by and then turned to watch her walk away—I saw that the cat was following us. This was a good omen, so I cracked the whip and gave a shout and felt joy bursting in my chest and began to sing for no reason at all—timidly, because I had never sung in my life before. In all those decades it had never crossed my mind that I might want to sing and now here I was singing, inventing words and sentences to fill in the places I didn't know, and the German shepherd began to howl, then sat down and let out a long wail, so I gave him a piece of salami and he rubbed against my legs, but I went on singing as if through the singing—not through the song, because all I could produce now were squawks—I was emptying out of myself drawers and boxes full of old bills and useless letters and postcards, as if fragments of tattered posters were blowing out of my mouth, posters pasted one on top of the other, so that when you rip them away you create nonsense signs, where soccer matches blend into concerts or where art exhibits get mixed up with brass-band tat-toos—everything that had accumulated inside me, like tar and nicotine in a smoker's lungs. And so I sang, and I felt as if I was hacking up and spitting out phlegm from clogged lungs, and I felt like the beer pipes the innkeeper cleans with a strong jet of water, like a room with all the wallpaper torn off, several layers of it, a room where a family had lived for generations.

I drove on through the countryside, and no one could hear me, and all I could see from the hilltops was forest, because what was left of man and his works was slowly and surely being swallowed up again by the trees. The small fields were disappearing beneath rocks and grass, and bushy undergrowth had moved into the buildings, and black elder branches were prying up cement floors and tiles, rolling them over, spreading leaves and tangled branches above them, because a black elder has more power in it than a lever, than a hydraulic lift or press. Following piles of gravel and ballast, I arrived at a large building. I walked around it and realized that I would feel good here, beside this road. Although I'd been told that my job was to mend the road and maintain it, so far no one was using it, and no one was likely to, because the road was maintained only in case of emergency and for carrying out logs in the summer. Suddenly I heard something that sounded like a human lament, the music of a violin and then a lilting cry, so I walked along the road toward the voice without noticing that my little horse, whom I'd unhitched, attaching the reins to his harness collar, and the goat and the German shepherd were all following me, and I came upon a group of three people. They were gypsies, the people I was supposed to replace, and what I saw was miraculous, the unbelievable come true. An old gypsy woman was squatting by a small fire like all nomads, stirring a pot that rested by its handles on two stones, and as she stirred it with one hand, she leaned her other elbow on her knee and held her forehead in her hand. An old gypsy sat in the road, his legs apart, pounding neatly piled stones into the roadbed with powerful blows of his mallet. A young man in boots and black trousers that fitted tightly around the hips and with cuffs that flared out in a bell was leaning over him, playing a passionate and elegiac melody on the violin, a gypsy song. The music must have made something in the old man's life seem more intense, because he wailed and complained in a long melancholy cry and, moved by the music, tore fistfuls of his hair out and threw them into the fire. Then he went back to pounding the stones while his son, or maybe it was his nephew, played the violin, and the old woman went on cooking her food. And I saw before me what I could expect, that I would be here alone, with no one to cook or play the violin for me, with no one but the little horse, the goat, the dog, and the cat, who was still keeping a respectful distance behind us. I coughed, and the old woman turned around and looked at me as though she were staring straight at the sun, and the old man stopped his pounding, and the young man put his violin down and bowed to me. I said I was here to start work, but the old man and woman stood up, bowed, shook hands with me, and said they were all ready, and I could see now that they had in the bushes a light gypsy cart with large rear wheels. They said I was the first person they'd seen in a month, and I said, Is that so? But I didn't believe them. The young man took an instrument case from the cart, opened it up, and like putting a baby in its cradle he very carefully laid the violin inside, then covered it even more carefully with a small piece of velvet cloth embroidered with initials and notes and the words to a song. Then he looked at the violin and stroked the velvet cloth lovingly, closed the case, jumped up onto the cart, and took hold of the reins while the old road mender sat down. They put the old woman between them and drove off the partly mended road to the house from which they carried out blankets and eiderdowns and several pots and a kettle. I tried to persuade them to stay for another night, but they were in a hurry and could hardly wait, they said, to see another human being, to see other people. I asked them what the winter was like here. *Ai ai ai ai*, wailed the old gypsy, very bad. We ate our goat, our dog, and our cat. He raised his hand and held up three fingers in the sign of an oath and said, Three months there hasn't been a soul here, and snowed in we were, sir. The old woman cried and repeated, And snowed in we were. Then they both began to cry, while the young man took out his violin again and played a melancholy song and the old gypsy shook the reins and the little horse leaned into his traces while the young man played standing up, his legs wide apart, with powerful motions, the languid expression of gypsy romance in his face. The old woman and the old man wept and quietly said, *Ai ai ai*, nodding to me, their faces full of suffering and wrinkles, letting me know with a gesture that they felt sorry for me and rejected me at the same time, because they shooed me away with both hands, not from themselves, but from life, as if they were digging my grave with those hands and laying me in it. When they reached the top of the hill the old man stood up and pulled out another clump of hair, then the wagon disappeared over the brow of the hill, and all I could see was a hand tossing the hair away, perhaps as a sign of the great despair and pity he felt for me. I went into the large hall of the abandoned inn to look at where I'd be living, and as I walked through the building and around the stables, the woodshed, and the hayloft to the pump for water to wash myself, the horse, the goat, the German shepherd, and the cat walked gravely behind me. I turned and looked at them, and they looked at me, and I saw that they were afraid I might abandon them, and I laughed and patted each one of them on the head in turn, except the cat, who wanted me to pat her too but the power of her own shyness made her scoot away.

The road I maintained and patched with rock I had to crush myself—that road resembled my own life. It was filling up with weeds and grass in front of me. Only the section I happened to be working on at the moment showed traces of my own hand. Cloudbursts and steady rainfall often flooded the work I did and covered it with deposits of earth, sand, and pebbles, but I didn't curse my fate, I went about my work patiently in the long summer days, carrying away the sand and the rubbish, not to improve the road but simply to make it passable for my cart and horse. Once after a rainfall a whole section of the roadbed was washed away and it took me almost a week to build it back up to where I'd finished the week before, but I started work early in the morning with even greater concentration, and the goal I set myself, to reach the other side of the gap, made me feel less tired. A week later, when I was able to drive my cart over this section, I looked proudly at my work, though it seemed as if I'd done nothing but restore the road to its former state. No one would have believed I'd done it or praised me or given me credit for sixty hours of work, except the dog, the goat, the horse, and the cat, and they couldn't have testified to it. But I didn't want to be seen by human eyes anymore, or praised for what I'd done—all of that had left me. For almost a month I did practically nothing but labor from sunup to sundown, just to maintain the road in the state it had been in when I'd taken over, and the more I worked, the more I saw that the maintenance of this road was the maintenance of my own life, which now, when I looked back on it, seemed to have happened to someone else. My life to this point seemed like a novel, a book written by a stranger even though I alone had the key to it, I alone was a witness to it, even though my life too was constantly being overgrown by grass and weeds at either end. But as I used a grub hoe and a shovel on the road, I used memory to keep the road of my life open into the past, so I could take my thoughts backward to where I wanted to begin remembering. When I finished work on the road, I would tap the blade of my scythe into shape, cut the grass on the hillsides and dry it, and on afternoons when the weather was good I would carry the hay into the hayloft and get ready for winter, which they told me lasted almost six months here. Once a week I hitched up the little horse and set off to buy food, going back along my mended road, then turning off and slowly going down an untraveled path. When I looked behind me I could see the tracks left by the cart wheels and, after a rain, the hoofprints of the little horse. Then, after passing two abandoned villages, I would finally arrive at a decent road where I could see ruts left by transport trucks and, in the dust of the shoulders, tracks left by bicycle and motorcycle tires, the vehicles used by the forest administration workers and soldiers on their way to and from work or guard duty. After I bought cans of food, salami, and a huge round loaf of bread in the store, I would stop off at the pub, and the pubkeeper and villagers would come and sit down at my table and ask how I liked it here in the mountains, in all this solitude. I was enthusiastic and told them stories of things that no one had ever seen before but were actually there, and I told the stories as if I were only passing through by car, or had come for two or three days, I talked as though I were on vacation, like a nature lover, like a city person who babbles romantic drivel whenever he comes to the country about how beautiful the woods are and the mountain peaks in the mist, and how it is all so perfect that he would like to settle here for good. And I talked in a jumbled way about how beauty had another side to it, about how this beautiful countryside, like a round loaf of bread, was all related to whether you could love even what was unpleasant and abandoned, whether you could love the landscape during all those hours and days and weeks when it rained, when it got dark early, when you sat by the stove and thought it was ten at night while it was really only half past six, when you started talking to yourself, speaking to the horse, the dog, the cat, and the goat, but best of all to yourself, silently at first— as though showing a movie, letting images from the past flicker through your memory—and then out loud, as I had done, asking yourself questions, inquiring of yourself, interrogating yourself, wanting to know the most secret things about yourself, accusing yourself as if you were a public prosecutor and then defending yourself, and so arriving, in this back-and-forth way, at the meaning of your life. Not the meaning of what used to be or what happened a long time ago, but discovering the kind of road you'd opened up and and had yet to open up, and whether there was still time to attain the serenity that would secure you against the desire to escape from your own solitude, from the most important questions that you should ask yourself.

And so I, a road mender, sat in the pub every Saturday till evening, and the longer I sat there, the more I opened myself up to people. I thought of my little horse standing outside the pub, of the wonderful solitude of my new home, and I saw how the people here were eclipsing what I wanted to see and know, how they were all simply enjoying themselves the way I used to enjoy myself, putting off the questions they would have to ask themselves one day, if they were lucky enough to have the time to do that before they died. As a matter of fact whenever I was in the pub I realized that the basic thing in life is questioning death, wanting to know how we'll act when our time comes, and that death, or rather this questioning of death, is a conversation that takes place between infinity and eternity, and how we deal with our own death is the beginning of what is beautiful, because the absurd things in our lives, which always end before we want them to anyway, fill us, when we contemplate death, with bitterness and therefore with beauty. I became a laughingstock in the pub by asking each one of the people where he wanted to be buried. At first they were shocked, but then they laughed till they cried at the idea, and then they would ask me where I wanted to be buried—that is, if I was lucky enough to be found in time, because they hadn't found the last road mender but one until spring, by which time he'd been eaten by shrews and mice and foxes, so all they had to bury was a small bundle of bones, like a bunch of asparagus or beef trimmings and soup bones. But I was delighted to tell them about my own grave, and I said that if I was to die here, even if they buried only a single ungnawed bone of me or a skull, I wanted to be buried in that graveyard on top of the little hill, at the highest point, with my coffin right on the divide, so that when what was left of me decomposed, it would be carried away by the rain in two different directions: part of me would wash down the streams that flow into Bohemia, and the other part of me down the other side, under the barbed wire of the border, through the brooks and streams that feed the Danube. I wanted to be a world citizen after death, with one half of me going down the Vltava into the Labe and on into the North Sea, and the other half via the Danube into the Black Sea and eventually into the Atlantic Ocean. The regulars in the pub would fall silent and stare at me, and I would always rise to my feet, because this was the question the whole village looked forward to. Whenever I came, they would ask me this question in the end, and I always answered the same way. Then they'd say, What if you died in Prague? Or in Brno? And what if you died in Pelhřimov, and what if the wolves ate you? And I would always tell them precisely what it would be like, just as the professor of French literature taught, that man's body and spirit are indestructible and he is merely changed or metamorphized. Once the professor and Marcela analyzed a poem by a poet called Sandburg about what man was made of, and it said man contained enough phosphorus to make ten boxes of matches, enough iron to make a nail to hang himself on, and enough water to make ten liters of tripe soup. When I told the villagers this, they were frightened—frightened of the idea and of me as well—and they made faces at the thought of what awaited them, which was why they preferred being told what would become of them when they died here. One night we went to the graveyard at the top of the hill and I showed them the empty spot from which, if I were laid in the ground there, half of me would reach the North Sea and the other half the Black Sea. The main thing was to make sure the coffin was lying crosswise in the grave, as if balanced on the peak of a roof. Then I went back home with my shopping. On the way I'd think things over, talk to myself, go over everything I'd said and done that day, and ask myself whether I'd said or done the right things. The only right things were the things I enjoyed—not the way children or drinkers enjoyed things, but the way the professor of French literature taught me, enjoyment that was metaphysical. When you enjoy something, then you've got it, you idiots, you evil, stupid, criminal sons of men, he would say, and he'd browbeat us until he got us where he wanted us, open to poetry, to objects, to wonder, and able to see that beauty always points to infinity and eternity.

Just before winter set in, when I couldn't take it anymore and began to long for someone to be with, I bought some big old mirrors in the village, and some of them I got for nothing. People were glad to be rid of them, because when they looked into them, they said, Germans would appear. So I packed the mirrors in blankets and newspapers and took them home. All day long I pounded pegs into the walls of the taproom that doubled as a dance hall and then screwed the mirrors into the pegs, and I covered a whole wall with mirrors—and I wasn't alone anymore. On my way back from work I would look forward to seeing myself coming out to meet myself, and I started bowing to myself in the mirror and wishing myself a good evening. Now I wouldn't be alone until I went to bed, because there would always be two of me here, and it didn't matter that our movements were the same. When I left, the one in the mirror would turn his back too and we'd go our separate ways, though I would be the only one really leaving and walking out of the room. I had trouble understanding this, and couldn't think through why it was that when I left I couldn't see myself leaving, and that when I turned my head I could see my face again but never my back. The unbelievable came true whenever I returned from Saturday shopping with my pay and stopped below the graveyard on the hill and walked down to the little brook that was fed by the springs and rivulets on the hill. In this country- side even the rocks shed water, and each time I washed my face in the brook, the water was cold and clear and I could see the juices from the people buried in the graveyard above flowing down into this little brook all the time, distilled and filtered by the beautiful earth that can turn corpses into nails to hang myself on and pure water to wash my face in, just as many years from now somebody somewhere will wash his face in me and someone will strike a match made from the phosphorus of my body. I drank the water from the spring below the graveyard, savoring it like a connoisseur of wine, and just as a connoisseur of Bernkasteller Riesling can detect the smell of the hundreds of locomotives that pass by the vineyards each day, or of the little fires that the vintners make in the fields each day to heat their lunches, I too could taste the dead buried long ago in the graveyard up there. And I tasted them for the same reason that I had got the mirrors, because the mirrors held the imprints of the Germans who had looked into them, who had departed years ago, leaving their smell behind in them, in the place I gazed into for a long time each day and where my double walked. As with the departed in the drinking water, I rubbed shoulders with people who were invisible, but not invisible to someone for whom the unbelievable had come true, and I kept bumping into young girls in dirndls, into German furniture, into the ghosts of German families. Just before All Souls', my countryfolk, who made me a gift of these mirrors in exchange for letting them see into the mirror that was waiting for them in the graveyard, shot my German shepherd. I had taught him to do my shopping—or, rather, he had taught himself, because one day he took the basket in his mouth to show me that he wanted to go shopping with me, but I knew he could find his way to the village on his own, so as an experiment I gave him a list of what I needed and off he ran, and two hours later he returned and set the basket with the shopping in it down in front of me. So instead of taking the little horse I would send the German shepherd every other day with the basket to fetch supplies, and once, when the villagers were waiting for me in vain and saw the dog carrying the basket, they shot him, to get me to start coming to the pub again. I cried a week, mourning for my German shepherd, and then I hitched up the little horse. The first snow was falling, and I set out for my pay and a large amount of supplies for the winter, and I forgave the villagers, because they had really missed me. They didn't make fun of me now, and if they did, it was a different, higher kind of fun, because they couldn't live any longer without having me come to the pub. They told me they had nothing else to look forward to, and they certainly weren't looking forward to my death. They wanted me to come once a week to see them, because it was a long way to the church and I was a better talker than the pastor. My German shepherd managed to make it home. They shot him in the lung, but he ran back with the basket of supplies, and I patted him and brought him a lump of sugar as a reward, but he wouldn't take it this time, he laid his head in my lap instead and slowly slipped away. Behind me the little horse leaned over us and sniffed at the dog, and the goat came as well, and the cat, who slept with the dog but had never let me pat her except at a distance. I would talk to her, and she would lie on her back and wriggle and twist and show me her claws and send looks at me as though I'd actually been scratching her under her chin or stroking her fur, but whenever I reached out my hand, the savage force of her shyness would make her scramble out of reach. Now the cat came up and cuddled against the German shepherd's fur the way she used to, and I held my hand out, but she was looking into the dying eyes of the German shepherd. I stroked her, and then she looked at me, and it was so awful for her to have me stroking her, to have overcome her shyness while her companion was dying, that she closed her eyes and pushed her head into the dog's fur so she wouldn't see what terrified her and filled her with longing at the same time.

One late afternoon, when I was walking up the hill to the well for water, thinking, I first sensed and then saw, at the edge of the woods, leaning against a tree, Zdeněk, and he was looking straight at me. I had served the Emperor of Ethiopia, so I knew he'd come on purpose, just to see how I was doing, and it seemed not that he didn't want to talk to me but that he didn't need to, that all he wanted was to see how I had taken to this isolated life. Zdeněk was now a big man in the political world, surrounded by a lot of people, yet I knew he was probably just as alone as I was. Pumping the water while the animals watched me work, I felt Zdeněk following my every move, so I took great care to pump as though I hadn't seen him, though I knew that Zdeněk knew that I knew he was standing there in the woods. Then slowly I bent over and grabbed the handles of the wooden buckets, allowing Zdeněk time to move a little, because at a distance of several hundred meters I could hear every movement and every sound, so I asked Zdeněk if there was something he wanted to tell me. But he didn't need to tell me anything, it was enough to have seen me and confirm that I was in the world, and to let me know that he missed me, just as I missed him. I lifted the two buckets and walked down to the inn, and behind me walked the little horse, and behind the horse the goat, and then the cat, and though I trod carefully, the water splashed out of the buckets onto my rubber boots, and I knew that when I put the buckets down on the stoop and turned around, Zdeněk would no longer be there, that he would go away satisfied, back to the government car waiting somewhere on the other side of the woods to take him back to his work, which was certainly more difficult than my escape into solitude. I thought about how the professor of French literature had told Marcela that the only true man of the world was one who could become anonymous, who could shed himself. And when I put down the buckets and turned around, Zdeněk was gone. Later that day it began to snow, with flakes as large as postage stamps, a peaceful snowfall that by evening became a blizzard. In the cellar a stream of clear, cold water flowed constantly into a trough cut in stone. The stable was in a corridor next to the kitchen, and the horse manure, which I had left in the stable on the advice of the villagers, was warm enough to heat the kitchen as though it were central heating. For three days I watched the moving snow, which hissed like tiny butterflies, like mayflies, like small flowers falling from the sky. My road was gradually buried, and on the third day the snow was so deep that the road blended in with its surroundings and no one could have guessed anymore where it went. On that day, however, I pulled out an old sleigh and found a set of bells, and I shook them and laughed, because jingling the bells gave me the idea of hitching the little horse to the sleigh and driving along above my road, floating above it, separated from it by this pillow of snow, this feather bed, this thick white carpet, this billowy white that blanketed the countryside. So I repaired the sleigh, and the snow now reached the windowsills, and then it climbed higher, halfway up the windows. The moment I looked out and saw, to my surprise, how high the snow had reached, I saw my cottage with the animals in it suspended on a chain hung from heaven itself, a cottage banished from the world and yet full to the brim, just like those mirrors with their buried and forgotten images, images that could be summoned up as easily as the images I put in the mirrors, as the images I littered and lined my road with, covered now by the snow of the past, so that memory could find it only by touch, the way an experienced hand feels the pulse under the skin, to determine where life has flowed, flows, and will flow. And at that moment I began to be afraid, because if I died, all the unbelievable things that had come true would vanish, and I remembered that the professor of aesthetics and French literature had said that the better person was the one who expressed himself better. And I longed to write everything down just as it was, so others could read it and from what I said to myself paint all the pictures that had been strung like beads, like a rosary, on the long thread of my life, unbelievable beads that I had managed to catch hold of here as I looked out the window and marveled at the falling snow that had half buried the cottage. And so every evening, when I sat in front of the mirror with the cat behind me on the bar, butting her little head against my image in the mirror as though the image were really me, I looked at my hands while the blizzard roared outside like a swollen river, and the longer I looked at my hands—and I would hold them up as though I were surrendering to myself—the more I saw winter ahead of me, and snow. I saw that I would shovel the snow, throwing it aside, searching for the road, and go on, every day, searching for the road to the village, and perhaps they would be looking for a way to get to me too. And I said to myself that during the day I would look for the road to the village, but in the evening I would write, looking for the road back, and then walk back along it and shovel aside the snow that had covered my past, and so try, by writing, to ask myself about myself.

On Christmas Eve the snow fell again and covered the road I had worked so hard all month to find and keep open. It was a wall of snow, a trench that came up to my chest. The snow sparkled in the evening like glitter on a wall calendar, and I decorated a tree and baked some Christmas cookies. I lit the candles on the tree and brought the little horse and the goat in from the stable. The cat sat on the tin countertop beside the stove. I got out my old waiter's outfit and put it on, but the buttons kept slipping out of my callused fingers and my hands were so stiff from work that I couldn't tie my white bow properly. I took the oxfords out of my trunk and polished them, the ones I'd bought when I was a waiter at the Hotel Tichota. When I put the blue sash over my shoulder and pinned the star to my side, the star shone brighter than the tree, and the horse and the goat stared at me and grew so alarmed I had to calm them down. Then I got supper ready, canned goulash with potatoes, and I made a Christmas present for the goat by slicing an apple into his mush, and the same for the horse, who ate with me as he did every Sunday, standing by the long oak table, taking apples from a bowl and munching on them. The horse followed me wherever I went, because he had a fixed notion that I was going to go away and leave him here. The goat, who was used to having the horse around, followed him, and the cat, who depended on the goat for milk, followed the goat's udder, and wherever the goat went the cat went too. We'd go to and from work that way. In the fall, when I went to cut the second growth of hay, they all followed me, and even when I went to the bathroom, there were the animals, making sure I wouldn't run off on them. The only time I had actually left them was in my first week on the job, when the girl from the Maršner Orion chocolate factory appeared to me and I wanted to see her, wanted to know if she was going to work in the chocolate factory with books under her arm, and I missed her so badly that I packed a few things and before the sun came up set out for the village to wait for the bus. When the bus drove up and I was just putting my foot on the first step to board it, I saw the horse galloping toward me from my road, and the dog behind him, and then the goat hobbled into view, and they made straight for me, those animals, and stared at me, silently pleading with me not to leave them, and when they had formed a circle around me, the cat showed up and jumped up on the platform where they put the milk cans. So I let the bus go without me and went back with my animals, who from that time on never let me out of their sight. They tried to cheer me up, though, and the cat would leap and scramble about like a kitten, and the goat would try to play the ram and for a joke he would dance about with me, trying to butt heads with me. The little horse was the only one who had nothing he could do, so he would take my hand in his soft lips and look at me, his eyes alive with fear. Every day after supper the horse would curl up by the stove and sigh happily, the goat would lie down beside him, and I'd go on writing out my pictures. At first the pictures were unclear and I even wrote out some that had no point to them, but then suddenly the writing began to flow, and I covered page after page while the pictures in front of my eyes went by faster than I could write, and this gap between the pictures and the writing kept me awake at night. I no longer noticed whether there was a blizzard outside or whether the moon was shining or whether it was so cold the windowpanes cracked. Day after day I would shovel snow off the road and think of the journey I'd be taking that evening when I set the nib in the pen and began to write, and each day I had it worked out in advance, so that by evening all I had to do was write down what I'd been thinking about as I worked on the road. The animals looked forward to the evenings as well, because animals like peace and quiet, and they would sigh happily, and I sighed too and wrote on, and put another stump in the stove, and the flames purred quietly, and the wind sighed in the chimney and crept in under the door. At midnight on Christmas Eve lights appeared under the window. I put my pen down, and the unbelievable came true. I went outside, and there on a sleigh outfitted with a plow were the villagers—they had pushed their way through to me from the other side, those same wretches who sat around in the pub missing me so much they'd shot my German shepherd—and now here they were with a snowplow and a sleigh. I invited them into the inn, and when they looked at me, I saw they were alarmed. Where did you get that? Who gave it to you? How come you're dressed up like that? And I said, Sit down, gentlemen, now that you're my guests. I used to be a waiter. As though regretting they had come, they asked, What's that sash and that medal all about? I said, I was given them many years ago, because I served the Emperor of Ethiopia. And who are you serving now? they asked, still uneasy. My guests, as you can see, I answered, and pointed to the horse and the goat, who had stood up and wanted out, butting their heads against the door. I opened it for them, and they filed out and walked down the corridor to their stable. But my tuxedo and the sparkling medal and the blue sash upset the villagers so much that they just stood there. Then they wished me a happy holiday and invited me to come for dinner on the Feast of Stephen, and left. I saw their backs in the mirrors, and when the lights of the lanterns had retreated into the distance beyond the windowpanes, and the jingling of the bells had faded, and the plow had fallen silent, I stood in front of the mirror alone and looked at myself, and the more I looked at myself, the more alarmed I became, as though I were with a stranger, with someone who'd gone mad. I breathed on myself until I was kissing myself in the cool glass, and then I raised my arm and wiped the fog from myself with the sleeve of my tuxedo, until I stood once more in the mirror holding out a burning lamp like a glass raised for a toast. Behind me a door quietly opened, and I stiffened, but it was just the little horse coming in, and behind him the goat, and the cat leaped up on the tin countertop by the stove, and I was glad the villagers had come all that way through the snow to see me, glad they'd been alarmed by me, because I must be something rare, a true student of the headwaiter Mr. Skřivánek, who served the King of England, and I had the honor to serve the Emperor of Ethiopia, who decorated me for all time with this medal, and the medal gave me strength to write this story out for readers, this story of how the unbelievable came true.

TRANSLATOR'S

ACKNOWLEDGMENTS

Bohumil Hrabal's work, Czechs say, is untranslatable. This book is my response to that challenge.

Josef Škvorecký, Antonín Vodseďálek, Jana Převratská, and Vratislav Brabenec guided me through some of the more puzzling intricacies of "Hrabalovština"—Hrabal's special way of using Czech—and Bert and Eva Jarsch of the Two Goblets Restaurant in Waterloo, Ontario, helped with the terminology of catering. I wish to thank Jan and Ivana Pavelka for their generous hospitality and, as always, my wife Helena, my daily lifeline to the Czech language.

To my mother and father I dedicate this translation.

Paul Wilson
Toronto, 1989

New Directions CLASSICS

please visit our website at www.ndpublishing.com